WEREWOLF ASYLUM

Roxanne Smolen

Published by: moonRox, Inc.
Cover Design: Y. Nikolova at Ammonia Book Covers

ISBN 978-0-9915673-2-4

Contents

ONE

April 8, 2008 Loxahatchee, Florida

When I shifted into my wolf form that balmy April night, all I wanted was to escape the hassle of the day. You know, romp through the sawgrass, maybe chase a rabbit or two. I never expected to run into a bear. But there it was, up on its hind legs like it wanted to give me a big hug.

I froze, staring, my teeth bared in greeting. I knew there were black bears in Florida. I lived in the northernmost region of the Everglades. We had panthers, gators, pythons, and bears. But I'd never seen one before. All my fur stood on end, trying to make myself appear bigger, but the bear had me on weight alone.

It swatted me with one frying-pan-sized paw, catching my shoulder. I yelped and tumbled. At that point, any sane person would have run. Unfortunately, the wolf in me took offense. With a low-pitched growl, I leaped at it.

Here's the difference between bears and wolves. Bears fight with their claws, and for good reason. They're like a fist-full of daggers. Wolves fight with their teeth. I caught its forearm in my jaws and clamped down. The bear roared. It swung around, trying to shake me off. My backend swished through the air. Blood filled my mouth, hot and slick. I lost my grip and flew against a tree trunk.

Floridian forests aren't like the forests up north. Back home in Massachusetts, I remember feathery grass, carpets of pine needles, and smooth-barked trees. Down here, we have porcupine palms and saw-palmetto. The ground is spiked with spiny cones. I struck an Australian pine, which isn't a true pine tree at all, and slid down the trunk. The bark felt like concrete wrapped with razor wire. Tufts of fur scraped off as I fell–which only served to make me madder.

I launched myself at the bear, my jaws snapping at its throat. It batted me away with the strength of a major leaguer. I sprang again, this time spinning in mid-air and striking its chest with my hind legs–a move sure to impress any ninja warrior. My attack staggered it, and it came down on all fours. I climbed aboard, biting the back of its neck. My fangs penetrated the heavy fur. The bear rolled to knock me off, exposing its soft underbelly. I dodged its weight and went for its gut. My teeth caught something strange. I pulled back with some sort of belt in my mouth.

As if it were melting, the bear morphed into a kid. My jaw dropped, and the belt hit the ground. The boy scrambled to his feet. His expression went from shock to alarm and then to determination as he took a fighting stance before me.

My wolf chuckled at that, but my human side filled with questions. Who was he? How did he shift into a bear? I couldn't wait to tell Brittany, the girl I secretly loved. I started the change back to human before I even made a decision to do it. My muzzle flattened painfully, sinking into my face. My fangs receded. With a liquid sensation, my ears slid down the sides of my head. My transformation was not as smooth as his, but moments later I got to my feet as a sixteen-year-old boy.

His eyes widened, and he took a step back. He looked like he feared me more as an unarmed kid. Then he squared his shoulders and lifted his chin. He was about my height with a weight lifter's build. Probably had twenty pounds on me. He looked a bit older than I was. We faced each other, and it was weird because we were both naked, yet we weren't in the shower room at PE or anything.

"Hi." I tried to sound nonchalant. "I'm Cody Forester."

"William." The boy eyed me warily. "I never met a werewolf before. I thought your kind only changed on the full moon."

I felt a twinge of panic. True, most werewolves only change with the moon. My ability to change at will made me an oddity. A super wolf, my Uncle Bob called it. And a super danger if it got out. Like gunslingers of the Old West, everyone would want a piece of me.

I shrugged, then motioned at the blood dripping down his arm. "Sorry I hurt you."

Anger flared on the kid's face. "You didn't hurt me."

"Well, you hurt me." I rotated my shoulder, wincing at the score marks. With a grunt, I picked up the bear hide belt and sat on a nearby log. "So, what are you, like a were-bear?"

William gave an indignant snort and raised his chin even higher. "I am a medicine man, like my father before me. We are able to change into many animals."

"With this?" I held out the belt.

His eyes flashed, but then he seemed to deflate. He took the belt and sat at the other end of the log.

After a few moments, I said, "Medicine man, eh? What tribe? Miccosukee?"

"I am half Navajo," he said as if challenging me to deny it.

A creepy feeling crawled into my stomach. My uncle's best friend was a Navajo medicine man. Without looking at him, I said, "Who's your father?"

"Howard Shebala."

"Garage Sale Howard?" I blurted.

He jumped up, face dark and hands clenched. "My father is a great man."

"Chill," I said. "I just know him, that's all. He's my uncle's best friend."

"Then speak of him with respect."

"Does he realize you're out here turning into a

bear?"

William shook his head and slumped back down on the log. "He was voted out of the tribe. An outcast. The tribal council says I cannot see him or make contact."

"That stinks." I knew all about being an outcast. My parents banished me to Loxahatchee the first time I showed fang and fur.

William said, "Now my mother has taken up with another."

"Top knot guy." I met Howard's rival during a trip to the *Miccosukee Indian Village* in the Everglades.

"Joseph Achak," William said with a scowl. "I hate him."

"No doubt," I said. "But why are you here?"

"I left. Wanted to be nearer my father. Sometimes I see him."

"So you live here? In the woods?" I remembered news reports about bear sightings in the city. "Hate to see the media blitz if Child Services finds out."

"Do I look like a child?"

"Okay," I said, "so you get hungry and you turn into a bear to eat. I get it. But where do you sleep? You can't be a bear all the time."

"I found an old fishing cabin in the Glades," he said, then looked sorry he told me. "That's a secret. I don't want anyone to come looking."

I nodded. Now we both knew secrets about each other. "You could stay at my house. I live with my Uncle Bob. Howard stops by pretty often."

"No." He stood. "No contact."

"So you'll defy the tribal council enough to run away from home, but you won't risk seeing your dad?" I rose to face him, royally ticked off. How could he act like that? I would do most anything to see my dad again.

"Don't comment on what you don't understand." With a scowl, William stomped off into the trees.

All I could do was watch him go.

TWO

The next morning dawned blue and breezy. Since I was out late the night before, I overslept my alarm. I made a Cap'n Crunch sandwich to eat in the truck as Uncle Bob drove me to school.

Uncle Bob had steel gray, over-the-collar hair and a thin build. He was known as the *Fix-It Guy*, a handyman who did odd jobs around town. In his spare time, he was a werewolf, although not many people knew that. I'd lived with him for only four months, but I felt pretty comfortable. He didn't try to replace my parents. He was more like a close friend looking out for me.

Seminole Bluffs High School seemed blindingly white under the bright sun. Its expansive concrete courtyard had small holes cut out for trees to grow through. The only grassy area was the football field. Home of the Hawks.

As we pulled into the drop-off area, I noticed Maxwell and Lonnie hanging around. They looked decidedly nerdy in their button-down shirts. It made me smile. At my prep school back in Cambridge, all the kids looked nerdy. I wondered what they'd think if they saw me now in my garage-sale t-shirt and jeans.

I hopped out of the truck and circled around to pull my bicycle from the back. I'd have to bike it home. My uncle drove me to class most mornings, but he was rarely able to pick me up again. Usually I made plans with Brittany after school. We were study partners, but in my head, we were more. Since she had just gotten out of the hospital, however, she'd probably take off a few more days.

My wolf sense seemed to be on high; I could hear laughter and conversation as far away as the buses. The stench of car exhaust assaulted me, mingled with a miasma of hair gel, perfume, and cigarette smoke.

I bounced my bike onto the curb and raised a hand in farewell. Uncle Bob drove away as Maxwell and Lonnie approached.

"Hey, where you been, man?" Maxwell asked.

I was ready for that. I'd missed the past two days of school, and I'd concocted a story about having the stomach flu, complete with illustrations. But Maxwell didn't give me time to get into it.

He said, "Is it true your girlfriend was kidnapped by a serial killer down by the old rock quarry?"

"B-Brittany?" I spluttered, not knowing how to answer. I couldn't tell him the whole story, that the serial killer in question was actually a murderous werewolf, and Brittany was kidnapped to punish me for not joining the pack.

Lonnie said, "Don't try to deny it, man. It was all over the news."

"No," I said, "I mean, she's not my girlfriend." Not officially, my thoughts added.

Maxwell blinked and gave his glasses a shove. "Really? I thought you were together."

"I'd like to be, but–"

"Hi, Maxwell," a female voice purred. Alitia Carpenter smiled over her shoulder as she walked by, her blonde curls ruffling in the breeze.

"Later, man," Maxwell told me.

"Seeya," said Lonnie.

I grinned, shaking my head. As I walked my bike to the rack, I thought about Brittany being my girlfriend. It would be too good to be true. She once told me that she loved me, but I couldn't count that. We were running for our lives from the pack of werewolves at the time. However, when I visited her in the hospital on Monday, she kissed me. In front of her mother, no less.

Did that mean we were together?

I glanced at the student parking lot. Brittany's lime-green Volkswagen Beetle wasn't there. Her car was wrecked in the kidnapping. I felt as responsible for that as I did for her safety.

No. I wouldn't tell anyone that she was my girl. I didn't want to jinx it by blabbing it around school.

I left my ratty old bike unlocked, certain that no one would bother to steal it, and headed to Trig. As I had been absent for two days, I was a little behind and had to pay attention in class. It was torture. Mr. Varney had to be the most boring teacher in the world. But I was rewarded for my efforts when I got to World History an hour later and found Brittany there.

She was stunning. Her hair was black and streaked with purple today, and her lips were deep violet. Her dark tank top showed off her pale shoulders and long slim arms. Her miniskirt accented her perfect legs. My heart skipped in circles as I stood there watching her. She was surrounded by a group of chattering, giggling girls. Perhaps they thought she was cool for having her life threatened. She looked up, saw me, and rolled her eyes. I smiled and let her have her moment of fame.

I didn't see her again until lunch. She sat at our table with her customary tray of yogurt and an apple. I felt so relieved to see her there. It was like everything was back to normal. I picked up a bag of chips and a couple of *Dews*.

"Hi," I said as I reached her.

She motioned at the chips. "Is that all you're having?"

"Hey, it's potatoes. It counts as a vegetable." I sat across from her, basking in her smile. Her long bangs trailed into her eyes, not completely hiding the *Band-Aid* over the stitches on her forehead.

"What?" She laughed, and I realized I'd been staring.

"I like your hair. Much better than the pink."

"Oh, I only did that for my mother."

"Your mother likes bubblegum hair?"

"No." Brittany grinned. "She hates it."

I opened my *Dew*. "I'm really glad to see you, but don't you think you should have taken off a little more time?"

"I couldn't stay at home with Grandpa Earle hovering over me. He means well, but..." She cut a slice of apple with a plastic knife and handed it to me.

Earle Meyer was old but a decent guy. He took in Brittany, her little brother Butt Crack, and their mother after a messy divorce.

"Anyway," Brittany said, "I feel much better. Except my stitches are beginning to itch."

"Hear anything about the car?" I remembered the panic I felt when I first saw Brittany's Beetle at the bottom of the cliff at the old rock quarry. Double that when I realized she wasn't inside.

"It's not totaled or anything. The bumper is dented, and the trunk is dinged. One headlight is smashed." She took a bite of apple, leaving purple kisses on the skin. "Because it's a bug, they had to special order everything. They've already got the windshield in. They tried to talk me into the tinted kind, but that didn't suit Baby."

"Baby?"

"Yeah, as in come on Baby, you can do it."

I chuckled. I never knew she named her car.

"The real problem is that the tie rod is broken, and it will take time to get the part in," she said. "Mom got a loaner from the insurance company, but she won't let me drive yet. She's making Grandpa chauffeur me around like a little kid. Parents can be such pains."

"Speaking of parents," I said, "did you know Howard had a son?"

"He does?"

"I met him last night. I was–"

"Hi, Brittany," a girl said.

Brittany looked up. "Oh, hi, Katie."

"I couldn't believe it when I heard about you on the news," Katie said. "Are you okay?"

"I'm fine," Brittany said. "Glad it's over."

I smiled and nodded as Katie walked away. "Anyhow, I was in the woods and I came across this bear. Only it wasn't a bear, it was–"

"Brittany, I'm so glad you're all right."

Two more girls stopped at our table.

One of them asked, "Were you scared?"

Stupid question. I closed my eyes and rubbed my forehead.

"Maybe we can go to the mall after school today," the other girl said.

"I'd better not," Brittany told them. "I still get really tired."

"Oh," they both crooned and patted her back.

After they left, Brittany said, "So, you met a bear in the woods."

"William the Bear," I said.

"He talks?"

"No. He turned into a boy. He uses some sort of magic belt."

She nodded. "A hide belt. Remember? We read about those when we were researching werewolves."

"Ohmygod, Brittany, you were kidnapped?" a girl squealed as she led three more to our table. "Was he cute?"

"No, Amber. What are you thinking?"

"What kind of thing is that to ask," I said, my voice rising. "Get out of here. Leave her alone."

"Well, check out Mister Jealous," Amber said, although she seemed more amused than miffed.

They walked away.

Brittany said, "Don't look now, but you have an admirer."

I glanced around and saw Efrem Higgins sitting at a nearby table. I hated Eff. He hated me, too. Enough to call his football-playing cronies together to play piñata with me. When Eff posted pictures of the beating on MySpace, his coach found out and turned him in. The courts saddled him with one-hundred and twenty hours of community service. And he was kicked off the school football team.

"Yeah," I said, "he was hanging around in PE, too. All his friends seem to have abandoned him."

Brittany muttered, "Serves him right, the psychopath."

"It's no fun being alone."

"You're too forgiving," Brittany said. "Anyway, I

didn't know Howard had a son, and I think he would have told us. After all, he introduced us to his ex-wife. Maybe we should talk to him about it."

"Yeah," I said, and finished my Dew.

Lunch ended, and I reluctantly said goodbye. I kept Brittany in my thoughts the rest of the day–the crinkle of her nose when she smiled, the tilt of her head to keep her bangs out of her eyes. It was almost as good as having her with me.

My last hour was Shop. I dreaded taking the class at first, but I found that I liked working with wood. Besides, all you had to do was show up and you got a passing grade.

I joined Maxwell and Lonnie at their worktable. We'd finished making birdhouses and had progressed to decorative mail caddies, the kind you might set on the kitchen counter to hold the day's bills.

"No, stupid," Maxwell told Lonnie as I sat down. "The top is supposed to look like waves, not pumpkin teeth."

"So," Lonnie said, "my waves are just a little choppier than yours."

Maxwell jostled him. "Let me fix it."

"No." Lonnie pushed back.

"What do you think, Cody?"

I studied the misshapen box. "If you paint it yellow, it would look like the sun. You know, the way little kids draw it. Your mom would love that."

"Yeah." Lonnie smiled, his eyes lighting as if with

fresh inspiration.

Just then, an annoying tone crackled from the intercom, and Vice Principal Overhill said, "May I have your attention, please."

Maxwell gave Lonnie another shove. Lonnie hip-checked him, sending him staggering. They laughed in hissing whispers.

"Boys," said Mr. Conklin, the Shop teacher.

"Due to recent tragic events," said the intercom, "grief counselors will be available to all students for individual sessions from eleven until two. We encourage everyone to make an appointment."

In an undertone, Lonnie said, "I'll be grief stricken if it gets me out of class."

"Right," Maxwell said. "Our poor, dear friend Brittany. She might have been killed."

I smirked. "You guys don't even know Brittany."

"We know she's hot," Maxwell said.

"Double hot," said Lonnie.

"Besides, what do you care if we get to know her better? Seeing how you two aren't together."

"Yeah, man. Study partners. Lunch buddies. You better make your move."

I nudged him with my shoulder. "I'm working on that."

Eventually, class ended. I hung around in front of school hoping to wave goodbye to Brittany, but in the crowd I must've missed her. Disappointed, I hopped on my bike and pedaled down the street.

I didn't feel like going home to an empty house,

although you'd think I'd be used to it. I grew up that way. Both my parents are doctors, and they were never home when I lived with them. Now that I was older, I had choices, so I headed toward Howard's house.

Howard Shebala lived on a street lined with pink and aqua houses. Between drought and water restrictions, the usually immaculate lawns looked brown, the flowerbeds sparse and wilted. In Howard's front yard, the shaggy grass lay in worn out lanes between rows of tables. The *Garage Sale* sign was a permanent fixture.

As I pulled my bike up the driveway, I noticed only one shopper, a woman with a small boy. The kid kept reaching up on tiptoe to drag items off the tables. I leaned my bike against the garage door and walked to where Howard sat with his customary lemonade. He stood as I approached, his ponytail swinging onto his shoulder. He was short and stocky–and a Navajo medicine man.

"Howdy. Good to see you." He shook my hand. "I'm sorry to hear of your recent trouble. Is Brit all right?"

"She's amazing," I told him. "So brave."

"The rest of the pack got away?" He said it as if he thought they were a danger, but I knew they weren't. They were followers. Sycophants. They wouldn't be back.

"The sheriff has the leader," I said. "He'll never get out. Brittany plans to testify against him, but even if she doesn't, they still have him on the other murders."

Howard shook his head. "The wolf in him cannot be incarcerated. Come the full moon, who knows what will happen?"

My face grew warm. This was the first time Howard spoke openly to me about werewolves. It was a touchy subject, not only because he knew my secret but because I should have realized he knew. His pet name for me was Mai Coh, which meant shape shifter.

I said, "Between you and me, I don't think that wolf will be coming out any time soon. You see, your wife, er, ex-wife, Chelsea, told Brittany and me about a potion to change a wolf back into a man. We used it on him."

Howard stared at me. Then he threw back his head and laughed. Great resounding guffaws. I'd never seen anyone laugh so hard.

When he quieted, I said, "I didn't tell my uncle that part." I hoped Howard would take the hint and not mention it. I didn't want to have to explain to Uncle Bob that I'd been trying to cure my own lycanthropy; he seemed quite content with his werewolfism.

Howard wiped his streaming eyes and slapped me on the shoulder. "A wise decision. So, young Mai Coh, what brings you to these parts?"

"Socks. I'm running low."

He nodded and led me through tables of neatly

folded Levis and stacks of t-shirts. He stopped at an open box. "I know I saw socks around here somewhere." He pulled out belts by the handful and draped them over the table, trying to peer to the bottom of the box. "Nope. Not this one."

As I watched him replace the belts, I said, "What would you do with all this stuff if it started to rain?"

"Not likely. Worse drought I've seen in many years."

"Has it ever happened?"

"Certainly. But not often. Florida weather is predictable. It hardly rains in winter, and in summer it rains everyday like clockwork. I just set my alarm clock and clean up when it goes off."

I shook my head, gazing over the many tables. "You need an assistant."

Howard grunted and moved to another box. The lone shopper waved to him and, kid in hand, walked off without buying anything. They left a trail of fallen Tupperware and paperbacks on the grass.

Howard said, "She never picks up after him."

"Do you have kids?" I said as if just thinking about it.

He buried his nose in the box. "Why do you ask?"

"The first time I saw all this stuff, I thought you must have a whole slew of kids to have so many castoffs."

Howard grunted again. "EBay."

"Excuse me?"

He looked up. "I'm running a business here. Most

of my inventory comes from EBay. I stock the items I figure I can sell, up the price a bit for profit, and make a living."

"No kids, then."

Howard sighed. "I have a son."

"Really? What's he like?"

"Dead."

I blinked, not sure if I should apologize or call him on it. Before I could respond, he held up two white socks bundled with a thick rubber band.

"How many do you need?" he asked.

"Five or six pairs."

He pulled more socks from the bottom of the box. Some had red or blue stripes on the tops and some were plain white. "Two dollars a pair."

I grimaced. "But they're used."

"No, they aren't," he said. "My friend's an amputee, gives me all his left-handed socks."

I pulled a five-dollar bill out of my pocket. "This is all I have."

"The magpie flies even in rain." Howard muttered one of his indecipherable sayings and took the five. "Don't tell anyone I gave you such a good deal. They'll all want something."

He walked back to his lemonade, pulled a plastic *Publix* grocery sack from under the lawn chair, and placed the socks inside.

"Thanks," I said, accepting the bag. "See you later."

"Tell Bob my Rummy cards are lonely."

I slung the bag of socks over my handlebars and took off, feeling bemused. I didn't really need socks, but I knew there was no getting information from Howard without buying something. Only I hadn't gotten much information. All I knew was that either Howard or William were lying to me. Maybe both.

It was late when I got home. My uncle and I live in a small, two-bedroom house with almost no furniture. It's set back from the road, surrounded by woods. The neighbors can't see or be seen. It's a perfect den for a couple of werewolves.

I dumped my bike in its usual spot on the grass. As I clomped up the wooden steps to the porch, Uncle Bob arrived. He parked his truck on the gravel drive and climbed out with several *Publix* bags of his own. His held groceries–chocolate milk, instant coffee, bread, and what smelled like a family-style fried chicken dinner.

I opened the door to the house and held it for him, and my stomach growled as he passed. It smelled great.

We didn't often cook in my new home. Of course, my mother, the brain surgeon, rarely cooked either. Our housekeeper, on the other hand, could've been a Japanese chef. Lots of greens. Fresh seafood. I missed the comforts of my home. But I was pretty much a vegetarian then. I couldn't go without meat now.

I followed my uncle into the kitchen, and we sat down to fried chicken, potato salad, and baked beans. A breeze blew through the open window, flapping the curtains. Uncle Bob insisted on keeping the window open regardless of the heat, a habit I was coming to appreciate.

"Heard you go out last night," he said as if reading my thoughts.

"I just needed to unwind."

"Have you heard from Brittany?"

"She was at school today. Looks great."

"Good. Now you can stop worrying about her." He poured me a tall glass of chocolate milk.

Glasses were a recent addition to the household. I guess Uncle Bob felt more domestic now that we both decided I would stay. The adjustment period was as difficult for him as it was for me. I hated Florida at first, but now I couldn't imagine living anywhere else. I would never run away.

Which made me think of William.

"I stopped by Howard's today," I said, tossing chicken bones into the empty bag. "I asked him if he had any kids, you know, with all the junk he has around, and he said he had a son but he was dead."

"Willie." My uncle nodded. "I suppose he *is* dead, figuratively speaking. I don't know if Howard told you this, but he's a full-blooded Navajo. He lived among the Miccosukee for many years. When his wife divorced him, the tribal council banned him from their land."

"They can do that?"

"Guess so. Willie was thirteen at the time. A

tough age. A tough situation for both him and his father. He must be seventeen, now. Lives with his mother. Howard never talks about him."

I took a long pull of milk. How could Howard neglect to mention he had a son? Was he happy to disown William, or was it too painful to think about him? I wondered if my dad ever spoke about me. Did he tell people I was dead? "What would happen to Howard if he defied the council and visited his son anyway?"

"Who knows? Maybe they'd excommunicate the entire family." Uncle Bob got up to make a cup of instant coffee with hot tap water.

I watched him for a moment, then shook my head. "That's brutal. What did Howard ever do to them?"

"There was an incident," my uncle said, slurping his mug.

When he didn't elaborate, I knew the subject was closed. I gathered the trash from dinner and carried it to the garbage can behind the shed. My unofficial chore. The sun was down, and the surrounding trees looked black against the pink sky. I listened to birds settling in for the night. Field mice scampered through fallen leaves. Farther off, I heard peacocks calling, making the place sound like the set of a movie.

For a moment, I wanted to slip out of my clothes and into the wolf, romp through the trees and swampland. But that was a dangerous habit to get into. Just because I could change into a wolf anytime I wanted didn't mean I should. After all, I had a human side, too. I couldn't be a wolf all the time.

I wondered about William living in the woods as a bear. Why would he refuse to see Howard when clearly he loved his dad? It wasn't like he had parents like mine. My parents banished me to Florida without a clue. They never told me that lycanthropy ran in my family or what to do if I suddenly turned into a wolf, like I had in that restaurant in France. They were all about secrecy. From their neighbors, from society. From their only son. I would never forgive the way they abandoned me. Still, I wished I could see them, if only to tell them that.

When I went back to the house, I found Uncle Bob in his beat-up old recliner in front of our twelve-inch black-and-white television. Watching *Jeopardy* was one of his nightly rituals. We exchanged nods, and I hurried to my room to call Brittany. *My* nightly ritual.

She picked up on the second ring. "I wondered when you would call."

I smiled as I always did when I heard her voice. "Did you miss me?"

"Always," she said, "but that's not it. I have to tell you that I won't be at lunch for the next few days because I have appointments with the school grief counselors at that time."

I winced as if she'd slapped me. "You're still that upset?"

"Not me. It's my mother. She thinks I'm repressing the horror of the ordeal and need to let it out. Her words."

I groaned. "I feel so responsible."

"That's silly. You couldn't know what would happen. Maybe you should talk to a counselor, too."

"Yeah, I can see it now."

"Don't make fun. I wonder if they have werewolf therapists or werewolf doctors."

"Why would they? There's no such thing as werewolves, remember?"

"Or were-bears."

"Now who's poking fun?" I said. "I'm telling you, he's out there. He said he's living in an old fishing cabin."

"I know where that is. At least, I might. There's a fishing cabin in the Everglades out on State Road 80, kind of community property. Grandpa took Butt Crack and me there when we first moved down. The original owner must be long gone. Of course, you can't really own anything in the Everglades."

"Howard told me his son was dead. That really bothered me."

"Because he lied to you?"

"Sounds kind of harsh, that's all."

"I can't imagine how anyone can live by themselves in the woods," Brittany said. "We should take some groceries to him."

"Whoa," I said. "I'm not sure that's a good idea. I was supposed to keep the whole thing a secret."

"It's no big. I'll just raid the pantry."

"But–" My mind whirled, searching for a way to derail her. "You aren't driving yet. How are we going to get there?"

"Maybe my friend, Eileen, can take us."

I frowned. "Does she go to our school?"

"No, she's homeschooled. Eileen Beamer. I've known her since I moved down. She lives at the Sunspot."

"A fulltime nudie?" I blurted. The Sunspot Naturist Resort bordered Brittany's house. I had a quick image of Brittany's grandfather sitting with his pellet gun, shooting nudists who strayed from the nature trails into his yard. "I thought only tourists stayed at the Sunspot."

"Not all the residents are tourists," Brittany said. "Remember the fortuneteller we went to? She lives on the resort."

"The grandmaster. How could I forget?" The grandmaster scared the life out of me by predicting that I would sacrifice Brittany for the greater good.

"Then it's settled," Brittany said. "Let's plan a trip to the old fishing cabin on Saturday morning."

I ran my hand over my face. William the Bear wouldn't be happy.

THREE

School the next day was miserable. Brittany and I barely had time to say hi in World History. I saw her a few times after that, but always from afar. I wanted so much to be with her, to hear her laugh, to touch her hand. Fat chance. What made it worse was she apparently didn't feel the same way. Whenever I saw her, she was either talking to someone else or rushing to get to class. She was never craning her neck to catch a glimpse of me.

As a result, I was in a foul mood as I rode my bike across town toward home. It was sunny and hot. Sweat rolled in rivers down my back. Instead of sapping my strength, though, the heat seemed to invigorate me. I turned down Southern Boulevard, passing several cars before I realized how fast I was going. I had to keep my wolf super-speed in check. How would I explain getting a traffic ticket while riding my bike?

I left Southern to follow a blacktopped road that cut through the many ranches and pastures surrounding the city. Rich scents of dung and hay filled the air. A couple of riders passed going the other way. The horses shied from me, so I rode in the gutter to keep out of their way. I didn't want my wolf to spook them. It must be hard enough for them to amble along when all they wanted to do was run.

At last, I turned down the dirt road that led home. The ground was dry, and my tires sank into sand. I was grateful to reach our long gravel driveway. I gathered speed, then skidded to a halt. My uncle's blue pickup was in front of the house. I tensed, ears perked like a hunting dog. Why was he home so early? Was something wrong? But as I approached, I noticed a white, late-model Lexus with out-of-county plates parked beyond the truck. Probably a rental.

We had company. For a moment, I hoped it was Rita, my uncle's werewolf mate. The last time I saw her, she had a bullet wound, and I wanted to know she was okay. But Rita drove an old, beat-up van. It wouldn't be her. I dumped my bike and climbed to the porch. Hair dripped on my forehead.

Uncle Bob met me at the door. "Where you been, boy? We've been waiting for you."

He smiled, but it didn't reach his eyes. I wanted to ask what was going on, but he walked away so fast it was like a cartoon character with the feet that spin around. I lifted my nose and caught a familiar scent. *Oh no.* Filled with foreboding and disbelief, I followed him to the kitchen.

There at the coffee-stained, aluminum-legged table sat my parents.

I blinked and backpedaled until I slammed into the doorjamb. "Mom? What are you doing here?"

"Cody." My mother smiled as if she hadn't sent me away, as if she hadn't made me feel like dirt. Arms outstretched, she stepped toward me and caught my face in her hands. "Goodness. You've grown. And you need a shave. Look at this, David. Your son has stubble."

"How have you been?" My dad moved in to pump my hand.

I felt like I was suffocating. I pushed them away, perhaps a little abruptly, and stood next to my uncle at the sink, grateful for the breeze of the open window. "This is a surprise."

"I know, darling," Mom said. "We should have called."

"You wouldn't return my calls. You wouldn't speak to me at all."

"That's all in the past. Like it never happened." She smiled. "We want you back."

"What?" I clutched my chest as if she stabbed me. After all the times I dreamed of hearing her say those words. How dare she come for me now? Now that I had a new life. Now that I had Brittany.

"We want to take care of you. Be a family again."

"Just like that?" I said. "Don't you realize what you put me through?"

"Cody, how about some nice, cold milk?" Uncle Bob said. "You don't have to make up your mind now. We can talk about this after you've had a chance to get used to the idea."

"No, Bob," Mom said. "Let him speak."

"Marie, please. You're my sister and I love you, but sometimes you are as subtle as a lead pipe. Sit down. You, too, David. Let's not crowd the boy."

Something cold pressed into my hand. A glass of milk. I stared and, honestly, I couldn't think of what to do with it. "Home," I murmured. But this was home. With Uncle Bob. And Brittany. I couldn't leave. I tried to imagine life without Brittany beside me, without touching her hand or seeing her smile. "I can't." The words drew a fight or flee response. My muscles knotted and burned. Breath hissed through my teeth.

"What do you mean, you can't?" my mother blurted. "We're your parents. You belong with us."

"And you think that gives you the right?" I shouted, my voice husky. "To lie to me? To keep me in the dark all my life and never warn me about what I might become? You banished me. You turned your back on me when I needed help. You didn't even tell me Uncle Bob was a werewolf, too."

"I admit we might have handled things better."

"Argh!" I spun about. The glass of milk smashed into the sink. Hair sprouted from my knuckles. I was losing control, shifting into a wolf before them. It would serve them right. Let them see their beloved son.

A hand cupped my arm. "Cody," my uncle said.

His tone was both sympathetic and stern, and I knew that I would disappoint him if I turned into a wolf and leaped slavering and howling onto the kitchen table. It would be impolite, a black-mark upon werewolves everywhere. The thought brought a strangled chuckle that, to my horror, turned into sobs. My shoulders hunched and shook. Tears streamed down my face. I hated it. This was worse than letting them see me as a wolf.

In a low voice, my uncle said, "The two of you should leave."

"We certainly will not," said my mother. "Cody, stop this nonsense and get your things."

"I don't have *things*." I looked at her. "You took them from me, remember?"

"Fine. Then let's go."

"I'm not going anywhere with you. You ruined my life. I won't let you do it again."

"Ruined." She stepped back as if I'd slapped her, eyes wide and moist. "Yes. I ruined your life. I knew there was a chance the curse would touch you. But I was selfish. I wanted you so bad. Oh, I never should have had you."

"That makes me feel so much better," I said.

"Enough of this," she snapped. "You're coming with us."

I turned to my father sitting at the table. "Don't you have anything to say? An opinion? A suggestion? You give in to her on everything."

"Hold on there," he said.

"How can you let her do these things to me?" I shouted.

Dad got to his feet. "You're upset. I don't blame you. We'll go now." My mother gave a surprised yelp as he took her arm and ushered her into the living room. "Just think about it, son. Don't make rash decisions. Like we did. We'll see you again soon."

And just like that they were through the front door and out of the house. I wanted to throw something at them. Smash something. Instead, I stormed to my room and dove onto my bed. The frame creaked and swayed. I thudded my fist against the mattress. How could they do this to me? How could they take my life away and then offer it back four months later? I hated them.

After a while, all that anger turned inward. I threw my arms over my face as if I could shield myself from my own recriminations. I failed them as a son. They wanted me to become a doctor, wanted to be proud of me. How could they be proud now? I was a mess. The amazing wolf boy.

With a pang, I realized I missed my old life. I had everything figured out then. Who I was. What I was going to be. Now I had no idea of what would become of me.

All I knew was that I loved Brittany. She was my mate. I would stay with her or die trying.

From my doorway, Uncle Bob said, "Pizza Barn is here, if you're hungry."

I opened my eyes, surprised to find my room dark. Head throbbing, I shambled into the kitchen. Pizza covered the table. Beneath the aroma of pepperoni and sausage, I smelled my parents. They'd sat right at that table and told me all was forgiven. All I had to do was give up everything. Again.

I sat down, folded a slice down the middle, and took a large bite. My uncle pulled out the chair across from me. We ate in silence for half a pizza.

Then he asked, "Do you want to go with them?"

"No." I looked at him, shaking my head. *Please don't send me away.* "This is my home." All at once, I realized it was true. My place was in Loxahatchee. I didn't feel torn between two homes any longer. That part of my life was behind me.

"I'm glad to hear it. Things wouldn't be the same without you."

"What do we do now?"

"We tell them. No problem." He tapped a quick drumroll on the tabletop. "Your mom loves you. She's not about to take you by force."

"Yeah." What was I worried about? My mother loved me.

The next day was just as miserable as the day before, but I was in a better mood. Probably because it was Friday. After school, I was in my room doing homework on my laptop when I heard a knock. My thoughts went immediately to Brittany. She must know how lost I felt without her. Convinced she came to save me from my loneliness, I rushed through the living room with a smile on my face. My smile died when I opened the door.

"Hello, Cody," Mom said. "May we come in?"

"Um, sure." I stepped aside. "Uncle Bob isn't here." With a start, I realized the sun was setting. Where was Uncle Bob? Where was dinner?

"That's all right, son," Dad said. "We came to see you."

"First, your father and I want to apologize for our behavior last night," Mom said. "Tempers ran a bit high."

"Oh." I blinked at them. What was going on? My mother never apologized. I motioned at the recliner and the kitchen chair arranged around the old black and white. "Would you like to sit down?"

"Actually, we'd like to take you to dinner," Dad said. "Some place relaxing so we can catch up."

"Well, I don't know." I took an uneasy step away. Uncle Bob's words came back to me–she's not about to take you by force. But why did they want to get me alone? "I'll have to leave a note. Where are we going?"

"Pistache. It's a French restaurant in West Palm Beach," Mom said. "Have you been there?"

"No. We usually eat in Loxahatchee." I tore off a corner of newspaper, wrote down where we would be, and left the note under a coffee cup. I didn't add that I wished he would join us. Maybe, he would get the hint.

My father smiled. "All set? Off we go, then."

We went to their rented white Lexus. I climbed in back, hoping my uncle would arrive home in time to block us in. I wasn't comfortable being alone with my parents. I didn't want to be yelled at or persuaded. I knew from experience that my mom had the ability to brainwash people.

As we pulled out of the driveway, I said, "Nice car." No one answered. Was it possible they were just as uncomfortable being with me? Maybe they wanted me in a public place so I wouldn't make a scene.

Before long, we were in downtown West Palm Beach with the Lexus' GPS chiming directions. We headed for Clematis Street and finally reached the Pistache. It overlooked Waterfront Park on the Intracoastal. I knew of the Intracoastal from my visits to Miami when I was a kid. It was a canal running parallel to the ocean deep enough to accommodate yachts. Expensive homes and fancy dockside eateries decorated its banks.

We sat on the restaurant patio because Mom said it was such a pleasant evening. They ordered a bottle of white wine. I drank water.

"How is school?" Dad asked.

"Fine," I said. "Pretty much like any other."

"Your grades are good?"

I nodded and shrugged.

There was a lull in the conversation, then he said, "It must be difficult to switch schools mid-term."

"Yeah." Especially when you're dumped without

warning, I wanted to say.

"Have you made many friends?"

"Some." There was Maxwell and Lonnie, but I didn't hang out with them. William the Bear, but he'd rather not see me again. The only person that mattered was Brittany, and I wasn't about to bring her into the conversation.

"You seem to have hit it off well with Bob," Mom said after a couple minutes.

I shifted in my seat. "Yeah, he's great. Really makes me feel welcome." It was a relief to know Uncle Bob didn't want me to leave, either. He wasn't in on the conspiracy to ruin my life.

We dined on a variety of cheeses and duck mousse from the bistro menu. Mom told me about her Valentine's Charity Ball. She was always organizing stuff like that. It all felt so normal I started to relax.

"So how are things in Massachusetts?" I asked. "Anything new happening?"

"The same old grind," Dad said. "Life goes on."

"How are my friends? Do you ever hear from anybody?"

"We had quite a few calls when you failed to return to school," Mom said as she sipped her wine, "wondering where you were, what you were doing. But they've tapered off."

"What did you tell them?"

"Simply that you were exploring other avenues of your life."

"Oh." I ran my fingers over the condensation on my glass. "I'm not saying I'm going back or anything. But it sure would be nice to see everybody."

"Oh, darling, you misunderstand," my mother said. "We aren't taking you back to Massachusetts."

I stared, feeling as if something bad was crashing down upon my shoulders. "No?"

"Of course not. That would never do."

"Actually, we've found a remarkable facility in Sweden," my father said. "The Lindgren Institute. It's a sort of werewolf retreat."

"It's run by Dr. Torhild Saarsgard." My mother opened her purse to pull out an actual brochure. "In the Fjallen Mountains."

I picked it up. It showed a posh resort with people by a pool in one shot, playing Ping-Pong in another. My mouth went dry. I croaked, "You want to institutionalize me?"

"No," my father told me, "it's a retreat. They're searching for a cure."

My mother said, "Even if they don't cure you, you will be happy there. You'll be with your own kind."

I slid the brochure back to her. "Are you sending Uncle Bob, too? He's my own kind."

"Bob is not my responsibility," my mother said. "Besides, he's set in his ways. I don't think he wants to be normal."

"Take me home," I said, my voice sounding far away. "I want to go back. To Uncle Bob's place."

My mother slapped the table. "You would rather

live in squalor? Look how beautiful this is. I thought you'd be delighted."

"You did?" For a moment, I couldn't recognize my own mother–her eyes were narrowed, lips curled in a snarl. I turned to my father. "Take me home now."

"Of course." He placed his napkin on the table and motioned for the waiter.

We drove back to Loxahatchee. The GPS was the only one talking. I stared out the window at passing traffic. I couldn't believe my parents wanted to send me to Sweden, hide me like I was some sort of leper. I thought they loved me, but they only wanted to protect themselves.

I was never so relieved to see my uncle's truck in the driveway.

"Do you want to come in and say hello?" I asked.

"Not at this time," Dad said. "We need to pack up and head home."

"Oh." I let out a slow breath. "Well, thanks for dinner."

"We'll do it again soon, Cody," Mom said.

Not if I can help it, I promised silently.

Uncle Bob stood on the porch as I climbed out of the car. Headlights washed over him. He looked angry, and I thought I might get an earful. I stepped beside him, watching my parents drive away.

He clapped me on the shoulder. "Did they give you trouble?"

"Just more wheedling." I wanted to tell him about

the werewolf asylum, but it was like admitting my parents were Nazis.

"Brittany called twice. She said your phone was turned off."

I nodded. "Guess I better call her back."

I went to my room and sat on my bed, staring at my phone. For the first time, I didn't want to talk to Brittany. I didn't know what to say. After a couple minutes, I punched in her number.

She picked up right away. "There you are. What's going on?"

"Not much."

"Are you okay? You sound weird."

I ran a hand over my face. I was more than weird. I was numb.

"Your uncle said you went to dinner in West Palm somewhere."

I winced. "Did he say who with?"

"No. Who?"

"My parents."

"Really? That must have been a surprise."

"They're evil. They want to hurt me. They're going way out of their way."

"Oh my God. They want to take you home?"

"Worse." I felt tears coming again and blinked them away. "They want to send me to a place in Sweden where I will be locked up for the rest of my life with other werewolves."

"There's a place like that?"

"They had brochures and everything. It was like

a concentration camp with Ping-Pong."

"That's horrible."

"I don't know what I'm going to do."

"Don't go."

"Yeah, right."

"Think about it. Even if they try to physically force you to go, all you need to do is turn into a wolf and run away. You could live in the woods. With William the Bear. And I could bring you Cheese Doodles."

I sat up straight. "I like Cheese Doodles."

"No one can make you do anything against your will again. You're like the luckiest guy alive."

"Yeah. You're right." Because I have you.

"So this place actually had brochures?"

"They showed people eating in a ritzy cafeteria and lounging around a pool, and they had a group therapy room to teach you how to deal with being a werewolf."

"And those were the good points. They probably have a dog run out back. What do you think?"

I laughed.

"Were the people in the brochure all hairy and everything? Wouldn't that be funny? Catch them when they're just starting to shift, with their fangs out and their bodies covered with fur, sitting in a lounge chair with sunglasses on."

The image brought me chills. "Yeah, heh. That's pretty funny."

"You don't have anything to worry about. I don't blame you for being upset, though. You must feel like they betrayed you all over again."

"I sat there at dinner and felt like I didn't know them. I never did."

"You're just seeing them in a different light," she said. "So are we still on for tomorrow? Eileen said she could drive but it would have to be early because she has things to do later."

I frowned at the quick change in subjects. Then I remembered we were taking food out to William. "Sure. What time?"

"Pick you up around nine. Don't stare at Eileen. That won't do any of us any good. Bye."

I closed my phone and leaned back on the bed, grinning. She was right. My parents didn't have power over me. No one could ever make me leave Brittany.

I wondered what she meant about not staring at Eileen. There was something different about her, but I couldn't remember what it was. Maybe she had a big nose or something.

FOUR

Brittany and her friend, Eileen Beamer, pulled up as I waited on the porch. Eileen drove an old Chrysler wood-paneled station wagon. She was so petite, all I saw was her head. I bounded down the steps, waved to Brittany in the passenger seat, and stopped at her open window. She smelled like coffee, peanut butter toast, and strawberry hair gel. With a smile, she leaned out for a kiss. A tingle spread as our lips met.

My breath caught in my chest, and I sighed, "Morning."

She smiled. "This is Eileen."

"Nice woody," I said to Eileen, then wished I hadn't said that.

Eileen was naked. All over naked.

"You're...You're..." I sputtered.

"I'm a naturist," Eileen told me. "I live at the Sunspot Naturist Resort."

"But, you can't...can't..."

"I can in the privacy of my own car," she said, then added quietly, "long as I don't get pulled over."

I remembered Brittany telling me not to stare. I

thought Eileen had a big nose or something. She didn't have a big nose. She had sun-streaked hair in tangled curls to her shoulders, and dimples when she smiled. Which she was doing. Her teeth were bright white against her tanned skin, and she had the bluest eyes I'd ever seen. And she was naked. Smooth and slim like in a magazine.

Don't stare.

"Well, hop on in," she said, her smile widening.

I stepped back, my face hot. I could see her through the glare of the windshield. Her boobs were small and firm, her nipples like little pink acorns. *Quit staring*. Tripping over my big feet, I stumbled toward the backseat.

Brittany opened her door. "I think we can all fit in here." She scooted across the bench seat.

I slid next to her, my long legs crammed against the dashboard. I became aware of Brittany's warmth against my thigh. In what I took to be a smooth move, I raised my arm to drape across her shoulders. At the same moment, Eileen leaned her arm on the seat to look behind as she backed down the drive. My hand brushed her boob. Yikes!

"Oh!" she said.

"Sorry." I withdrew my arm as if I'd been burned.

She didn't answer, but continued driving. My thoughts whirled. I touched a strange girl's bare boob. It was soft and supple. Like a marshmallow. Had Brittany seen what I did? I banged my head against the window frame.

Eileen said, “Sorry for the lack of air conditioning and all, but I promise the breeze will cool us just fine once we get moving.” Her words had a lazy southern twang to them.

The two friends seemed total opposites. Brittany was pale, while Eileen was tan. Brittany had straight, dark hair. Eileen had free-falling blond curls. Brittany wore tons of make-up, while Eileen didn’t wear any at all. Brittany wore clothes...

“We’re just glad for the ride,” Brittany told her.

“No problem. I’ve had friends stay out at the old cabin, too. It’s a good place to fish.”

We turned onto Southern Blvd. I wanted another glimpse of Eileen. I steeled myself to lean forward to turn on the radio. As if reading my mind, Brittany reached to turn it on.

“All you have is AM?” she asked.

“Yep. There’s a nice oldies station I listen to. All Sixties all the time.”

I recognized an early Beatles tune.

“Ooh, grandma music,” Brittany said. She and Eileen sang along to *She Loves You.*

I gazed at the traffic, wondering how many other drivers were naked. There must be loads of fulltime nudies at the Sunspot. When I first moved down, I checked out Loxahatchee on the Internet. There was a photo of a town council meeting with naturists sitting in among the clothed folks. Protesting in their birthday suits. I considered going to the next meeting.

Then Brittany cuddled my arm, driving out all thought of nudies and Eileen's boobs.

"I didn't know you had a grandma," I said.

Brittany nodded. "She was great. I only knew her for about a year. Heart attack. Grandpa Earle was devastated."

"I'm sorry for you both," I said, imagining how hard it would be to lose a mate.

Eileen said, "Is she the one who taught you to crochet?"

I feigned shock. "You crochet?"

"Only when I'm upset. It calms me. Sometimes I feel like she's sitting there beside me."

"Now I'm beside you." I kissed the top of her head.

I suffered through a few do-wap tunes. The best thing about Sixties music was that all the songs were short.

Eileen said, "Anything new about that guy who kidnapped you?"

"Pascal," Brittany said. "I'm supposed to be at some sort of preliminary hearing or arraignment on May the ninth."

"Really?" I blurted. She hadn't told me that. Why would she volunteer information to Eileen but not to me?

"That's a Friday," Brittany continued, "which is good in a way because maybe it won't take so long then. Everyone will want to go home for the week-end."

Eileen said, “I’m just glad you’re going through with it. Too many people back off when they realize there’s nothing in it for them.”

“I’m not interested in compensation,” Brittany said. “Just doing my civic duty.”

I tried for a witty quote I’d heard, bungling it. “It’s not that the world is full of evil people, it’s that it’s full of people who won’t do anything about it.”

“Exactly,” Eileen said, making me smile.

The radio crackled as we went under some power lines. Brittany snuggled against me. I put my arm around her, drawing her close. It felt perfect.

“Brit, have you been practicing?” Eileen asked.

“Sure have.” Brittany looked at me. “Eileen’s been teaching me Wiccan rituals. Every morning, I welcome the sun. It’s really awakened my spirit.”

“Oh.” What else could I say? I didn’t know much about spirits. The only things my parents believed in was their abilities as doctors and the inevitability of death.

The two girls carried on about candles and something called smudging. I watched the road. We followed State Road 80, going past Belle Glade. Sugar cane fields dominated the area, making the air sickly sweet. We reached the southern bank of Lake Okeechobee and headed toward a town called South Bay. Then we took 27 to Okeelanta, which was an absolute ghost town. Buildings stood deserted, windows broken or boarded. I expected to see tumbleweeds cruising through.

Once there, we turned onto a dirt road and traveled under cover of trees for a while. Then we rode past fields of scrub, and under trees again. The old station wagon jostled and creaked.

Eileen said, "I haven't been here for a while."

"Me, either." Brittany leaned forward, peering out the windshield. "Everything's so dry. The last time I was here, this road was flooded in areas. I remember splashing through."

The landscape changed to a sea of tall brown sawgrass. It smelled like an old wicker basket. I wanted to get out and run. Clusters of trees rose like tiny islands in a tan ocean. One of those islands turned out to be a wooden cabin on stilts. The road petered out before we reached it.

Eileen turned off the car. "Want me to come with? I brought boots."

"Sure!" I said hopefully.

But Brittany said, "No, that's all right. It doesn't look like anybody's home. We'll check and be right back."

I opened the door and offered my hand to help her out. I heard the ping of the cooling engine, the hiss of a warm breeze in the grass. Overhead, a couple of turkey vultures soared with the clouds, their red heads plain to my enhanced sight.

Brittany opened the back door and pulled out two plastic grocery sacks packed with non-perishable items such as granola bars, cheese doodles, and Oreos. I took one and led the way toward the cabin.

The grass grew in thigh high clumps, dragging against our pant legs like serrated knives. Eileen would never have made it through, but Brittany and I wore heavy jeans. Brit also wore a long-sleeved shirt despite the heat. I envied it. Each of our steps kicked up clouds of insects to swarm around us.

We approached the silent cabin. Thick beams formed sturdy-looking walls, but the roof consisted of gray and curling wood-shake. It probably leaked. Posts held the floor three feet up from the dry swamp. There were no stairs, but a large boulder at one side gave access to a westward-facing porch.

Brittany said, “It used to be you could row your boat and dock it right up to these pilings.” She climbed the boulder and peered through the cracks of a shuttered window. “William isn’t here.”

“Yes, he is. He’s behind that group of trees.”

“I don’t see him.”

“I smell him,” I said. “Stay here.”

I set my bag on the porch and ambled toward the trees, gazing around as if not knowing where he was. The breeze tousled my hair, bringing with it William’s scent. With a start, I smelled open wounds, and realized he hadn’t recovered from our fight a few nights ago. Evidently, were-bears didn’t have a werewolf’s recuperative powers.

“That’s far enough,” William said. He spoke quietly although there was distance between us, perhaps trusting my ears to pick him up.

I halted, careful not to look directly at the copse

where he hid.

He said, "You weren't supposed to tell anybody."

"Brittany's good at keeping secrets."

"And the other girl?"

I looked back at Eileen. The car door was open, and she stood upon the frame, only her head and bare shoulders visible. "She thinks we have a friend out here fishing. We didn't tell her your name."

"What do you want?"

I hesitated. Why *was* I there? To get in good with Brittany? "I wanted to invite you again to stay at my house. I know you don't want to see your dad. We can work something out."

"No."

I grimaced at his stubbornness, biting back a tirade. He had issues with his dad. I got that. But becoming a hermit was stupid. "I also wanted to warn you that there's been bear sightings on the news. You don't want any trigger-happy ranchers to form a posse."

"I hear you."

"All right, then. The groceries are yours. See you around." I walked back to the log cabin with Brittany's eyes upon me.

As I neared, she whispered, "What happened?"

I put my hands about her waist and lifted her off the porch. She felt small and fragile, like a precious bird. "We're going."

"But I wanted to meet him. Couldn't you talk him into coming out?"

I shook my head.

"What about the food?" she asked.

"He said thank you. That it was very kind."

She gave a little smile and took hold of my arm.

We retraced our steps, my wolf eyes picking out the faint path we'd left through the grass.

"No luck?" Eileen asked.

"No, he must be fishing somewhere," Brittany said. "We left the groceries so he'll know we stopped by when he gets home."

"You are a good friend." Eileen got into the car. After Brit and I settled in, she pulled a U-turn and headed back along the dirt road.

Brittany hummed with the radio. Despite the wild goose chase, she seemed in a great mood. Why was she so interested in meeting William the Bear? I watched the dry brush, unable to shake a pall of foreboding.

Around noon on Sunday, as I was making myself a nice grilled ham and cheese, Howard stopped by. He looked anxious and stressed, like he hadn't slept well. I figured he wanted to speak to Uncle Bob alone, so I asked to be excused and took my sandwich into my room. Their voices were low, and I tried not to listen.

But when Howard hollered, "He's my son," my ears perked.

I was about to walk to the door to eavesdrop when Brittany called on my cell.

"Hi," I said, smiling. "How are you?"

"Fine, just fine. Great, in fact." Her nose sounded stuffed, like she'd been crying.

"What's wrong?" There came a long pause. I sank onto the bed, listening to silence, clutching the phone as if I could force her to speak. "Brittany? What's going on?"

In a high-pitched voice that sounded nothing like her, she asked, "Can you come over?"

"Yes. When?"

"Right now. I need you."

I snapped the phone shut and hightailed it out of my room. Howard and Uncle Bob had moved onto the porch, most likely to keep me from hearing what they were saying. They looked at me, their expressions grave, and for an instant, I wondered if something had happened to William. That thought would have to wait.

"Could you drive me to Brittany's house? She's upset about something." I motioned with the phone to prove the seriousness of the situation.

"I'll take you," Howard said. "I remember where she lives."

I vaulted the steps and ran to his rusty old pickup. Howard followed, moving like five hundred pounds were strapped to his shoulders.

"Let me know what you find out," my uncle called.

As one, Howard and I said, "I will."

I ducked my head, deciding that he probably wasn't talking to me.

Howard climbed into the cab and started the engine. Howard's truck looked like it was falling apart, but that was deceiving. The rebuilt engine produced enough torque to uproot a tree. I felt the rumble in my chest as we drove away.

"What's up with Brit?" he asked.

I shook my head. "She was crying."

"That's not like her."

"No." I drummed my fingers on my thighs, wishing he would drive a little faster. A string of feathers, beads, and neck bones swung from the rearview mirror. Ostrich, I decided, although I had no way to tell if it was true.

"Why did you want to know if I had kids?"

"Um, what?" I nearly choked. I couldn't tell him that I knew William. I'd promised to keep it secret. "I just thought you had a lot of cast-offs, that's all."

Howard sighed. "Last night, my ex-wife called to tell me that my son has disappeared. My Willie Shiye. He's been gone since March seventh and she's just now calling me about it. Do you believe that?"

"W-Willie Shiye?"

"My name for him. Shiye means son in Navajo."

"You must be worried."

"Yes, but–" He shrugged. "He's run away before. Many times, actually. I think he can take care of himself."

My stomach clenched. All of a sudden, I felt like an accessory to a crime. "Did she call the police?"

"It's not our way to get outside authorities involved. The tribe is searching for him. In the past, they've found him in the Miami area. But not this time. Chelsea says she's looked everywhere."

I watched him as he spoke. His words were light, but his expression was strained, like he still fought that weight on his shoulders. I felt guiltier than ever.

"When was the last time you saw William?" I asked.

My heart stopped as Howard gave me a sharp look. I could have kicked myself. I should have called him Willie. Now Howard knew I was hiding something. He knew I lied by omission.

Howard said, "As a matter of fact, I caught a glimpse of him last month, that day I took you and Brit to the Indian Village. Maybe he saw me, too. Maybe that's why he ran."

I remembered Chelsea telling Howard that *he* was there, and Howard saying he saw *him*, but at the time I thought they referred to topknot guy. Joseph Achak. Howard's rival. "Why didn't you stop to say hi?"

"I'd love to speak with him, but it's forbidden. The child belongs to the woman, and she can deny visiting privileges. Besides, I'm banned from Miccosukee land. I wasn't supposed to be there."

"Why?"

"There was an incident."

And just like that, the conversation was over. I gazed out the window as we turned onto the long dirt road leading to Brittany's house. I felt like a turd, letting Howard worry about his son when I knew where he was. Especially since what William was doing was stupid and reckless. What if he tangled with a panther? Or another bear? But a promise was a promise. I couldn't rat him out now.

We reached a large, two-story clapboard home with an overhanging roof and a screened-in porch. Tangled woods surrounded the property. I murmured my thanks for the ride and got out of the truck. As I crossed the shaded yard, I watched for Brittany's dog, Haff, but the mutt didn't show. Maybe he was hiding from me. Dogs didn't like me much now that I was a werewolf.

I climbed the steps to a porch that was larger than my living room. Oversized white wicker furniture made it feel cramped. A pair of ceiling fans stirred the air with a gentle whap-whap. I knocked at the front door. Voices came from inside.

Brittany shouted, "You've got to be kidding!" A moment later, she yelled, "How can you do this to me?"

Grandpa Earle opened the door. He was stooped and wrinkled, but his bright eyes always looked like he was on the verge of laughter. He believed in flying saucers and Bigfoot. And he had a fierce love for his grandchildren.

"Hello, sir," I said. "May I speak with Brittany?"

"Might be I'm not doing you a favor," he said as he held the door wide. "It's a little noisy here today."

I walked through a darkened living room into a bright yellow kitchen. Brittany and her mother, Dalia Meyer, faced each other in the center of the room. Brittany's younger brother, Butt Crack, sat at the table along the far wall. He gave me a little wave.

I said, "Hello, Missus Meyer. Is everything okay?"

Without taking her eyes off her mother, Brittany said, "No, it's not okay. My mother has invited my father here to live."

That stunned me. I understood that the divorce was well deserved. I blurted, "Here in this house?"

"No, here in Florida," her mother said. "He wants to be nearer to the family in light of Brittany's recent experience."

"As if *that* would have made any difference."

I took a few quick breaths, hoping to clear my head enough to dredge up what I knew about Brittany's father. All I remembered was he lived in Georgia and worked on a road crew.

Her mother sighed and leaned against the stove as if drained. She addressed me. "Dean was upset. He heard about the ordeal on the six o'clock news, for heaven's sake. He just wants to be closer."

Brittany shouted, "I don't want him to be closer. Don't you remember what it was like?"

"Brittany, please."

"He used to beat us," Brittany said.

Her words struck me like a sledgehammer. I

suspected her father had hit her, but she'd never admitted it before.

"He's sober now, has been for over six months," her mother said. "He seems to be a changed man, more like he was when we first met."

"How gullible of you."

I started to hyperventilate. If I didn't distance myself, I'd yell at her mother, too. How could she allow a violent drunk near her daughter? But it wasn't my place to join the argument.

Trying to be invisible, I sidled across the room and sat beside Butt Crack at the table. Sweat popped out on my forehead, and my fingers curled into fists.

Brittany said, "If he moves nearby, I'm leaving home."

"You are so selfish," her mother yelled. "Do you know how hard things are for me? I'm tired of working two jobs. I could use a little help."

"He hasn't sent a cent of support money since we moved here, even though the courts ordered him to. He isn't likely to start helping now."

I wanted to applaud her insight. Instead, I murmured to Butt Crack, "How do you feel about all this?"

"Well." He drew a deep breath. "I have to admit, he was scary. But sometimes he was nice, too. I kind of miss him, you know? He's still my dad."

I nodded, although I didn't agree. Dean Meyer didn't deserve to be a dad. He beat his family. He hit

Brittany. I wouldn't give him a chance to hurt her again.

"Enough!" her mother roared. "This isn't your decision. He's already quit his job in Georgia. So you better make peace with the idea, because ready or not..." She stormed from the room and up the stairs.

Brittany looked thunderstruck. She covered her face with her hands. I stood and put my arms around her. I felt her tears through my shirt.

"It's all right," I said. "I'm with you."

"Why can't she understand?"

"Let's get some air." I drew her out to the porch. We sat together, holding hands. "That must have been a surprise."

"Yeah. I guess we've both had a shock this week."

"Instead of problem children, we've got problem parents."

She sniffled.

"I'm still your bodyguard, right?"

"Yes."

"Then you have nothing to worry about."

With a chuckle, she said, "What are you going to do, change into a wolf in front of him?"

"Darned right. I'll scare him so bad he won't even look at you."

"You'd do that for me?"

"I'd do anything for you. You're my–" I wanted to say mate, but I was afraid she'd laugh at me. Instead, I said, "Best friend."

She leaned her head against my shoulder. "You're my best friend, too."

Right then, I knew I wouldn't let her father touch her, even if I had to kill him.

When I went to school on Monday, I felt like a dark cloud hung over me. Too much was happening at once, and I didn't feel I had a handle on any of it. When Brittany joined me at lunch, however, all my cares flit away. I couldn't help but grin as she sat across from me at our table.

"All done with the school's grief counselor?" I asked.

She nodded. "More than done."

"That's good."

"I tried to talk to her about my dad, and she just kept saying to stay on topic. So I walked."

"The topic being the kidnapping?"

"Yeah. I mean, what good is having a counselor if you can only talk about one certain thing? I thought I was supposed to be able to confide in her."

"How about I get you an apple?"

"No." She sighed. "I'm not hungry."

"You look exhausted."

She shrugged and gazed across the room. After a few minutes, she said, "Look, are you my boyfriend or not? Because if you're not interested–"

I took her face in my hands and planted a kiss

right on her lips, in front of God and everybody. I pulled back an inch and said, "I am your boyfriend, your best friend, and your confidant. I'll be there for you. Always."

"Always," she breathed.

After that, she seemed more relaxed. Of course, word of the kiss spread through school like wildfire. When I walked into Shop, Maxwell punched me on the arm.

"Finally made your move, eh?" he chortled.

"'Bout time, dude," said Lonnie.

For the next hour, I endured their good-natured ribbing. By the end of the day, I was almost sorry I'd kissed her.

But that kiss filled and carried me on the long ride home. I replayed it, thinking of dozens of ways I could have made it better. I promised myself that next time it wouldn't be so public. Next time I would make it last.

As I rode up the driveway, I saw a white courier van parked by the house. The driver had a legal-sized envelope for Uncle Bob. I signed for it and went into the living room, turning it over in my hands. There was no return address, just the word confidential stamped in red beneath my uncle's name. I frowned, wondering if there was a way to open it without anyone knowing.

Just then, there came a knock at the door. I dropped the envelope onto a pile of newspapers and glanced out the window. A strange car sat in the drive. I groaned, expecting to find my parents on the porch. When I opened the door, however, I saw Brittany.

"Hi," I said, unable to keep the astonishment out of my voice.

She looked embarrassed. "I told Grandpa we had a study date."

"I'm glad you did. I could really use your help." I leaned out to wave at Grandpa Earle.

The tan Toyota backed out of sight. I closed the door. Then I slid my hands around Brittany's waist and pulled her close. I kissed her slowly, just as I imagined. Her mouth tasted like raspberry lipstick. Her body melted into mine, each curve filling an empty spot. My fingers buried in her hair, cupping her neck as I bent her backward, my lips pressing harder. Her arms twined around my neck.

Moments later, I realized I couldn't hold my breath any longer. What was I supposed to do? I didn't think it was cool to exhale in her face. Someone should write a guidebook.

I pulled away, murmuring, "I'm happy to see you."

"Hmm?" She smiled, her eyes half-mast.

With tremendous willpower, I released her. "Let's sit in the kitchen."

"All right." She seemed a bit dazed as she followed me from the living room. "I'm so glad you were home. I had to get out of that house for a while."

"Isn't your mother at work?"

"She's not the problem. I just feel so outnumbered." Brittany sat at the table. "Butt Crack is looking forward to seeing Dad again. And Grandpa, well, we're talking about his son. Of course, he wants to forgive him."

"How about a cold glass of chocolate milk?"

"That sounds good."

I set our drinks down and sat beside her. "Do you still plan to leave home?"

"Absolutely. I can't be anywhere around him."

"Because I thought maybe you could move in here."

"You mean live with you?"

"With me and Uncle Bob." My cheeks went hot. "You could have the bedroom, and I'd sleep in the living room. My uncle loves you. I'm sure he'd agree to it."

"Well, I don't know."

"Unfortunately, you couldn't bring all your stuff. It's a small room. But we could paint it purple, and you could put your Captain Jack posters on the wall."

"And it's not like it would be forever anyway," Brittany said. "Just until my mother realizes that I'm serious."

"Yeah." I looked away. I was thinking it *would* be forever.

"I might take you up on that." She put her hand over mine. "I'm still hoping my mother will come to her senses. It's like she's desperate for him to change. But people don't change." She pulled her hand away and took a long drink of milk. "My father used to do the weirdest things. Like he said the television was his and we weren't allowed to watch it. So when he wasn't there, he'd pull the batteries out of the remote."

"But couldn't you just turn it on and change the channels manually?"

"I know, right?" She shrugged. "So one day he came home unexpectedly, and there I was watching television. He hoisted that TV over his head and heaved it at me. It wasn't a flat screen or anything. It was heavy. It missed my head by inches, smashed into the wall and made a gaping hole. I would have been a little smear of brains. My mother came running out of the kitchen, yelling for him to stop, that she was the one who did it. He started pounding her, blood flying, and the whole time he kept looking at me and saying, 'See what you did, this is your fault.' I was thirteen years old. I just wanted to watch TV."

"What happened?"

"My brother was standing in the hallway with his eyes bugging out. I grabbed him and ran out of the house. I didn't know if Dad would start on us after he was done with Mom. We ran next door and called 911." She sighed and shook her head. "When the police got there, Mom was unconscious. He was standing over her, still yelling. They arrested him. But because I had never called the cops on him before, there was no track record. The judge ruled that it was a first time offense. Dad got ninety days. We moved down here while he was in jail."

"And your mother is willing to overlook that?"

"I don't know," Brittany said. "But I'm not."

The wolf in me growled. Neither was I.

FIVE

School cut into my daydreams. I alternated between fantasizing about kissing Brittany again and punching her father's lights out. In Trig, Mr. Varney yelled at me for doodling when I should have been listening. I could have laughed, since I was acing his class. I'm not super smart or anything; I'd just already covered the material in my school up north.

At last, it was lunchtime. My heart soared when I saw Brittany sitting at our table in the back of the room. I bought a turkey on rye and a couple apples, then headed toward her.

"Hi." I sat across from her. "I'm glad to see you. How are you feeling?"

"Just tired." Her eyes showed deep circles even her make up couldn't hide. "Can you come over on Saturday?"

"Sure. What's up?"

"My father is moving down this weekend." She sighed. "I don't want to face him alone."

I took her hand. "Don't worry."

"Silly, I know. It's not like this is the first time I've

seen him. He visited twice before. I'm always in charge of finding him a room."

"I can help with that. There are probably a few hotels in West Palm that will take him."

"Or Miami. He can stay down there." Her smile was fleeting. "I guess I'm kind of scared."

That sent my *Protect 'O Meter* over the top. "We'll handle it together."

She nodded, and then opened her yogurt. I unwrapped my sandwich and wolfed down half of it.

Brittany motioned with her chin. "How's your shadow?"

I glanced to the side and saw Eff sitting alone two tables over. "How the mighty have fallen."

"He sure looks different without his fan club."

"Maybe I should ask him to join us."

Her eyes sparkled over a sudden smile. "Don't you dare."

"Yeah. Come on. It will cheer you up." I moved as if to stand.

She grabbed my arm, giggling. "Cody."

I loved seeing her laugh. "So beautiful." I looked down at the table, embarrassed that I had said it aloud.

"You're too much." She finished her yogurt and stuffed a napkin in the container. "So, it's report card day."

"I thought that was Tuesday."

"This *is* Tuesday." Her nose crinkled with her smile. "You get good grades in your old school?"

"Fair." I shrugged. Actually, my grades had been slipping. I missed a lot of school because of unexplained fevers–which I now suspected had something to do with becoming a werewolf. "Are you expecting your usual B average?"

"That's the plan."

"You know, you don't have to keep throwing your grades. You could do better."

"I'd rather be invisible."

"Said the girl with purple streaks in her hair."

She smiled and got to her feet. "I'd better get to class. Talk to you tonight."

"You bet." I watched her walk away, feeling like the luckiest guy in the world.

Apparently, Uncle Bob hadn't forgotten it was report card day because he took off early for the occasion. He practically threw confetti as I walked through the door.

"You did great, boy. I'm proud of you." He clapped my back, brandishing a slip of paper. "You even passed Shop. I never saw what you built."

"It was just a birdhouse. No big." I hoped it would stay hidden in the back of my closet. I squinted at the paper he waved in front of me. The top of the form said my grade average was 4.0.

"This calls for a celebration." Uncle Bob grinned. "We'll go anywhere you want for dinner. The sky's the limit. How about that restaurant you like? What's it called? Outback?"

A thick steak sounded good. Or a nice rare hamburger. But what if Brittany showed up again? I wanted to be home in case she needed me. "How about we eat in? We haven't had Chinese in a while."

"Chinese it is." His smile widened.

The setting sun found us in the living room balancing a variety of cartons on our knees: Chicken Lo Mein, Kung Pao Shrimp, Mongolian Beef. Uncle Bob bought enough to feed a dozen people.

As we ate, we watched the local news. The weather girl predicted a sunny and dry tomorrow, as usual, and there were no traffic tie-ups. Then the newscaster reported more bear sightings near the city.

I nearly dropped my Lo Mein. I leaned forward, trying to catch every word. Eyewitnesses described the bear. Park rangers showed off their tranquilizer rifles. A garbage man decried the existence of unlocked garbage can lids.

Then a wildlife authority told the reporter that animals hibernate even without the presence of snow or frigid weather. In Florida, bears come out of hibernation in late March and early April. He said the best course of action was to steer clear, because they could be deceptively fast and decidedly grumpy.

That sounded like William. I wondered if he was the bear Butt Crack followed into the Everglades the time he nearly got himself eaten by a gator.

"Can Howard turn himself into a bear?" I asked.

"What?" Uncle Bob put down his carton to stare at me. "Why would you even ask that?"

"Brittany's grandfather told me that Howard was a medicine man. In school the other day, I read that medicine men could turn into animals. They said it was a myth, but then so are werewolves."

"Oh." He hesitated so long I knew the answer even before he told me. "Yes. Howard can become a bear. Other animals, too, I guess, but I only saw a bear. It's an ancient Navaho ritual, one not to be taken lightly."

"Could that be him on the news?"

"No. Of course, not. He's not about to change just to knock over a few garbage cans. Look, don't mention any of this to him. It's supposed to be a secret."

I nodded. "I'm good with secrets."

The local news turned into the evening news. I leaned back, rubbing my Buddha belly. We'd left the door open to let in the breeze, and I heard a vehicle outside that sounded like Howard's truck. Boots clomped up the steps.

Howard said, "Can I come in?"

"Grab a chair." My uncle motioned at our smorgasbord. "Have something."

"No, thanks. I've eaten."

"Kung Pao." I held up the container.

"Well, maybe just a little." Howard pulled a chair from the kitchen and dug in.

"What's up?" asked Uncle Bob.

"Not enough," he said. "I've been on the phone all day with homeless shelters and the like. They say they only report minors. Willie's a big boy. He could pass for older."

"What do you want to do?"

"What else can I do? I'm going to check them in person. Maybe I'll get lucky. I was hoping you'd keep me company."

"Let me get my shoes." He looked at me. "Do you need help cleaning up?"

"No, I've got it," I said. "Good hunting."

After they left, I turned off the television and stared at the blank screen. What was it with fathers? Brittany hated hers, William refused to talk to his, and mine was driving me crazy.

I pulled out my cell to call Brittany. "Hi. How's everything going?"

"Oh." She groaned. "You know."

"Wish I were there," I said as I carried leftovers to the refrigerator.

"What are you doing?"

"Cleaning up. Did you get your report card?"

"Yeah. You?"

"I aced every subject," I said. "Uncle Bob wants to nominate me for student of the decade."

She laughed. "Let me talk to him. I'll add my vote."

"He's not here. He went with Howard to search homeless shelters for William."

"That's not good."

"I don't get it. First Howard tells me his son is dead, then he goes on a quest to find him. He's really worried."

"Maybe you should tell him where William is."

"I can't. If I ran away, I wouldn't want anyone to rat me out."

She hesitated. "Yeah. Me neither."

"I hate lying to him, though."

"Maybe it will blow over."

I said, "Yeah," but I didn't think it would. The best way for it to end was for William to go home voluntarily.

After we said our good nights, I stared unseeing out the kitchen window. I went over the route we took to the cabin. The road took us north, west, south, then west again. I would save a lot of time just running through the woods in a straight line.

Before I could talk myself out of it, I walked out the front door and into the jungle encroaching upon our yard. The cool night welcomed me with flower scents. And the smell of mold. And dung. I walked through the crisp, fallen leaves. My favorite tree was a short distance away. I stripped and hung my clothes on a broken limb. Then I searched for the pull of my lunar mother.

It was getting easier to shift into a wolf without a full moon. Before I had to will the beast into existence. Now I just tap into the moon's power and ride it into my essence.

My wolf stirred at once. My chest expanded, and

my shoulders drew back. Hair sprouted from my knuckles and prickled over my arms. My muzzle grew, making my teeth ache and my eyes water with pain. At the same time, my ears slid to the top of my head with an almost liquid sensation.

And there I was, a wolf. The only thing to distinguish me from a real wolf was my negligible tail. That and the fact that I weighed one-fifty.

I bounded through the woods, ears perked, tongue lolling. I loved running through the badlands, feeling the swampy muck beneath my paws. The sounds of crickets and frogs, mice and raccoons surrounded me. Usually I chased a rabbit or two. Tonight I had to focus on finding William the Bear.

Within twenty minutes, I picked up the musky odor of bear hide mixed with the too-sweet scent of man. I smelled wood smoke even before I reached the sea of sawgrass.

The cabin on stilts jutted upward, a blot upon the starlit sky. I might have passed it, but the campfire gave it away. Crouched in the grass, I watched the shadow of a man move against the orange glow. After a moment, I approached.

He leaped up when he saw me, stumbling back over the log he'd been sitting on. He held out a staff as if it would protect him. It had feathers tied to its end. I grinned. He hadn't heard me, hadn't smelled me. His senses were no better than any man's.

I moved nearer the campfire. Smoke made me sneeze.

His eyes narrowed, and his posture relaxed. He wore pants that were laced not sewn and beaded moccasins. His chest was bare but for a medicine pouch on a rawhide cord. After a moment, he hopped onto the porch and disappeared inside the cabin. What was he getting? A rifle? Maybe a bow and arrow?

When he returned, he threw a ratty towel in my direction. At first, it offended me; then I understood. Feeling as if I was climbing out of mounds of fur, I shifted back into a boy. I wrapped the towel around my waist.

He said, "Why do you keep bothering me?"

"Just want to talk."

I sat on the log beside the campfire. The fire was small and surrounded by a double row of rocks. Neither it nor the log had been there when I visited previously. I smiled, noticing Brittany's grocery bags to the side.

"Your father knows you're missing," I said. "He's crazy with worry."

He shouted, "You told him! I knew it! None of you can be trusted."

"None of *us*?"

"You gave your word."

"And I kept it. If I told on you, your dad would be here right now instead of searching homeless shelters in West Palm."

"He's looking for me?"

"Everyone is. Your dad, my uncle. Your mother

brought Howard into it after the tribe turned Miami upside down."

He stared for a moment, then nodded. "I'm sorry they're upset. It is not my intention to hurt anyone. But this is something I have to do. I'm learning–"

"What? How to become a proper hermit?"

"I am living as my ancestors lived."

Right. Except for Brittany's Cheese Doodles. "Don't you care about your father?"

"I'm doing this for him as much as for me." William sat on the boulder leading to the porch. "He shamed us. Disgraced my family."

"What did he do?"

William gave me a hangdog look. "I wasn't there. My information has been pieced together from several sources."

"All right."

"My father was a Navajo living as a Miccosukee. He begged the tribal leaders to let him take his wife and son back to Arizona. But my mother is Story Keeper. Her loss would diminish the tribe. In despair, my father began to drink."

"A common story."

"But my father is not a common man," William said. "He is a medicine man with a responsibility to behave with decorum."

"A medicine man with the Navajo Nation."

"Exactly." He nodded. "His place within *his* tribe was just as important as hers. Friction wore between my parents. My mother needed advice, so she turned to my father's best friend."

"Joseph Achak," I said with sudden inspiration.

"Late one night, the barkeeper called our home to tell my mother he had taken the car keys away from my father. She couldn't go get him because he had the car, so she asked Joseph to bring him home. When Joseph walked into that bar, my father was drunk and belligerent. He accused Joseph of plotting against him and of having an affair with his wife. Words turned into blows. Somewhere in the midst of it, my father put on his bear pelt belt."

I drew in a sharp breath. "He turned into a bear right there in the bar?"

"He did. There was mass panic. People were injured trying to get outside; others were hurt trying to subdue him. Joseph has scars down the length of his back." William sighed. "The council ruled that because my father had the belt in his pocket, it was a premeditated act. They banned him from Miccosukee tribal lands. My mother's choice was clear. She could either betray her post with our people, or she could divorce him."

"Tough choice."

"So you see my shame. My father is a strong and powerful medicine man. He had courage enough to transform in a bar, and he could have done so again in the council chambers. Yet he did nothing to keep his family together. He sat meekly and allowed them to pass judgment upon him." William stood abruptly and threw a stone at the night. "I will never be meek.

I will become the world's most powerful medicine man. I will take back the respect of my tribe."

"So that's why you're out here communing with nature?"

"I try to." His voice cracked as if he was holding back tears. "I came to speak with the spirit of my grandmother. Sometimes I almost hear her voice in the trees."

"Why do you need to speak with her?"

"She was Story Keeper before my mother. Ninety years wise. Before she died, she was teaching me what she knew about the old ways."

"Can't you go to the local library?" I didn't understand all this Story Keeper stuff.

He shook his head. "The Miccosukee have no written language. Everything is verbal."

"Weird."

"Still I am making progress. I can put my being into a hawk and ride along as he flies. I can't control him as yet, but I can see through his eyes."

I shrugged. I didn't want to seem too impressed. "Cool."

"And I can summon nature. Watch." He picked up his staff and walked onto the dry lakebed. Chanting something indecipherable, he scratched a circle in the hard muck.

Immediately, the wind picked up. The campfire guttered. Sticks and leaves pelted my back as if caught in a whirlwind.

He was a shadow within a shadow of swirling

wind and debris. His voice fell to a deep rumble. "To me."

I sensed movement around me, something running. My nerves prickled. I stood.

He gave a final wordless cry. It echoed into silence. The wind cut like the drop of a curtain. William held the staff overhead. Facing him on the rim of his circle was a variety of animals. Rabbits, raccoons, opossum.

"Bunnies?" I burst into laughter. "You summoned bunnies?"

He scowled. "Someday it will be panthers."

"You've got this medicine man gig all wrong. It's not about bending things to your will. Howard works with nature to brew potions and stuff. He healed me when I was almost dead."

"I am a medicine man."

"You're a jerk, acting out fantasies in the woods. You'd be lucky to do half the things your father can do." I tore the towel from my waist and left it on the log. "Go home, William. Your mother is weeping."

Turning my back, I walked toward the woods, shifting into a wolf as I went.

SIX

"We should take some more food to William," Brittany told me as we walked slowly to the pick-up point in front of school.

I winced, glancing around, not wanting to talk about William the Bear in front of so many passing kids. School was over, and the entire student body spilled out the doors at the same time. "I don't think he wants us to do that."

"Why not? Who knows what he's eating out there."

"Let's not make it any easier for him. He should go home. His parents are worried."

"Then his parents shouldn't have made him run away. Besides he's our friend."

A hundred retorts came to mind–Friend? Where did you get that idea? Just because Eileen thinks he's our fishing buddy doesn't make it so. Instead I asked, "Hear any more about your car?"

A smile crossed her face, and her tone lightened. "All the parts are in. They are putting Baby back together now. I should have her soon."

"Good." I noticed a tan Toyota pulling up to the

pick-up area. "There's your grandpa."

"I better go. Call me tonight." She took several steps away, then bounded back and kissed me. It wasn't a passionate kiss, but it was enough to make me feel flushed all over and send my heart rate skyrocketing. "Bye," she said.

I smiled, feeling buzzed, and watched her get into the car. "Bye," I said belatedly.

I was so happy I wanted to whoop aloud. But that would be too weird, so I did it in my head. I hopped on my bike and took off for home. It was a perfect day. The sun was warm, and the breeze was cool. Flowers filled the trees. I couldn't imagine anyone not wanting to live in Florida.

Happy thoughts still filled my head as I turned onto my driveway. I skidded to a halt, staring at a white Cadillac parked near the house. Dad stood on the porch, and Mom rocked on the porch swing. My good mood curdled in my stomach as I walked my bike toward the house.

"Mom. Dad," I said. "What are you doing here?"

"Gah! It's so humid," my mother said. "I don't know how anyone can stand living in this state."

Then why did you come back? I dropped my bike on its appointed spot in the grass.

Just then, tires roared up the drive, skidding on the gravel. Uncle Bob jumped out of his truck, his face livid. "I told you, Marie. These unannounced visits will end. I will not have you hustling Cody off to be alone with you."

In less than a second, my mother was off the porch and streaking toward him. She looked like a banshee. "He is my son," she shrieked. "I will do as I please."

"You made me guardian," Uncle Bob bellowed.

"That can change. Didn't you get my paper-work?"

My stomach fell. The envelope the courier dropped off. Where had I put it?

"Your what? What paperwork?"

"Well, somebody signed for it."

I sidled around them, then snuck up the stairs, entering the house as quietly as I could. A cold lump formed in my throat as I stared at the metal TV table. The newspapers were gone.

"Lost the package, eh?" my father asked behind me.

I rushed around the recliner, checking between the cushions, looking on the floor. "I put it here. Then Brittany came and–"

"It's all right," he said in a soothing voice. "She'll just have more papers drawn up."

Outside, Uncle Bob yelled, "I will not give up custodianship."

Panic uncoiled in my gut. "Dad, I don't want to go. I like it here."

"We just want the best for you, son."

I pointed out the window. "All she wants is to hide me. The farther away the better. She doesn't want to risk a scandal. It might ruin her fundraisers."

"That's not true. We love you. And this doctor might be just what we need. If she can cure you, then you can come back here to live."

"What if she can't?" My voice wavered, and I bit the inside of my cheek.

"It's worth the risk, isn't it? Wouldn't you like to be normal again?"

I wondered what Brittany would say to that.

Uncle Bob burst through the doorway, my mother trailing. "No. Absolutely not. End of discussion."

"Then we'll see you in court," Mom snapped.

"I don't think threats are necessary," Dad said. "Let's all take a step back."

My mother looked furious. "David–"

"We didn't come here to argue," Dad said. "In fact, we planned to take you to dinner, Cody. Would you like to come along, Bob? We have reservations at Ruth's Chris in North Palm."

Mom spluttered. "Do you think that's all right? I mean, the restaurant expects–"

"I'd love to," Uncle Bob growled.

"Great." Dad smiled. "You'll need a jacket."

"Fine. I'll just be a minute. Don't go anywhere." His eyes burned into mine.

"I won't," I said, although I really didn't want to be alone with these two.

He stomped to the bathroom to wash up. I stared at my parents, trying to gulp the lump from my throat.

My mother fanned the back of her neck. "Whew. Don't you ever put on the air conditioning?"

"We will when it gets hot."

"Oh." She pasted on one of her fake smiles.

Why didn't I realize she was so shallow? Brittany said I was seeing her in a different light. I wondered if that was true or if she had changed.

"Have you been to Ruth's Chris before?" Dad asked me. "They're famous for their steaks."

"Sounds good," I murmured.

"You know, honey, you really should wear a jacket as well," said my mother.

"I don't have one."

"Of course, you do. It was in the box we sent."

"Mom, all those clothes were too small." By at least six inches, my thoughts added.

"Oh, of course." She looked embarrassed. "Well, do you have anything other than jeans?"

I frowned. I had what I dubbed my clown pants, the pink and gray flares I got at Howard's garage sale, but I wasn't about to wear them. I folded my arms. "No."

"He's fine." Dad hugged her shoulders. "Relax."

"This is an impossible situation."

"It wouldn't be if you'd just listen to me." My voice rose. "I don't want to leave."

She sighed, eyes closed. "How Bob could brainwash you in just four months–"

"He didn't," I cried. "I'm old enough to make my own decisions."

"We don't need to discuss this now," Dad said. "I just want to get through a nice calm dinner."

Uncle Bob entered the living room, dress shoes clicking. He wore a black suit and looked clean although unshaven. “Ready.”

“Excellent.” Dad beamed. “You’ll have to move your truck. You have us blocked in.”

“No problem. Cody, why don’t you wait on the porch?”

With a start, I realized he was afraid they might take me away while he was parking the truck. I grasped the porch railing with both hands. But no one tried to kidnap me. My uncle parked on the grass, and then the four of us got into my parents’ rented Cadillac. The backseat was spacious.

Our ride to North Palm Beach was uneventful despite the heightened emotions in the car. Uncle Bob seethed beside me. A potential for violence hung around him like a cloud, making my nose twitch. In the front seat, my mother was more anxious than angry. I smelled that on her, too. This ability to sense a state of mind in other people was new. It occurred to me that emotions were more than electrical impulses in the brain. They were chemical reactions, like hormones flooding the body, and my wolf was aware of them. I wondered what other powers I had that I didn’t know about.

Ruth’s Chris Steakhouse had a green roof that shone against the setting sun. The restaurant wasn’t much to look at from the outside, but inside it was all crystal and gold. Several patrons were already dining, although it was early, and the sound of silverware and plates grated against my nerves. A smiling hostess confirmed our reservation and told us we were in the Hobe Sound room. I wondered why we needed a private dining room.

We followed our guide, two by two. A thin sheen of sweat broke over me. I felt wary, like we were walking into a trap, and I glanced toward Uncle Bob, grateful to have him beside me. As we entered our room, I saw a large table draped in linen.

A woman sat there. She wore a ladies suit in an iridescent blue. The color reminded me of the glaciers I once saw during an Alaskan cruise. Her shoulder-length hair was as white as a frozen waterfall. She smiled and stood, holding her hand out to me.

"You must be Cody," she said with a funny accent. Scandinavian, I thought.

I stepped forward to shake her hand. I noticed her eyes were the same color as her suit, shifting between blue and gray. Her perfume covered any whiff of emotion my wolf could pick up. I smelled lavender and lemon grass and something deeper, something that reeked. A purple flower came to mind. Wolfsbane. I was certain of it. She wore wolfsbane so I wouldn't be able to read her. She knew about me.

"I am Dr. Torhild Saarsgard," the woman told me, "and I have come a long way to meet you."

I snatched back my hand. It *was* a trap. I glared at my parents.

My mother smiled. "Dr. Saarsgard runs the facility we mentioned. It's in Sweden."

"The Fjallen Mountains." The doctor nodded. "A beautiful place."

"What facility?" Uncle Bob asked.

Dr. Saarsgard turned an icy gaze toward him.

"Oh, excuse me," said my mother. "This is my brother, Bob. Cody lives with him for the moment."

"Then I assume I may speak freely?" She took her seat. "Come sit near me, Cody, so we may get to know one another better."

I'd just as soon sit by a snake, but I did. Uncle Bob sat on my other side and my parents across the table. As we settled, a waiter appeared with *pâté en terrine* and a chunk of Roquefort cheese. I remembered trying both during a recent trip to France with my parents. That was before my exile, when I was still the good son. I glared at the food, the memory offending me.

Another waiter poured a bit of blood red wine into the doctor's glass. Dr. Saarsgard sipped and nodded. "I took the liberty of ordering *hors d'oeuvres*. This dish is bland compared to *Leverpostej* of my homeland, but it is delicious nonetheless."

"Lovely," my mother said. Both she and my father accepted a glass of wine.

"Just water for me," I told the server.

"Water," Uncle Bob said.

He didn't smell as angry as before, but he definitely wasn't friendly. It wasn't like him. He knew almost everybody in Loxahatchee, called them by name, remembered whose kid just went to college or whose dog just had pups. He said it was good business practice. I swear if he ran for mayor he'd win, hands down.

After the waiters left the room, Dr. Saarsgard said, "Cody, I am pleased to speak to you about my mountain retreat. My wish is to assist people like you."

Uncle Bob bristled. "People like him?"

"Yes, Bob." She paused as if his name was funny. Actually, it *was* kind of funny the way she said it. "I speak of lycanthropes."

"A werewolf asylum."

"In one respect, yes. We currently have fifty guests. They live in comfort. All their needs are attended."

I thought of Brittany's crack about them having a dog run in back.

"What I offer is more than a common luxury spa, however," she said. "The Lindgren Institute is a medical facility. We have therapists and counselors to help the lycans accept who they are and why they are that way. In addition, we study the affliction. I am confident that we will have what we are looking for within a few years."

Uncle Bob stared at Mom. "Where did you find this woman?"

"We met by chance over twenty years ago at a medical convention in Akron." She sipped her wine, avoiding his gaze. "It wasn't easy to track her down again."

"No matter." The doctor laughed. "The important thing is I'm here now."

I wondered what kind of convention my mother would attend that would attract someone like Dr. Saarsgard. Then I remembered hearing that the reason Mom got into medicine was to find a cure for her wayward werewolf brother. Did that mean the doctor knew about Uncle Bob as well? No, I didn't think so. True to her word, Mom hadn't turned her brother in. As she said, he wasn't her responsibility.

"Did you bring the literature?" Mom asked.

"Yes. Of course." Dr. Saarsgard reached into a briefcase to pull out a folder full of financial reports and graphs. And brochures.

I groaned. More propaganda. She handed me a thick, full-color glossy booklet. I passed it to Uncle Bob without looking.

"Your institution has been in existence for a while?" my uncle asked as he turned the pages.

"Since 1941."

That perked my ears. I'd thought my parents were acting like Nazis, but I didn't really mean it. This woman, though... I sent her a covert glance. She was old, probably my mother's age, but not ancient. She couldn't have anything to do with Nazis, could she?

"All the guests shown here are werewolves?"

"Lycans," she said. "As you can imagine, it is an exclusive club. I would like to extend an invitation to Cody."

"Not interested," I said.

"I understand your reluctance," the doctor said. "You are yet a child. You need the security of what you know. Familiar places and possessions. I assure you, however, there is nothing to fear. You were meant to be with us."

"And my parents and friends can visit me?"

"I'm afraid not. Once admitted to the facility, you can have no contact with the outside world."

"You didn't tell us that," Dad said.

"It's the same in any rehabilitative center." She spread her hands. "I'm sure you understand."

My father looked toward my mother, who busily spread *pâté* on a triangle of black bread.

Uncle Bob turned another page. His increasing silence made me nervous. He was my only ally in all this. If they won him over...

Waiters swarmed the room, refilling our glasses and taking our orders. We three guys ordered Filet, rare, with potatoes au gratin. My mother ordered a stuffed chicken breast, and Dr. Saarsgard asked for Portobello mushrooms.

The food arrived quickly. Dad moaned about how good the steak was, but I barely tasted mine. For dessert, both my mother and the doctor ordered the Chef's Chocolate Selection, and Dad and Uncle Bob asked for cheesecake. I didn't want anything. I sat back in my chair, arms crossed, and waited for the ordeal to be over.

At last, Dad said, "I'm glad we had this chance to spend some time together. Cody, perhaps now you understand our intentions."

I said, "I'm not going."

He smiled. "You should at least tour the facility before making up your mind."

That thought made me squirm. If I went in for a tour, I doubted they would let me back out.

The ride home was more relaxed. Dad made small talk with Uncle Bob–how was work, did he like the area, did he worry about hurricanes? My mouth was so dry I couldn't have joined in the conversation if I wanted to. I kept glancing at the booklet lying on Uncle Bob's lap, and each time my stomach swooped.

Everyone was against me. No one understood. Running away to the Everglades seemed my only hope.

SEVEN

I tossed and turned that night. When morning came, part of me was happy to end the charade of sleeping, and part wanted to give it one more try. My fate was decided when my phone rang. I rolled out of bed, looking for the pair of Levis I left on the floor, fumbling for the cell phone in the pocket.

It was Brittany. “Morning. You up?”

“Pretty much,” I said. “Everything okay?”

“You didn’t call last night.”

“Oh.” I rubbed my eyes. “Yeah. I was–”

“Don’t bring your bike to school today. I can drive you home.”

“What, you mean–”

“Baby’s back.” Her voice smiled when she spoke of her car.

I flashed to her face; eyes sparkling, nose crinkling in the way that I loved. “That’s really–”

“We should celebrate.”

“Sure. What do you want to do?”

“I thought we could take more food to William.”

My shoulders sagged. I’d hoped never to see him again. “Nah, let’s not do that. There’s that new ice cream place. I'll buy you a milkshake."

"Come on. It'll be fun. Maybe he'll be home this time. I'm dying to meet someone who can turn into a bear."

"I really don't think–"

"Okay, well, I've got to go. See you at lunch."

"Yeah, but Brittany–"

She hung up. With a sigh, I closed my phone. Why was she so focused on William? He was the last person I wanted to see. Maybe I could talk her out of it. Or maybe he had gone to his real home and wouldn't be at the fishing cabin at all.

I slipped on my pants, found a clean tee, and headed for the kitchen. Mom had complained about the heat and humidity. It *was* pretty warm. I stood with the refrigerator door open, pouring a cold glass of chocolate milk, when Uncle Bob said, "Who was on the phone?"

The events of the night flooded back to me–Uncle Bob thumbing through the booklet, silently soaking in everything the good doctor had to say. I put the carton away and closed the refrigerator door. "It was Brittany. She got her car back."

"Good." He sat at the table. "Have a seat."

I grimaced, then covered it by taking a long swig of milk. In my gut, I knew he was about to tell me to pack my bags. I slouched in the chair, my long legs stretched into the center of the room.

"You didn't tell me your parents were badgering you about this werewolf retreat."

"I told them I wasn't interested. I thought that was the end of it."

"Obviously, it wasn't."

I gulped the milk, then closed my eyes, bracing myself.

"Cody, don't be sucked in by pipedreams. There is no cure for lycanthropy."

"What?" I stared. "But the booklet, the brochures."

"Trust me. I've tried it all. That Saarsgard woman is... wrong."

An image of a bubbling cauldron came to mind. Brittany and I had concocted a potion that turned a werewolf serial killer into a man so we could have him arrested. "They say that Indians can–"

"Oh, I went that route. How do you think Howard and I met? I went out to Arizona looking for the best. And he is the best. He can do amazing things. But he couldn't cure me." He leaned forward. "If you want to give this retreat thing a try, I won't stand in your way."

"I don't," I blurted. "I want to stay here. But Mom won't listen."

A knock came at the door.

My uncle stood to answer it. "Who could that be?"

For a moment, I hoped it was Brittany, wished she'd come to rescue me. My head swam with confusion. I'd been so sure the doctor had convinced my uncle to send me to Sweden. Now that I knew he had my back, I should be relieved. But all I felt was dread.

Uncle Bob returned to the kitchen with a grim expression and an envelope. He set it down as if it were a bomb. "Summons. My loving sister wants to terminate my custodianship."

My jaw dropped. "She's taking us to court?"

"Looks like it."

"We need a lawyer."

"I don't know any."

"She does," I said. "Expensive ones."

"Look, this is just a hearing. If it goes any further, I'll get a lawyer."

I dug my fingers into my hair. "This can't be happening."

"Forget it. I've got it covered. Why don't you get something to eat? We're running late."

I didn't want to eat, didn't think I'd ever want to eat again. How many times could my own mother betray me? Nothing was the way I thought it should be.

When I got to school, all I could think of was talking to Brittany, telling her all about the custody hearing and my mom. But, a funny thing, when I finally sat with her at lunch, I couldn't find the words. It was like if I spoke about it, it would become real. And I didn't want it to be real.

"How's your car?" I asked.

"Perfect." She smiled. "The trunk even opens easier. Remember how the hinges used to creak?"

"Good. Good."

"The color match isn't smack on, though. More

chartreuse than lime."

"That's great."

"And they attached bunny ears to the roof."

"Ah."

"Cody." She laughed. "Where were you?"

"Hmm?"

"Last night. You were supposed to call."

"Oh." I shrugged. "My parents showed up again. Remember that retreat they were going on about?"

"In the mountains?"

"Well, they brought the doctor to speak with me. She's kind of spooky."

"Like mad scientist spooky?"

"Exactly. She kept saying I'd be happier with my own kind."

"Would you be?"

I blinked at her. How could she ask that? "No."

"Then don't go."

I nodded. *What if I didn't have a choice?*

"We'll have to pick up some food on our way out to see William," she said. "Not much in our pantry."

"Come on, Brit. I'm really not up to this."

"You don't want me to go by myself, do you?"

I really didn't.

"It's all good," she said. "I just thought we could talk, that's all. Things we can't say here."

I sighed in defeat. "All right."

After school, I hurried to the parking lot to find Brittany leaning against her lime and chartreuse Beetle.

She spread her hands. “Ta-da.”

“Hey, it looks great.” I remembered the last time I saw the car, with its front end smashed and its windshield webbed with cracks. “You can’t even tell.”

“Hop in.” She climbed behind the wheel, then leaned across to pop the door for me.

The interior of Brittany’s car was like no other. Nearly every inch was *decoupaged* with bumper stickers: *The gene pool could use a little chlorine; Give me ambiguity or give me something else; Sure, I’ll share the road, you can have the part behind me.* She started the engine, then put Tool on the radio. I smiled, feeling that life was back to normal.

We stopped at Walgreens to pick up some food. Brittany chose a bag of shoestring potatoes, extra spicy beef jerky, and cheese in a can. Then she looked for a gallon jug of ice tea. When she put everything on the counter, I said I’d pay. I added a key ring with a plastic fairy on it.

“Aww.” She smiled.

“What are you grinning about,” I asked. “It’s not for you, it’s for Baby.”

“She’ll love it,” she said. “And so do I.”

She hugged my arm, causing my heart to flutter. I carried the bag, feeling like my head was a balloon bouncing along on a string. The trunk opened without a creak.

“See?” she said. “Easier.”

I nodded. Brittany made everything easier. I set the bag in the trunk. Then we climbed in the car and headed toward the Everglades.

"All right," she said. "I know you're dying to ask, so I'll just tell you. I got my father a room at the Sunshine Motel, the same place where those werewolves were holed up."

"He's still coming on Saturday?"

"Rain or shine."

"How are you dealing with that?"

"I'm not happy. But I've decided not to leave home." She glanced at me. "Yet."

"You don't deserve this. You had such a crummy childhood with the guy."

"You don't know the half of it. We were always moving. I never had any friends." She turned down the volume on the tunes. "My dad had these buddies. Real estate types. We used to live in empty houses that his buddies owned so they could prove residency until they got around to renovating or whatever. Some of them were rundown and spooky. I'd love it now, but I was like six at the time. It creeped me out."

"Sounds like an adventure."

"I remember this one house was really big and old, and we stayed there until the very last moment. I woke up one morning to see a crane and a wrecking ball in our front yard. We had like two minutes to pack up and get out. We stood on the sidewalk and watched them demolish our home. All of a sudden, I realized I forgot my doll inside. I started crying and saying we had to save her. Dad backhanded me across the face so hard I went flying. One of the construction workers came over to stop him, saying it wasn't right. That was the first time I wondered if my life was different. Up to then, I thought that all daddies bloodied their little girls."

I felt the wolf stir in my gut. A burning sensation. "I won't let him hit you again."

"*I* won't let him hit me," she said. "His reign of terror is over."

I clenched my fists, my lengthening fingernails biting into my flesh. I took a few sharp breaths to get myself under control. Every time Brittany talked about her father, I wanted to rip out the man's throat. Unlike her, I looked forward to his arrival. I wanted to face him, monster to monster.

We bounced along the dirt road toward the fishing cabin. I was distracted and only half listening to Brittany's chatter. She'd found new crystals to hang over her door, and her friend, Eileen, was teaching her a repulsion spell. Apparently, she hoped to build a psychic force field around her room.

As she turned off the engine, I gazed across the sawgrass at the shack on stilts. It looked as abandoned as ever, but I knew William was there. I smelled him.

I pulled the snack bag from the trunk and forged a path through the grass. Brittany followed, smacking insects from her legs. She wore black knee-high boots and a miniskirt to school that day. I focused on getting her through the clumps of vegetation and didn't notice William step onto the porch.

"Back again?" he called.

Chagrin swept over me. I stood there with my stupid Walgreens bag and had no clue why we were there. "This is Brittany. And this is William."

"Hello, William. It's n-nice to meet you." Brittany stammered and blushed, and I did a double take. She grinned at him like he was a rock star. "We brought food."

"Come on up," he said. "Less bugs in here."

He moved to the boulder that served as stairs and stretched out his hand. Brittany took it with a little giggle. My jaw dropped, and I cocked my head, staring. William helped Brittany onto the porch. He was shirtless, as usual, and his body-builder muscles rippled when he moved. I hadn't thought he was particularly good looking, but Brittany's reaction told me different.

"Do you like living here?" she asked in a voice that sounded way too shy.

"It's comfortable. Keeps the rain off my head. If we had any rain, that is."

She laughed as if he'd said something amusing. With a hand on her back, he guided her inside. I heard her say, "Where do you sleep?"

A growl filled my throat. I scrambled up the boulder and stomped to the doorway. Through the shadows, I saw a single room, shelves along the far wall, and a heavy wooden table with two chairs. Brittany and William stood together.

"It must be cold at night," she said.

"Usually, I sleep during the day and go out at night. I'm warm enough."

"Bear skin." She smiled, her nose crinkling in the way I thought was only for me.

"Here are your snacks," I said.

She appeared startled, as if she'd forgotten I was there. "A housewarming gift. We didn't know what you liked."

"Anything is appreciated," he said. "What I could really use is drinking water. With the drought–"

"We'd be happy to bring you some tomorrow."

"I don't know, Brit," I said.

She looked at me. "You don't have to come. If you're busy."

That's how I found myself at the fishing cabin after school on Friday.

William met us at the car as we arrived. Brittany wore another miniskirt, and so he carried her, actually *carried* her across the sea of sawgrass and over the threshold. I was left to lug two cases of Zephyrhills spring water and a freaking sleeping bag Brittany found in storage.

I slid my burden onto the dock and scrambled up from the dry lakebed. Their quiet conversation drifted from inside. I took a deep breath then stepped across the porch, hands on my hips, filling the doorway.

Brittany and William sat together at the table. They took no notice of my super hero entrance.

"Don't you worry about living out here alone?" Brittany asked. "It would make me nervous."

"None of us are ever alone." William motioned like a magician on stage. "There are spirits all around us. Protecting us. Showing us the way. People have learned not to listen."

"What if you get sick?"

"I don't get sick. I have these." He went to the shelves and took down a few items: a turtle-shell rattle, the pouch I'd seen him wear, and a pestle and mortar with two fat cigars sticking out of it.

Brittany gasped and glanced at me. "Cody didn't mention you were a medicine man."

"He doesn't believe I am."

"Who trained you? Is there, like, a medicine man school?"

"Training is ongoing, usually passed from father to son. I'm alone, so I've taught myself."

She touched the rattle reverently as he set it before her. Then she pointed at the pouch. "What do you keep in there?"

He opened the drawstring top and dumped the contents onto the table. Out fell a stone, a stick, a figurine of a bear, and a cloud of yellow powder.

I said, "Brittany, don't–"

She ran her fingers through the powder, then looked at me with a cocked eyebrow. "Corn meal."

"Mixed with corn pollen," William said. "If I feel ill, I breathe in a pinch, or if I am wounded, I rub a bit onto the injury."

"Magic," she breathed.

"We know magic." I crossed my arms. "We brewed an anti-werewolf potion in a cauldron we got from the garden shop."

"Oh?" William showed his teeth. They were bright white and even–like a flipping movie star.

Brittany said, "We meant to use it to turn Cody back into a boy, but poured it on another werewolf instead."

He spread his hands. "Why?"

"He was a serial killer." My voice rose as I pointed. "He kidnapped Brittany."

"I have to go to court about it, and then it will be over." She shrugged as if embarrassed. "Anyway, the potion worked fine. It turned him into a man and knocked him out."

"I've heard of potions like that." He stared my way. "But I'm surprised you meant to use it on yourself. Like me, you have a calling. Can you defy your nature so easily?"

I jutted out my jaw. Of course, I could. I looked at Brittany. I would do anything for her. Anything to keep us together.

Brittany motioned to the pouch. "What's the rest?"

"Cypress bark to bind my past, river rock for new beginnings." He picked up the figurine. "I carved this from the neck bone of my bear."

"Yours?"

"My spirit guide. I bested him in combat, claw

against knife. He gave me this." From the highest shelf, he withdrew the hide belt that allowed him to turn into a bear. The pelt was thick and dotted with bits of grass.

Brittany unfolded it. "Fascinating."

I wasn't impressed. Hands in my pockets, I walked along the shelves. There wasn't as much garbage as I expected. Evidently, this place was more a hostel than a designated party spot, and those who sheltered here respected it enough to pick up after themselves.

The shelves held cobwebs, leaves, and neat stacks of fishing magazines dated ten years ago. There were also rows of rusty-capped mason jars. They smelled like gasoline, probably meant to fuel a motorboat before the lake went dry.

"How do you do it?" Brittany asked. "Turn into a bear."

"Study and practice." William put the belt back upon the shelf. "I was fifteen years old when I first took my shape. I've learned much since then. My heritage is both Navajo and Miccosukee, and I have the advantage of drawing wisdom from both."

"So, you're kind of a sukee-ho?" I asked.

He looked at me as if I were a cockroach climbing the wall. I set down the fishing magazine I'd been thumbing through and took a step forward, my shoulders square.

"Tell me about these," Brittany said, picking up the stogies.

She said it hurriedly, as if she were trying to distract us. But I wasn't going to start a fight. Not unless he kept pushing me with his stare.

"Smudge sticks," he said.

"Oh, I have those," Brittany told him. "I got some from my friend. She's Wiccan. Do you use sage?"

"Mangrove leaves, sawgrass blossoms, a little sage." William smiled and sat across from her. "Has your friend taught you the proper way to smudge?"

"She just said to wave the smoke at the walls."

He shook his head. "In the wheel of life, there are four directions. Life begins in the east. The teenage years are in the south. Mid-life is in the west. When we finally reach north, we have done our many deeds on Mother Earth. We are ready to go to the Spirit World. Keep this in mind as you smudge. Start in the east, then move to the south. When you reach north, snub out the stick, but leave the ashes there. North is but the beginning of our next journey. The cycle continues in the Spirit World."

Brittany sighed. "I'll remember that."

"Are you cleansing a room or a house?"

"Room. My room, actually. I'm trying to ward off evil." She gave a crooked smile. "It's for protection."

I stepped forward. "I told you, I will protect you. I won't let him–"

"But what if you aren't there?" She looked at me, and for the first time I saw more fear than anger at the mention of her father. "I need to learn how to protect myself. If William can help, well, I'm a willing student."

William's chair creaked as he leaned back, teetering on two legs. He smirked as if he'd won this round.

I hated him.

EIGHT

Uncle Bob dropped me off at Brittany's house at noon on Saturday. I stood in the yard, my nose turned to the wind, trying to catch any unfamiliar scents. I didn't know if her father was there yet, and I didn't want to walk in unawares. Instead of smelling him, however, I caught a whiff of Brittany. I crossed the wide expanse of drying, tangled grass to the side of the house and then continued through the brush and trees out back.

I found Brittany staring at her little brother's club-house. At least, it had been his until some bees claimed it for their hive. Grandpa Earle tried to smoke them out with smoldering newspapers, but he didn't know about the stash of comic books inside. The place went up in flames. Now there was only a stinking, charred mess.

"You okay?" I asked.

She turned slowly, blinking as if coming out of a trance. She wore no makeup, and her eyes were puffy from either crying or lack of sleep. "I'm glad you're with me."

I wrapped my arms about her and kissed the top

of her head. She smelled of bath soap, toothpaste, and fabric softener. Beneath that, I smelled fear–not the panicked terror of a trapped deer, but the quiet certainty of a prisoner facing her executioner. "What are you doing out here?"

"Picking herbs." She opened her hand to show a fistful of crushed leaves.

I sneezed and took a step away, laughing. "What is that stuff?"

"Catnip, rosemary, chamomile, wormwood."

"Wormwood as in what we put in that potion? We went through all the trouble of buying it online and we could have gotten it in your backyard?"

"When Grandpa and Butt Crack put out the fire, they left the garden hose lying here. It's been dripping all this time–and the plants just sprang up. There's hyssop, oregano, sage, sorrel. Over there is cardamom and mint."

"Weird, huh?"

She looked at the burnt remains. "I found out about this place. You'll never guess what it was."

I moved a blackened plank with my toe. My nose twitched with the stench. I thought about the stacks of vintage comic books that met their demise in the blaze. "When I saw it, the walls were covered in vines. So maybe a garden shed?"

"It was a little girl's playhouse, all pink and white with gingerbread molding and shutters stenciled with flowers. Grandpa Earle built it in the seventies for his daughter. I never even knew my dad had a sister.

Aunt Lynette." Brittany shook her head. "Grandpa said there was a cobblestone walkway. My grandmother planted marigolds and dwarf geraniums along the edge. But when Lynette got older, she dug up the flowers and planted herbs. Green herbs. The kind you use in potions."

"Or in soup."

"She wouldn't need so many. These herbs are poisonous in large quantities." She looked at me. "I think my aunt is a witch."

What do you say to that? I pulled her close in a kind of all-purpose hug.

After a moment, she sighed and stepped away. "I have to get these to my room. He'll be here soon."

By that, I assumed the leaves were meant to protect her. It seemed foolish to think a plant could change her life, but no more so than the crystals and candles Brittany believed in, so I didn't say anything. We walked hand-in-hand to the house and entered the kitchen by the side door.

It smelled phenomenal. A pot roast was in the oven along with carrots, celery, onions, and potatoes. Three loaves of freshly baked bread cooled on the kitchen table.

From the living room, Brittany's mother cried, "Earle, please put these shoes away. You know how Dean likes a tidy house."

"He's my son," Grandpa Earle roared. "He'll like what I tell him to like."

Brittany dropped my hand. "I'm going to get

cleaned up. I'll just be a minute." She walked away, passing her mother without a word as the woman rushed into the kitchen.

I looked at her mother. *There* was the look of a trapped deer. Dalia Meyer wasn't just anxious as one might be for a drill sergeant's inspection. She was terrified. She lifted the lid from a pot on the stove and stirred what smelled like homemade apple butter.

I placed my hand on her shoulder. "Can I help?"

She flinched, and her eyes reddened. "Oh, thank you, Cody. You're such a good boy." She patted my cheek with fingers that felt ice cold, then lifted the spoon. "Taste."

It was spicy and smooth. I licked my lips. "He'll love it."

"For the bread," she said distantly. "His favorite. I better let it cool. Can you snap the beans? You're so good at that."

I washed to my elbows, then sat at the table with two pots and a bag of green beans. It felt good to be doing something. Mrs. Meyer bustled back and forth between the kitchen and the dining room, carrying plates and napkins. After a time, Butt Crack thundered down the stairs. He nodded to me, then pulled up a chair to help.

"You nervous?" I asked.

"It's hard not to be," he said, "the way everyone's acting."

From the next room, my super hearing caught Mrs. Meyer's murmured prayer. "God, help me through this day."

We were still snapping beans when a knock sounded at the door. The entire house stilled, as if the walls themselves were holding their breaths. I stared at the pot of bean stems hard enough to incinerate them. It occurred to me that it was the day before a full moon, and my wolf was itching to come out. Not a good day for an altercation.

Grandpa Earle opened the front door. "Hello, Dean. Come on in."

"Dad. Good to see you." There came the slapping sound of manly hugs. "Where's my family?"

"Cooking a scrumptious meal. Let's check the kitchen."

Footsteps moved toward us in the hall. Mrs. Meyer appeared in the dining room doorway, wide-eyed and pale, wiping her hands on her apron. I got to my feet, teeth clenched, and Butt Crack stood close beside me as if for support.

Grandpa Earle stepped into the silent kitchen, followed by Brittany's father. He was a tall man. Muscular–the type of muscle that denoted hard work rather than bodybuilding. Despite his size, or maybe because of it, he stood stoop shouldered in the center of the room.

My eyes narrowed as I sized him up. Here was the man who hit Brittany, the man who abused and terrorized her all her life.

Dean Meyer's gaze brushed mine but did not linger. "Something smells good."

In a tremulous voice, Mrs. Meyer said, “Dinner will be at one as you requested.”

“Thank you, Dalia. Will Dave and Jessica be joining us?”

“No. I told them you’d be here, but neither could make it. Busy lives.”

I remembered Dave and Jessica were Brittany’s older brother and sister. I wondered if this man had abused them, too. Were they also apprehensive about seeing him again?

“Where’s Brittany?” he asked.

“Upstairs getting ready. You know how girls are.”

Butt Crack said, “Hi, daddy.”

“Bartley.” His father spread his arms, and Butt Crack stepped hesitantly to his embrace. “Good gosh, boy, you’re bigger every time I see you. Are you into sports, yet?”

“I like volleyball.”

I nearly laughed. Butt Crack’s idea of volleyball was to sneak into the Sunspot and watch the nudies play.

His father motioned toward me. “Who’s your friend?”

“That’s Cody, Brittany’s boyfriend.”

I stepped forward, memorizing his stance, his thinning hair, the sweat clinging to his upper lip. I hated everything about him.

“He’s a good boy,” said Grandpa Earle. “Fixed my drippy faucet.”

“That so? Glad to meet you, Cody.” His gaze met

mine but I stared him down. He lowered his head. Submissive.

That's because he's a coward, my inner wolf snarled, still wanting a fight. My senses went into overdrive. I heard fear thrum in his veins. His heart beat like a rabbit's. The sweat rings around his armpits reeked. He was nervous and unsure, anxious to please. I frowned. Where was the monster that beat little girls?

Dean offered his hand, and when I took it, he didn't squeeze or try to exert dominance. Instead, he turned my hand over to look at my green fingernails. "Part of the family, eh? That's good. I'm... I'm glad she has someone."

Just then, Brittany entered the room. She looked beautiful with her eyes painted black and her lips blood red. The top of her hair was in orange spikes. Evidently, she used the method of ironing it with an orange crayon. She crossed the room to stand beside me. I was so proud I could have burst.

"Hello, dad."

"Brittany." He smiled. "You look... nice. I was so worried about you." He held out his arms to hug her.

She didn't move. "I'm fine. As you can see. No need to freak out."

"I should have been here."

"Why?" Her voice rose. "What would you have done? What could any of you have done to prevent it? Shit happens, and I got through because of my will and my wits. Me."

An uncomfortable silence filled the room. She was right. I'd done nothing to prevent it, although I should have known she was in danger. And it was her quick thinking that led the pack leader to our cauldron. I'd been little more than a distraction.

A distraction that saved her life, my wolf growled. Quit whining.

"Well, I'm here now," her father said in a low voice. "When you go to court, I'll be behind you."

Brittany stiffened, and I put an arm around her. *I'll be there, too*, my touch told her. *Don't worry*.

"Why are you all standing here in my kitchen?" her mother said with forced cheerfulness. "Go sit in the living room and be comfortable. Go on." As we filed out, she hissed, "Bartley, see to everyone's drinks."

I sat with Brittany on the couch. Her father took the chair, and Grandpa Earle sat in his favorite recliner.

Butt Crack said, "Who wants water and who wants Coke?"

"Nothing," Brittany said.

"I'm fine," I told him.

"I could go for a Coke, if you don't mind, son," said Mr. Meyer.

"Ditto," said Grandpa Earle.

Mr. Meyer leaned back, glancing around. "The old house hasn't changed much."

"It's a fine home," Grandpa said, "all thanks to Dalia and my two blessings. The yard could use some tending, though."

"I can help with that."

Brittany trembled. I took her hand and entwined our fingers. She didn't seem to notice. Butt Crack handed out two glasses of Coke, ice cubes clinking, then sat on my other side.

Grandpa Earle said, "So what are you planning to do for work now that you're here? Are you staying in road construction?"

"It's what I know." Her father shrugged. "Of course, laying asphalt in Georgia is not the same as laying it in Florida. That's due in equal parts to Georgia's swing in temperatures and Florida's rainy season."

So began a half-hour dissertation of the differing compositions of asphalt. I watched Mr. Meyer as he spoke. He was more animated and at ease talking about his profession. It was like work was his life, like he had nothing else. He was boring and pathetic "in equal parts."

"Brittany, dear, can you give me a hand in the kitchen?" her mother asked quietly when there was a break in the monologue.

"I'll come, too." Butt Crack jumped up.

"I can help," I said, moving to stand, but Brittany pushed me gently back down.

"You stay," she whispered. "Keep an eye on things."

"So, to make a long story short," Mr. Meyer said, "I have my application in with public works, and I hope to find something nearby."

"That's good. Good." Grandpa Earle grunted as he staggered to his feet. "Well, if you'll excuse me for a moment, son, I have to see a man about a horse."

I wasn't sure, but I figured that meant he wanted to use the bathroom. I was left alone in a room with the man I wanted to kill.

He took a swig of his watery Coke, the remaining ice tinkling lethargically, and looked around with feigned interest. After several moments, he asked, "Did you and Brittany meet at school?"

"Yes."

"She's a bright girl. Could probably get better grades."

I bit back a response. Brittany once told me that she was punished for good grades because he didn't want a snooty know-it-all for a daughter.

"I suppose she told you about me," he said.

"Some."

"I don't blame her for hating me. But the past is past. The best I can do is start over."

"Commendable," I said. "When did you have this change of heart? In prison?"

"Actually, it wasn't until several weeks after I got home. I'd get back from work, and the place would be empty. So quiet. One night it hit me. Family is important, and I hadn't treated mine very well."

I stared at him with narrowed eyes. He took another swig.

"I quit drinking cold turkey," he said, "but it was

hard. I had to join one of them support groups."

"Maybe you should have found something on anger management," I muttered. I surprised myself, saying it. I didn't usually spout off to adults.

"What do you mean?"

"Well, it's easy to stay calm in a silent house, but when you start hanging out with people and they don't do what you say..." I spread my hands, letting my words hang in the air.

"Yeah." He rested his forearms on his knees, swirling his glass. After several moments, he said, "It's just that she might have died, and I wouldn't have known about it until I heard it on the news. I just care about her, you know?"

I did know. What I wasn't sure of was whether he could lie to my wolf. Because I didn't sense a threat from him. He was nothing. Prey.

"Dinner's ready," Brittany's brother said from the doorway.

I stood, stretching my back after sitting so long, then followed Butt Crack from the room, leaving Mr. Meyer alone. As I reached the kitchen, Mrs. Meyer shoved two baskets of freshly sliced bread into my hands.

"One on each end of the table, please."

"Mmmm. Smells good." I gave her an encouraging smile and carried the baskets into the dining room.

Food loaded the table: pot roast and gravy, roasted vegetables, green beans with almonds.

Brittany stood beside Grandpa Earle at the head of the table. I took my place, making sure to stand between her and her father. Butt Crack and his mother moved to the other side, leaving the end for Mr. Meyer.

When he finally showed, we sat simultaneously.

"It looks wonderful, Dalia," he said.

"Dean, will you say grace?" she asked.

Relief swept through me. Last time, I was the one to say grace. It didn't turn out as well as I'd like. I took Brittany's hand and bowed my head.

Mr. Meyer cleared his throat. "Lord, we thank you for these gifts aplenty, and for Dalia's deft hand at cooking. And I thank you for the blessing of my family, and that Brittany is safe among us."

"Amen," Grandpa Earle said. He passed around the still-warm apple butter.

Dinner was solemn and uncomfortable. Grandpa Earle didn't tell one of his UFO stories. Butt Crack didn't talk about the latest happenings at the Sunspot. Brittany didn't speak at all and barely ate, although the meal was delicious.

I kept one eye on her father, my senses piqued. But even when Mrs. Meyer juggled the coleslaw and dropped the serving spoon, splattering creamy goodness all over his shirt, he didn't become angry. I relaxed. Everything was going to be all right.

After our dessert of triple chocolate cake and ice cream, Brittany's father said goodbye. Grandpa Earle and Brittany's mother walked him to the door while we kids cleared the table. There was a mountain of dirty dishes. I wanted to tell Brittany the good news that she didn't have to worry about her father anymore, but she seemed pre-occupied and moody, so I thought I'd better wait.

"Thank you, children." Her mother hustled into the kitchen, retying her apron. "I can take it from here. Why don't you sit on the porch? It's a lovely day."

"Is he gone?" Brittany asked.

"For the moment."

Brittany pulled me from the room.

Over my shoulder, I said, "Thank you for the delicious meal." I didn't hear her reply.

Brittany and I went outside and sat together on a white wicker loveseat that was so small it forced me to drape my arm around her back. The afternoon was sunny and warm, but a breeze kept the shady porch comfortable. I was fit to bust, wanting to tell her what I learned.

I said, "That was anti-climactic."

"You think so?"

"Sure. You saw him. There's no aggression left. He's just a lonely old man."

"Lonely."

"I think you should give your father another chance."

"What?" She pulled back, although there was little room to do so. "You're taking his side?"

"I'm not taking anybody's side," I said through a

prickle of alarm. “But I was talking to him and–”

“You think one conversation gives you insight?” Her voice rose. “He’s a time bomb waiting to blow.”

“I understand, but–”

“You don’t understand anything. You have no idea what it was like to live with him, to dread going home, to wake up in the middle of the night and hear him hitting my mom.”

“But he’s changed. You’re safe. I thought you’d be happy.”

“And I thought you’d always be there for me. I thought you’d put my feelings first. I never thought you’d betray me like this.”

Betray? “You don’t understand. I was just trying to make you feel better.”

“Thanks for nothing.” She stood. “And besides, you’re a fine one to talk about giving parents a chance when you don’t even want to be with yours.”

“Not if they want to take me away from you.”

“Just go, Cody. I can’t look at you anymore.”

“Brittany–”

“Leave!” She went into the house and slammed the door.

NINE

I stood in Brittany's yard gazing at the house, fully expecting her to bounce down the steps, laughing at her little joke. But the door stayed shut. She really kicked me out. After a while, I lowered my head, tucked my proverbial tail between my legs, and headed home. I could have called Uncle Bob for a ride, but I needed time alone. What had I done to make Brittany so mad? I only wanted to help.

Birds sang as I followed the dirt road that ran alongside her house. The ground was so dry I tasted dust. Trees rustled overhead, sounding like paper crumpling, and there was a steady, slow rain of dead leaves.

I thought about Brittany's father, remembering everything I noticed about him: the slumped shoulders, the wimpy handshake, the sheen of nervous sweat on his upper lip. Was Brittany right? Was he faking? My wolf sense said no. But I was new at this reading emotions thing. Maybe I'd been too quick to judge.

The dirt road dumped me onto a flat, smooth, two-lane highway that stretched forever in either direction. This area was popular with joggers and horseback riders. In spite of that, cars roared by, traveling way over the speed limit. I wanted to chase one, just to see if I could catch it. I probably could, but that would be too weird.

With my hands jammed in my pockets, I walked toward home. I decided to wait until tomorrow to call Brittany. That would give her a chance to calm down. I felt certain that once she had a good night's sleep, she would realize I was right. Her father had changed. He wasn't a threat. She didn't need herb garlands or smudge sticks, and she didn't need William the Bear. Especially not William.

A rusty, old pickup pulled to the side and stopped next to me. I was so deep in thought it took a moment to realize it was Howard. He had a feathered staff sitting in a gun rack in the back window, and beads and bones hanging from the rearview mirror.

"Hey." I leaned in through the passenger-side window. "What's up?"

"I was about to ask you," he said. "A thundercloud hovers over your head. Do you intend to break this drought on your own?"

"As if I could."

He sighed. "You have friends, young Mai Coh. Burdens are not meant to be carried alone."

"I know, but–"

A silver limo drove by. It went real slow, probably because Howard wasn't completely off the road. As it passed, the back window opened partway. I couldn't see who was inside, the windows were tinted too dark, but a faint smell leached out.

Alarm shot through my rigid body. A million tiny hairs prickled in waves. I was in danger. I had to run.

"Cody! Peace!" Howard shouted.

I looked at my hands. My nails were thick and long, and my fingers left dents in the window frame. I relaxed my grip, staring at the receding taillights. "That car."

"Another limousine. It seems nowadays parents rent a limo for every minor event so their little girls arrive in style. They give the rest of us a bad name when we can't keep up."

That wasn't it. My eyelids fluttered as red haze faded from my vision. Where had I smelled that scent before?

"Are you all right?" he asked.

"Yeah. Sorry about your door."

"You could use a cup of tea."

My stomach knotted with the thought of Howard's snake blood tea. "I'll pass. Could you give me a ride home?"

"Hop in." He put the truck in gear. "I need to speak to Bob, anyway. I hope to join your excursion tonight. Maybe we could all look for William."

I frowned as I settled into the seat. Did that mean he planned to turn into a bear? I wouldn't mind seeing that. But I just didn't feel like going out for one of Uncle Bob's werewolf lessons. Or worse, a search for William. I had too much on my mind. "Can I ask you something?"

"Certainly."

"Have you ever heard of anyone using their wolf sense as a kind of lie detector?"

"What do you mean?"

"Lately, I've been sensing other people's emotions. You know, like if they're wary or confused, if there are things they aren't saying. I just wondered if these assumptions are trustworthy."

Howard paused before answering. "The wolf is wise and shrewd. Many of my people aspire to emulate them."

"Then you think my instincts are right."

"What do you think?"

My fists clenched. "I think Brittany's father is a pathetic coward who has crawled back into her life looking for mercy."

"Did you tell her this?"

"She wouldn't listen. She thinks I'm taking his side."

"The memory of sunset bleeds upon morning."

Another of his indecipherable sayings. I grit my teeth with impatience. "What should I do?"

He shrugged. "This close to the full moon, I would trust my gut."

I nodded, gazing out the window. Right then, my gut warned of impending doom.

When we pulled onto the driveway, Uncle Bob stepped outside. His smile faded when he saw me. "You're home early. Everything okay?"

"Cody and Brittany had a spat," Howard said as he climbed onto the porch.

"Sorry to hear that," my uncle told me. "Nothing serious, I hope."

"She'll come around." I stepped passed him, then stopped in the open doorway. "Listen, I think I'll stay in tonight. You go on without me."

My uncle looked incredulous. "But it's the night before the full. Come on. I'm sure it will make you feel better."

I doubted that, especially if they were going to look for William. "I'm not in the mood. I think I'll get some studying done." That always got him.

"Well, I can't force you, but–"

I walked away before he could finish, went to my room, and dropped on the bed. I didn't know what was more unnerving–Brittany's anger or that smell from the limo. But one thing was for sure. I wasn't in full control of my wolf. I almost shifted right there on the side of the road.

After a while, Howard and Uncle Bob moved into the kitchen, probably for some tap water instant coffee. They spoke in low voices, but my super hearing picked up every word. My uncle worried that I wasn't normal, as if being a werewolf was normal in the first place, and Howard reminded him that everyone was different and he shouldn't expect me to fit in his own category.

With a sigh, I pulled my laptop from under the bed and booted it. Best to look busy. I went to chat to see if Brittany was on–often on these cloudless days, she was able to pick up Wi-Fi from the Sunspot. But she wasn't online. I was almost glad. Didn't know what I was going to say to her anyway.

On impulse, I googled *Doctor Torhild Saarsgard.* I hoped for a personal website. No joy.

However, her name came up twice in the Newspaper Archives: once in an obituary for her son, Christoph, who died of leukemia in 1985, and again in 1990 when she reopened her father's research facility in the Fjallen Mountains. Now called the Lindgren Institute.

Was Daddy Dearest involved in all this? I cross-reffed Saarsgard and Lindgren and came up with Dr. Brynjolf Lindgren. There were about twenty articles about him in the Archives, but they were all in Swedish or Greek or something, so I looked him up on Wiki.

The article was short, and I scanned it quickly. Dr. Brynjolf Lindgren, known for his work in biochemistry with Ivar Wehler during World War II, left his fortune to his only daughter, Torhild, after his acquittal for war crimes in 1962.

What?

"Last chance." My uncle stood in my bedroom doorway. "Are you sure you don't want to join us?"

I blinked at him, surprised at how dark it had become. "No, I mean, yeah, I'm fine."

"All right." He tapped a drumroll on the doorframe. "See you in the morning."

I nodded, barely hearing him leave. War crimes. That had to mean Lindgren was a Nazi, didn't it? But he wasn't German. Maybe he was one of the scientists drafted during the war. I turned back to the article. Lindgren died in prison before they exonerated him. What was he accused of doing?

I looked up the Lindgren Institute but got no hits, so I typed in Lindgren's partner, Ivar Wehler. He warranted a much longer article. Wehler was a Danish scientist working with the Germans to build a super soldier by transplanting wolf glands into unsuspecting volunteers. He was considered the Dr. Moreau of the time. There were a few grainy photos of hairy mutants and paragraphs of medical jargon about his breakthrough work in hormones.

Was Saarsgard continuing her jailbird father's research? Was she trying to create some sort of human werewolf hybrid? That must be it. She wasn't running a posh retreat. It was a secret laboratory complete with mad scientists and gullible werewolf volunteers.

Did my father know about this? Was he aware of the kind of place he wanted to send his only son? Certainly, my mother knew. My mother knew all sorts of things she wasn't saying. She and Saarsgard probably met when my mother was still trying to cure lycanthropy. Maybe Saarsgard tried to recruit her for the Institute.

A ball of rage exploded in my chest. I slammed the laptop closed, barely containing the impulse to smash it against the wall. My fists clenched in my hair. I wanted to call my parents and confront them with all the horrible images in my head. I wanted them to be shocked, and appalled, and sorry, so very sorry. I wanted them to convince me they were innocent.

But what if they weren't? I stared at the phone in my hand. I needed to play dumb. If they realized I knew what they were up to, they might accelerate their plans. All I could do was to make sure Uncle Bob continued as my guardian. But how?

I needed Brittany. I needed to hear her voice, to have her calm words surround me. I punched in her number and listened to it ring. It went to voice mail.

"B-Brittany," I stammered, "it's me. Um, Cody. I really need to talk to you. Something's happened. Please call me back."

I tossed the phone onto my bed and stared at it. I imagined Brittany doing the exact same thing. She wasn't taking my calls. She didn't want to talk. It was over.

"Noooo," I cried, the sound rising into a garbled wail. I couldn't live without Brittany, couldn't face my screwed up life without knowing she was there rooting for me, believing in me.

But she didn't. Nobody did. I was a freak. The amazing wolf boy. Astound your family and mystify your friends.

Without warning, my muzzle grew. It felt like it would pull off my face. My teeth ached so bad I couldn't close my mouth. Drool spilled down my chin. I clawed my shirt, shredding it, my nails raking my chest. This wasn't right. I hadn't given the wolf permission to come out. I tried to stop, but it was too strong. My shoulders hunched, and my hips narrowed, throwing me to hands and knees. My back felt on fire as coarse fur popped through my skin.

The phone rang. I stared at it, slobbering and growling. I even reached out a paw as if to pick it up. But I was too far gone. I couldn't answer. The ringing stopped. Lifting my head, I howled.

A killer headache attempted to pull my brain out of my eye sockets. Morning sunlight danced on my head, making me cringe. I was naked and human, still in my room. The remains of my shirt littered the floor. My Levis looked okay. I slipped them on, then searched my bed for the phone. When I checked missed calls, my heart fell into the empty pit of my stomach. It hadn't been Brittany returning my call last night, just some guy who wanted to know if I wanted my carpets cleaned.

I covered my face with my hands. Why hadn't I been able to control the shift? I felt so superior before, turning into a werewolf on command. My uncle called me a super wolf. An alpha. Maybe I wasn't as special as he said.

At the thought of my uncle, I tested the air. He

was home. I could smell him. Embarrassment crept over my cheeks. I picked up the pieces of my shirt, hoping he hadn't figured what happened. But he would have. The stink of wolf in my room was pretty noticeable.

A car rolled up the driveway, gravel crackling under its weight. At first, I hoped it was Brittany, but this was no VW. I put on a clean tee and hurried to the front room, trying not to wake Uncle Bob. Through the window, I saw a silver limousine. The same limo I saw yesterday. A prickling sensation gathered at the back of my neck. My wolf warned me to run, but I wasn't too pleased with the wolf right then, so I smacked it back down.

I opened the door. The soft morning light stabbed like daggers, darkening my mood. As I stepped onto the porch, a pudgy little limousine driver got out, scurried around back, and opened the car door. Dr. Saarsgard appeared. I wasn't too surprised. She wore an expensive-looking off-white business suit, and her silver hair was in a bun. She reeked of wolfsbane, the scent I noticed earlier.

"Good morning, Cody," she said. "I see you are an early riser, like me. Can we sit and talk?"

She looked at me expectantly, but no way was I letting her into my house. I nodded at the porch steps. "Be my guest."

She didn't take me up on it, just stood on the walkway with me above her on the porch. "I know, of course, that tonight is the full moon. You must be frightened at the prospect of turning into a wolf against your will. It must be a terrifying and painful experience."

"Thanks for your concern. That's really nice of you. Was your father that considerate, you know, when he was dissecting werewolves?"

For a fraction of a second, alarm crossed her eyes. Then they hardened again. "My father was a brilliant scientist conscripted into Hitler's army by force. Yes, he was studying werewolves. Hitler wanted to create enhanced soldiers by incorporating the werewolves' heightened senses, strength, and healing abilities. The program is, of course, defunct. However, I am now continuing my father's research in the hope of acquiring a drug or vaccine that will grant ill children the ability to heal themselves." Her voice caught dramatically. "I lost my only son to leukemia."

"How noble. If you're done with the soap box, I'll just take it back to the laundry room."

"You don't believe my motives are pure?"

"Sure I do. And no werewolves were harmed in the making of this movie."

She gave a smile that had no humor in it. And just like that I knew: they *were* experimenting on people, maybe even killing them.

I growled, "I bet you aren't even a real doctor."

"Not a medical doctor, if that's what you mean. My degree is in psychiatry. I also have degrees in thaumaturgy and biochemistry."

"Biochemistry. Like your father."

"Enough about me," she said. "I came to warn you about your involvement with Native Americans. You spend too much time with that shaman. What is he? Seminole? Miccosukee?"

Was she talking about Howard? I didn't hang with him. Then it struck me. She meant William. She'd been spying on me. "Navajo," I said.

"You must be cautious around such people. They have no love for your kind. They practice the old magic. This one, this person you think is a friend. He wields much power and has no idea of the consequences."

My stomach twisted–the wolf squirming. *Either fight or flee*. "You actually believe in magic?"

Her eyebrows rose with her first true smile. "I've seen things you wouldn't believe." Without another word, she got into her limo. The driver closed her door and drove away.

Behind me, Uncle Bob said, "Seems she doesn't like Howard."

I knew she wasn't referring to Howard, but I didn't correct him. "She said she had a degree in thaumaturgy. What does that mean?"

"I don't know. Magic. Holistic healing."

I shivered as if ice filled my stomach. "She scares me."

"Well." He clapped me on the shoulder. "You didn't sound scared."

We went inside. I collapsed onto a chair at the

kitchen table. My head throbbed, and now it spun, too. What kind of experiments were they running at the Lindgren Institute?

Uncle Bob set a glass of chocolate milk before me, then busied himself with making instant coffee at the sink. "Do you have plans today?"

I gulped half the milk then set the glass down. "No plans."

"Good." He sat at the table. "I was hoping to spend some time together. We can grab some breakfast at the *Coffee Café*."

I groaned. "I'm not hungry. I had a bad night."

"Yeah." He nodded. "Me, too. Howard had me looking for Willie. For some reason he's convinced he's in the area."

I sat straighter. "You searched the forest?"

"The city. He had me in the back of his pickup hoping I'd catch a whiff of the boy. I don't need to tell you how difficult that is with exhaust blowing in your face."

"He must be really worried."

"Frantic. Made me think about how I'd feel if something happened to you." He shifted in his seat, making the chair creak. "Anyhow, maybe after we shower up and eat, we'll both feel a little more human. Then I figure we should head out to the mall and buy you some clothes."

"Wellington?" I grimaced. The last time I was there half the football team jumped me and beat me to a pulp. "Good times."

"I know." Concern showed in his eyes. "But it's the only place I can think of to get you a suit."

I blinked in surprise. "Off the rack?"

He laughed. "Where did you used to get things like that?"

"Angelo's." I smiled, remembering the cramped, lint-strewn shop. "He was a little pip-squeak of a guy, used to cluck his tongue as he measured me. A week later, I'd have my suit."

"Well, we can't afford Angelo, but you'll look just as good."

"Why do I need a suit?"

"The court hearing."

"Oh. Yeah." How could I forget? I lowered my forehead to the table, my head pounding harder.

But he was right; after I showered and shaved, I felt a little better. As I climbed into his truck, the sun was shining and the birds were singing enough to fool me into thinking it would be a nice day.

The *Coffee Café* was my uncle's favorite place to eat. He kept a running tab for me so I could stop in after school. When we opened the door, the place smelled like pancake syrup and bacon, and my stomach growled in spite of itself.

"Bobby," Anne, the waitress, called. "Nice to see you, hon. Sit anywhere you like. I'll be with you in a moment."

We took our pick of booths beneath the windows. Sunday morning was usually a busy time, but we'd gotten in before the church crowd.

Anne set a steaming cup of coffee and a cold glass of milk before us. "How are you two doing? Good? What can I getcha?"

"I'll have two scrambled and bacon," I told her. "No grits today."

Uncle Bob nodded. "The same."

"Coming right up." Anne bustled away.

I sipped my milk. I didn't really like milk, but my uncle maintained that it was good for a growing werewolf's bones.

He watched me for a moment. "Howard told me why Brittany was mad."

"She was more than mad. She kicked me out."

"I never met her dad. What's he like?"

"Nothing like I expected. After everything she told me about him, I thought he'd be this hulking monster, but he was wimpy. You know? Normal." I set down the glass. "Can I trust my wolf sense on this one?"

He blew out a breath. "The wolf will always be sizing people up, mostly to see if they're a threat. Kind of a territorial thing. In my experience, it's always right. The trick is in knowing if it's the wolf talking in your head or some nagging little voice of your own."

"So I could be wrong about him."

"Like I said, I never met the man."

"What should I do? Send her flowers?"

"That's good for a start. What girl doesn't like flowers?"

I leaned on my elbow, my chin in my hand. "I'm

going to have to apologize, aren't I?"

"When dealing with women, it's always best to apologize." He grinned. "Even when you're right."

He fell silent, and I stewed. It wasn't enough that I had to deal with my parents and their lousy custody hearing. Now I had to worry about a lunatic scientist spying on me. Top the list with Brittany suddenly hating me, and I was trounced. I didn't see how the day could get much worse.

Anne brought our order, and my uncle dug in. I picked at my eggs, barely tasting them. After a while, Uncle Bob got up and swiped a newspaper off the counter. He read the sports page while he finished his coffee. I decided to call Brittany as soon as I got home. Even if she wouldn't take my call, I'd keep leaving messages on her voice mail–I'm sorry, I'm sorry, I'm sorry.

When we got to the mall, the lot was already filling up, so we had to park a distance from the main entrance. The mall was bright and colorful, with escalators leading to the second floor and potted palm trees reaching for the skylights. It was a designated hangout, and kids stood around in groups along the walkways. My wolf sense hiked up a notch. I didn't expect anyone to jump me, but I hadn't expected it the first time, either.

We walked into Macys. I didn't go into department stores often, my mom didn't think they were cool, and I was impressed by how big the place was. It took some time to find the men's department, but when we did, Uncle Bob bought me the whole outfit: suit coat and pants, shirt and tie, even shoes. Maybe he was as nervous about the court hearing as I was. I insisted upon carrying the bags. It was the least I could do.

As we exited onto the second floor, my wolf sense prickled. I paused. Laughter and conversation swirled around me. Perfumes and aftershaves bombarded my nose. Over the railing on the first floor, I smelled the food court gearing up for lunch.

Then I saw Brittany.

At first, I thought I was mistaken. I rushed along the balcony, trying for a better view. She was really there. She walked with Eileen, heading for the escalators. Part of me noticed that Eileen wore clothes, an improvement over the first time we met. But a bigger part marveled at how beautiful Brittany was. Her dark hair was tipped in green and gelled to show off the angular cut. Her customary black t-shirt clung to every curve.

I took a breath to call to her, but my greeting died in my throat. I couldn't let her see me. She'd think I was stalking her.

I put my hand on Uncle Bob's back and hustled him into the nearest store. "Let's go in here."

"Wait! What are you doing?"

I rushed him deeper inside. "Just pretend to look around."

"May I help you gentlemen?" a salesgirl asked.

I stopped dead, the Macys bags slipping from my

hands. Oh my God. We were in a ladies underwear shop. I was surrounded by filmy, pastel nightgowns. Across the aisle was a table loaded with panties. Three for ten. My face turned so hot, I thought it would catch fire.

Uncle Bob said, “My nephew wanted to look at something.”

The salesgirl smiled. “A gift for your mother?”

Not likely. “I don’t want to buy anything. I just wanted to–” I took a step back, half turning, looking toward the door, and in the process banged smack into an armless mannequin sneaking up behind me. It wobbled, and I reached automatically to steady it, my hand closing over the cup of its bright pink bra.

“I’m afraid I have to ask you gentlemen to leave,” said the salesgirl, her face stern.

“But you can’t,” I blurted. “I’m trying to–”

“Is there a problem?” A woman, probably the manager, joined us.

“We were just leaving.” Uncle Bob picked up our packages and marched me toward the door. “What was that all about?”

I gasped. “You don’t understand.”

Just then, Brittany and Eileen crossed the store-front. Brittany’s eyes narrowed as she saw me.

“Hi, Brit,” Uncle Bob said.

With a growl that would chill a werewolf, Brittany said, “You’d better not be buying me anything, Cody Forester, because I am not interested.” She and Ei-leen strode away.

"Wow," said Uncle Bob. "She really is mad."

I hung my head.

We walked slowly toward the escalators. I thought of what my uncle said about all girls liking flowers. I doubted it would work. She'd probably throw them at me. Brittany believed I'd turned against her. I had to do something to prove she was wrong. But what?

Tears burned my eyes, and I swallowed hard. I couldn't lose her. It would destroy me. But more importantly she couldn't lose me. I would always be there for her. I promised.

Just then, we passed a jewelry store, and it clicked. A promise ring. Something that would remind her of my love every time she looked at it. I stepped to the display case in the store window. Spotlights glittered on diamonds and gems. I saw the perfect ring.

"What's up?" Uncle Bob asked.

"Hold on a minute." I rushed inside, moving down the glass cases until I found the one I wanted.

"How can I help you?" a woman asked. Her blond hair was teased up eighties-style, and the studs in her ears glinted.

"How much is this fairy ring?" I asked.

"A lovely choice." She unlocked the case and handed me a small box. The ring showed a fairy in flight with a teardrop-cut semi-precious stone in each wing. "One twenty-nine ninety-five."

I wondered if I had enough left in savings.

"This is a birthstone ring. When was your friend born?"

I nearly dropped the box. When *was* Brittany's birthday? Had she ever told me?

"November third," Uncle Bob said.

I chuckled. "Do you remember everything about everyone?"

He shrugged. "I helped Earle build a picnic table one year. They were having a birthday barbeque."

"Then you need a topaz." The woman took the box and replaced it with another. The golden fairy gleamed and sparkled with deep yellow wings.

"Perfect," I said. "Do you engrave here?"

"Certainly. Let me take you over to Charles. I believe he can help you with that right away."

Charles was an overweight man who looked grateful for something to do. "What would you like it to say?"

"Always. Cody." I leaned over the counter to watch him clamp the ring into a machine and type in the words. The machine whirred for a moment; then he removed the ring, blew on it to check his handiwork, and put it back in the box.

The woman smiled. "Check Out is this way."

My debit card went through without a hitch. Maybe my parents hadn't stopped my allowance money after all. As the woman placed the little box in a bright purple bag, I thought Brittany was sure to love the ring. Then a voice warned me that the last time I bought her a gift, I got my butt kicked.

TEN

By evening, I was so ready to turn into a wolf I was bouncing in my seat. Uncle Bob and I drove way out in the Everglades where no one would find us. He knew the dirt roads better than anyone did.

I was amazed to see the changes the drought had wrought in just the few months I had been in Florida. The swamp had receded, making the road appear elevated. The brush looked like tumbleweeds, the trees craggy and leafless. Even the sawgrass was shriveling, lying flat like it would never stand again.

The road petered out beneath a canopy of tangled branches. They looked black against the darkening sky.

"Going to be a nice night." Uncle Bob peered through the windshield as he shut off the car. Then he twisted around to remove his boots. "We can leave our clothes in the cab."

"Sounds good." I opened the door and stood in the cooling air. Piece by piece, I tossed my clothes onto the seat. I was anxious to get moving, but I knew Uncle Bob couldn't shift until moonrise. We sat naked on the warm hood of his truck. "Hear anything from Rita?" Rita was Uncle Bob's mate, a redhead with kind eyes and a wide smile.

"No." He shrugged. "She could be anywhere."

"Does she ever travel outside the country?"

"You mean like Europe or Asia? Sometimes. Why?"

"I wonder if she knows anything about the Lindgren Institute. You'd think there'd be rumors about what goes on there."

"What's to know? It's a fancy resort."

"Which Saarsgard runs out of the goodness of her heart." I hopped down. "Only once you go in, no one hears from you again. No outside contact, remember? The family keeps paying the doctor's exorbitant fees, never knowing if their werewolf is alive or dead."

"You're worried about your parents getting scammed?"

I didn't know how to answer that. "Let's walk. I can't hold still anymore."

We walked. The muck felt cold and firm beneath my feet. Insects chirped and buzzed, and before long, I was smacking at mosquitoes. We reached a hill that rose above the sawgrass.

"This is Tony's Mound, a burial ground," he told me. "Some people hike the hill. It's only about sixteen feet high. But that seems disrespectful to me. We'll go around."

I gazed at it. An invisible barrier surrounded the

mound. It was similar to the magic circle Brittany conjured when we were making the anti-werewolf potion. However, this barrier was so old and forgotten you could pass through with barely a shiver.

"I don't want to be here," I whispered.

As if in response, Uncle Bob made a gagging, choking noise. He fell to his knees. His face rippled and bulged. A muzzle grew, and his lip curled, showing blood-streaked fangs.

I looked at the black sky. Pinprick stars appeared. The moon peeked over the horizon, its pull strong. Closing my eyes, I let it take me. Red-hot agony shot through my spine. Every bone in my body seemed to shatter. Waves of coarse fur rode my skin. My shoulders hunched, and I lifted my head, screaming. It came out as a howl, long and forlorn. Lost.

My uncle shook himself from head to tail, his gray coat smoothing. He licked a forepaw. I nuzzled him then led away. I was hungry, and rabbit sounded good. But this wasn't the place to hunt; the deep thrum of the burial mound made my teeth ache.

I trotted through dead and dying sawgrass toward distant trees, and as I did, I felt my worries slough away like the clothes I left behind. It wasn't that I forgot my human self. Not exactly. Things just didn't seem urgent anymore.

My uncle wanted to play, and we chased each other and wrestled, coming up black with muck. Part of me was surprised we hadn't stumbled upon any rabbits, but a larger part was glad to get out and stretch. After a while, I heard frogs and knew there was a pond nearby. Fresh water. With my uncle on my heels, I dashed off to find it.

The frogs silenced at our approach. I hesitated at a strange odor. Not panther, I thought, running through the short catalogue of my experience. Not gator. The alligators likely moved south, fleeing the drought.

Cautiously, I approached the pond and dipped my snout for a drink. The stench of death was all around. Something touched my foot.

I leaped back to see a huge snake slither out of a hole. I froze in shock, images flashing before my eyes. I remembered my uncle telling me when I first moved down that there was a nasty population of python.

He barked a warning, but too late. The snake wrapped around my waist. It moved with a slow, hypnotic grace as if it had all the time in the world. I bit it and tasted blood. The coil tightened. Air whooshed out of me in a strangled huff.

The python was still coming out of its hole. My uncle pounced on it, biting, tearing out chunks. The back end looped around, trying to ensnare him, but he was too quick. He darted around and came at it again.

As if his attack was inconsequential, the snake's head rose before me. Its jaws opened. I knew that if it got its jaws around mine, I would lose my only defense. But I could barely breathe much less move. I snarled and pressed backward, digging with my hind legs, trying to squirm from its hold.

The snake struck faster than I could see, biting me twice in the shoulder. Pain flared like fire. I couldn't draw enough air to yelp. My uncle went into a fury, trying to tear the coil from my chest. My body went limp. The snake swayed, its eyes burning into mine, its jaws opening wide, wider.

My jaws opened wider still. I clamped onto its head, chomping down with all the strength left to me. I felt a crunch, then a snap. The pressure around my chest eased. Blood spurted into my mouth. The snake jerked and writhed. I refused to release my hold. As the coils fell away, my rage increased. I shook it like a chew toy, growling, grinding my teeth together. At last, I ripped its head from its body.

The effort left me staggering. I dropped the head into the grass, then turned around and kicked some dirt over it. Stumbling, I collapsed at the edge of the pond. My uncle nuzzled me, whimpering, but I was all right. I drank to get the taste of snake blood out of my mouth. I wasn't hungry anymore. That thought made me chuckle.

I got to my feet, feeling shaky. My shoulder bled freely. I thought that was a good sign. With a yip, I limped away. I wanted distance between the pond and me. I doubted there were other pythons in the area; it would've eaten them. I just didn't want a reminder of my stupidity. The signs of a predator had been there–the lack of small animals, the rank smell of death–I just wasn't paying attention. When would I learn?

By the time we reached the scalloped edge of the woods, the pain in my shoulder had simmered to an ache, and I felt stronger. My uncle and I played hide-and-seek around the trees. I caught an interesting scent–deer passed through recently. I lifted my nose, gauging their direction, and headed toward them with my uncle at my side.

Tracking deer was easy. There were three of them. Their scent cut a path like a dotted blue line. We crouched low, edging around bushes, pretending the hunt was more of a challenge than it was.

When we found them, they stood huddled together, skittish, as if waiting for us to make our move. Only we were careful to stay downwind. I didn't see how they knew we were there.

Then I caught a new scent–thick and musky. Something else stalked this prey. My fur stood in alarm, and a voice in my head warned me to back away. But my uncle was already nose to the ground, following the mysterious scent.

I joined him. The footprints were large and heavy. A bear, I realized. At that, my inner voice went wild, warning me to leave. But why should I? After all, I just killed a python. How much trouble could a bear be? We followed the scent around the clearing where the deer stood and stumbled onto the bear. He reared up, startling us as much as we startled him. Our eyes met. I recognized him.

It was William the Bear. No wonder my human side warned me away.

With a rising growl, my uncle leaped, going for William the Bear's throat. A massive paw batted him away. My uncle hit the ground rolling and sprang up for another go. I gave his ear a hard nip then ran in the opposite direction hoping he would follow. He did. We blundered into the clearing and scattered the deer. William the Bear roared. I took a moment to gain my bearings, then hightailed it out of the woods.

I hadn't gone far when the change hit like a cannonball in my gut, bowling me over. I lay on my back, whimpering as my limbs repositioned themselves and my fangs withdrew to my sinuses. My shoulder felt stiff and swollen. I touched the snakebites gingerly.

Uncle Bob sat up, his ear bloodied. "Hey, that hurt!"

"I had to get you out of there." I snapped at him, although I was angrier with myself. I shouldn't have let him see William. "Couldn't you feel the moon set? It would've been so not cool to change into a human in front of an enraged bear."

His face fell, and he nodded. "How's your shoulder?"

"It hurts," I said. "In fact, I hurt all over. Why is it that every time I go out with you I get beat up?"

"Because when you shift by yourself, all you do is stay in your room."

That struck me funny, and I burst out laughing.

Smiling, Uncle Bob gave me a hand up. “Come on. It’s a long walk to the truck.”

“Assuming we can even find it again.”

“I parked by Tony’s Mound for a reason,” he said. “We can home in on its vibrations.”

I sharpened my senses. “Ah, yeah. It’s right over there.”

“You’re learning, young grasshopper.” He started walking.

“You mean padawan.”

“Same difference.”

“Besides, I thought I was the alpha. You should be learning from me.”

He chuckled. “Every day.”

“Was that a smirk? I don’t like it when you smirk.”

Uncle Bob laughed. We walked to the truck through the dark sea of grass.

“I think you should stay home from school,” Uncle Bob said. “That looks painful. Maybe we should give Howard a call.”

My neck was stiff, but I managed to look at my swollen and discolored shoulder. “I thought you said those snakes didn’t have venom.”

“They don’t. But a python’s fangs are angled backward so its prey can’t pull out of its mouth. When it bites, it doesn’t puncture. It takes chunks.”

I considered staying home, but discounted it immediately. I had Brittany's ring. I wanted to see her. "I'll be fine. Can you bandage it so I don't ooze onto my shirt?"

"No problem." He took a self-adhesive pad from the first aid kit and covered the wound. "Ready?"

"Yeah."

We went out to his truck. I had trouble climbing into the front seat. I could barely move my left arm. But once I settled inside, I felt better.

When we got to the drop-off point in front of school, he said, "Do you want me to pick you up this afternoon?"

"No. That's okay." If everything went as planned, I'd be with Brittany after school.

But when I saw her during History, I lost all courage. I had the ring in my pocket, and my apology in my head, but I couldn't face her. I kicked myself about it all morning long. Who ever heard of a chicken werewolf?

At lunchtime, I stood at the cafeteria door, scanning the room until I spotted her. She was beautiful. Her shirt was so purple it was almost black. It read *Yes, I'm Deep Purple*. Her lips were also dark, making her skin look pale and perfect.

She sat at a table with a group of girls. I considered walking up and slapping the ring down before her, but that wasn't how I wanted it to play out. The ring meant a lot to me. I wanted it to mean a lot to her too.

My heart beat so hard my entire body throbbed. I took a breath to steady my nerves, then crossed the room toward her table. The girls seemed to be talking all at once. I paused, waiting for Brittany to notice me. She looked up, and her eyes narrowed.

"I'm sorry," I croaked.

A chuckle circled the table.

Brittany cocked her head. "Is that so? And what are you sorry *about*?"

My head filled with responses. *I'm sorry you overreacted. I'm sorry your father is not as big a jerk as you want to believe.* "I'm sorry I disappointed you."

"Fine." She leaned back, staring.

Another chuckle ran through the group. Their faces were amused, all eyes on me. I waited, hoping Brittany would say something more, but she was finished. With the fairy ring hot in my pocket, I walked away.

I sat at *our* table with my back to her. I couldn't stand to look at her. A tsunami of noise crashed over me. I wanted to leave, wished I could call my uncle for a pick up. My shoulder felt wet, and I worried that I was bleeding again.

As I twisted to check it, I caught sight of Eff sitting two tables away. He stared openly. I wanted to yell at him to keep his eyes to himself. But he was as alone as I was. An outcast. I couldn't hate him, although I had reason to. He and his teammates nearly killed me. But he didn't matter anymore. Nothing did.

Closing my eyes, I willed the tension from my body. I imagined myself as a wolf running through the woods, wind in my fur, rabbit scent in my nose. Then a snake reared up, striking faster than I could see.

Someone rapped at the table. My eyes opened to see Brittany. I sat up so fast, I yelped with pain.

"Are we still study buddies?" she asked.

"Y-yeah."

"Fine. Then meet me at my car after school. We can go to my house to study."

"Okay," my voice squeaked. I cleared my throat and tried again. "Fine. I'll be there."

She walked away. I wiped sweat from my forehead and found that my hands were shaking. I felt like I'd narrowly escaped death.

For the rest of the day, I wavered between despondency and elation. I didn't know how I would get Brittany to forgive me, and I knew I had only one chance to try. By the time I got to my last class, I was exhausted. I snaked my way to the back of the room where Maxwell and Lonnie stood at our workbench. This week in Shop, we were learning about jigsaws. That was never a good thing.

"Hey there." Maxwell punched his glasses higher on his nose. "You look bummed."

"Brittany and I had a fight."

Lonnie sang out, "My girlfriend and me, we had a fight. Now I don't know how to put it right."

"What about?" Maxwell asked.

I shrugged. "She didn't like my opinion."

"What?" Lonnie chortled. "You just broke the Number One Rule, man."

Maxwell leaned toward me conspiratorially and said in a low voice, "This is the Number One Rule when dealing with women. Never offer an opinion."

"Even if they ask you for it," Lonnie said.

"The best thing to do is make non-committal sounds. Don't say *anything*," Maxwell told me. "But if they trap you, and your back is to the wall, say I understand how you feel and you have the right to feel that way. Say it with me now."

The three of us said, "I understand how you feel, and you have the right to feel that way."

"The Rule has been passed down for generations," Maxwell said. "Learn it. Believe it."

"How do you know so much?" I said. "Neither of you even have girlfriends."

"I have a sister." Maxwell nodded knowingly. "Once I learned the Rule, she stopped beating me up so much."

"Don't be a fool," Lonnie sang. "Remember the Rule."

"What's with the singing?" I asked.

"We're starting a garage band." Maxwell punched up his glasses. "I have a keyboard synthesizer and Lonnie's on drums. We're writing our own songs. Want to join? We could use someone on tambourine."

"Tempting, but I think I'll pass."

"Come on. It'll be fun."

"Fortune and fame, or maybe just lame," Lonnie sang.

I shook my head and laughed.

By the time school ended, my head was full. *Apologize even if you're right. Don't give an opinion even if she asks.* I walked toward the student's parking lot feeling like my shoes were full of lead.

I opened the car door, wincing with the effort, and leaned inside. "Hi."

"Get in," she said.

I slid into the cool silence, shutting the door. The little VW was like an island in a hurricane; kids ran about shouting to one another, engines revved, and cars pulled out in all directions.

"How's everything at home?" I asked. "You know, with your dad."

"He comes over every day. I keep waiting for the big blow up."

"It must be hard."

"The worst thing is how accommodating my mother is. It's as though nothing happened. She actually wants him here. I think she's still in love with him."

"No, she's not," I told her. "When I saw her on Saturday, she was scared half to death. She's just trying to make the best out of a bad situation. Like you."

Brittany looked at me. "So now you think you know my mother better than me?"

Warning! Warning! "I'm just saying that in my opinion..." Crap! What was I doing?

"Get out," Brittany said.

"But–"

She leaned over me and opened the door. "Now."

I stepped from the car. She started the engine and slammed it in gear before I shut the door. Dust and exhaust traced her escape from the emptying parking lot. I watched in disbelief. How could I be so stupid? How could things go so wrong?

A red Ford Ranger stopped beside me. The truck had a row of spotlights on the roof and windows tinted so dark you couldn't see the driver. The window slid down.

"Need a ride?" Eff said.

ELEVEN

Eff leaned out of the driver's side window, his brow cocked. I knew I shouldn't get into the truck with him. He could drive me into the woods where his cronies were waiting to hammer me again. Maybe that's what I wanted. Then I could turn into a wolf and scare the crap out of them. Or worse.

But Eff didn't have cronies anymore, and it was too hot to walk all the way home. I circled around and climbed in shotgun. The truck didn't have that brand new smell, but it was clean enough to be right off the lot.

Eff watched as I attempted to buckle in one-handed. My snake-bit shoulder ached to my finger-tips, and my neck was stiff. When I was ready, he pulled onto the street. He didn't have any tunes on, and the silence was oppressive.

After a few minutes, he said, "Brittany kicked you out?"

I gazed through the window. "She's mad about something. I don't get it."

He let that settle for a moment. "I always had a thing for Brittany. I don't get it either. I mean, she's pretty, yeah, but there's something else about her. Like she's got a fire inside her, you know? She'll tell anyone off. My mother. The school principal. I swear she'd lock horns with the President of the United States if she thought she was right. And she always thinks she's right." He turned onto Southern Boulevard. "But if she fell for you, she's not the right girl for me. You and me? We're on opposite ends."

I tensed, dialing up my wolf sense, thinking I heard a challenge in his words. "Where are your friends?"

"What friends?"

"I thought you owned this town."

"Yeah." He shook his head. "I used to think I was the most popular guy in school. Thought I had everything. I didn't have *anything*."

He fell silent then, and I went along for the ride. My wolf sense told me he wasn't a threat. For some reason, that ticked me off–if he wasn't dangerous, how come I got creamed?

When we reached my driveway, Eff turned to me. "So, are you going to tell me how you healed so fast after we knocked the spit out of you?"

I shrugged. "Healthy living, I guess."

"Right."

"Look, it's no big, okay? All the men in my family heal fast. Uncle Bob does, too. Why don't you beat him up and see?"

He sighed. "About that. I'm sorry. It never should have gone that far. I don't know what came over me."

I muttered, "Pack mentality."

"That's exactly right." He jabbed the steering wheel with his index finger. "A group of people will do things they'd never dream of doing alone."

"And now you're out of the pack."

He nodded and exhaled loudly. "One thing I learned, I don't have any friends. Never did."

We sat for a moment. Then my mouth opened and words fell out. "Do you know Howard Shebala?"

"Garage Sale Howard? Sure. Everybody does."

"He's an honest to goodness Navajo medicine man. Grows plants in his backyard I never saw before. Buys powdered snake blood off EBay."

"No way."

"It's amazing the knowledge the Indians had," I said. "They just came at life from a different direction. He's the reason I didn't die that night you beat me to a pulp." I looked at him. "Don't go posting that on MySpace. I don't think he wants it around."

Eff nodded slowly. "No one would believe me anyway."

I unbuckled my seatbelt. "I'm going in to make a grilled cheese and bacon sandwich. Want one?"

He hesitated, then said, "Sure." He turned off the engine and followed me inside.

I was uncomfortably aware of how empty the place looked. The middle of the living room held my uncle's recliner, a pile of newspapers, and a twelve-inch black and white television on a metal TV stand. That was it. No couches. No lamps.

Eff motioned at the television. "You're kidding, right?"

"At least no one's going to steal it. We need to get one of those HD converter boxes. Knowing my uncle, he'll wait until the last minute."

He shrugged as if he approved of procrastination. "You have until next year."

I led him through the empty dining room into the kitchen.

"Is that a pet?" Eff pointed at a bright green lizard about a foot long on the side of the cabinet.

It wasn't a pet, but I didn't want to tell him that. Lizards wandered the kitchen at will through the open window. When I first moved in, they freaked me out.

"He's on bug patrol. We used to have a bunch of those little black lizards, but they disappeared. Maybe he ate them." I turned on the heat under a cast iron skillet sitting on the stove. Then I pulled a tub of margarine, sliced cheese, and pre-cooked bacon slices out of the refrigerator. "You want some chocolate milk?"

"That's fine."

I poured a couple glasses and set them on the table. "Have a seat."

Eff sat. After a moment, he asked, "Your parents dead?"

"Nah. My mom's a brain surgeon. My dad's a heart specialist. They have a semi-mansion up in Massachusetts."

"Why do you live in Florida with your uncle?"

I flashed back to the first time I turned into a wolf–my father's horror and concern, my mother's disappointment. Like I'd done something wrong. Like it was my fault. Of course, she knew all along there was a chance I would become a werewolf–her only brother was one.

I flipped the sandwiches. "I guess they just got tired of having me around."

"That sucks."

"I hated it at first. Now, it's like I'm free, you know? I was going to be a doctor like my parents. It was expected. I had no choice. Now I can be anything." A fix-it-guy, a vagrant, a hermit in the Everglades...

Eff said, "I was supposed to be a football player. Like it was the only option open to me. Don't get me wrong, I love the game and I'm good at it. But that's not all I am." He accepted a paper towel wrapped grilled cheese with a nod of thanks. "Dad's going crazy trying to get me reinstated. Coach agreed to reconsider. He says I can try out next season with the rest of the wannabees. Just not sure I want to."

I sat with a sandwich. "You don't want to play?"

"I'd like to, but it would be different. They threw me under the bus. I don't think I'd ever feel part of the team again."

Retorts crawled up my throat. It was his idea, wasn't it? He was the one who got his teammates to pulverize me and post the pictures on MySpace. He got what he deserved.

But the pain of the beating had faded. Now I felt a little sorry for him. We ate in silence.

Then I heard my uncle pull up. Oh-oh. How would Uncle Bob react to Eff being there?

Uncle Bob rushed in with blood streaming down his arm. He went to the kitchen sink and turned on the water.

I jumped up. “What happened?”

“Nicked myself with the saw.” His voice tensed with pain as he ran his hand under the cold stream.

Eff said, “That’s a bad gash, sir. I’ll be happy to drive you to the hospital.”

Uncle Bob froze. He turned slowly and said, “Efrem Higgins. My nephew might have a forgiving soul, but I do not. I’ll thank you to get out of my house.”

“We were just talking,” I said.

Eff wadded up his empty paper towel and tossed it into the garbage can next to the refrigerator. “It’s all right. I don’t blame him.” Without another word, he left.

I leaned over my uncle’s shoulder and watched blood swirl down the drain. “What can I do to help?”

“Get the first aid kit, would you? I left it on top of the fridge after patching you up this morning.”

I grabbed the kit and some extra paper towels and sat at the table. “We’re a great pair. We spend more on first aid supplies than on food.”

“See if you can butterfly it.”

I shook my head at the wound. He practically cut off his thumb. It would take every butterfly we had to tape it closed. As I worked, I said in my best teacher voice, "You need to utilize basic saw safety protocol. I can send Lonnie and Maxwell over to give you a few pointers."

He grinned. "Can you set that up for me?"

"Seriously, though. You should probably stop over Howard's and have him hit you with some of his smelly salve."

"I'll do that. We're going out tonight anyway. Going to search for Willie." He flexed his hand, checking my handiwork. "Do you think it strange that we ran into a bear?"

My eyes widened, but I tried to act nonchalant. "No. There are bears in Florida."

"Just something about it." He looked thoughtful for a moment, then shrugged. "Anyway, Howard and I are searching points north of here. I hope we don't tangle with that bear. Howard's not in a very good mood. He's liable to rip its head off."

I gulped. "Do you want me to go with you?"

"I'd rather you stayed home. And don't go letting Eff in here while I'm gone."

"What's he going to do?" I scoffed. "I'm stronger. Faster. He isn't a threat anymore. My wolf says he's broken."

"There's wolf sense, and there's common sense. You need to listen to both," Uncle Bob said. "A broken man is dangerous because he harbors resentment. You don't know what Eff will do."

I slouched, pursing my lips. Maybe I *was* overlooking something.

Eff wasn't a problem, I was certain. But my wolf sure perked when I first met William. I remembered Dr. Saarsgard warning me about him: *He wields much power and has no idea of the consequences.* William had the markings of a true adversary.

And Brittany liked him.

Uncle Bob was in a foul mood as he drove me to school the next morning. He still smelled like wolf, and his eyes were red with lack of sleep. I didn't ask if he'd found William, didn't want to know what his reaction would be when he discovered I'd been withholding information.

As we pulled into the school drop-off, I half expected to see Maxwell and Lonnie hanging around hoping to hear how things went with Brittany. I did not expect to see Eff.

"Hey, there" I said as I hopped down from the truck.

"Hey." He stepped around me and peered in the window. "Good morning, Mister Nowak. I want to apologize for yesterday. It won't happen again."

"See that it doesn't."

"Yes, sir. How's the hand?"

Uncle Bob held up his hand. What had been a

gaping gash yesterday was now only a red welt.

Eff gasped and backed up.

As my uncle drove away, I said, "I don't think it will scar or anything."

Eff looked at me, his face etched with shock.

I nearly bust out laughing. "Like I said, my family heals fast." With a shrug, I walked into school.

Brittany was still ignoring me, so I focused on my studies. My uncle was so proud of my good grades; I didn't want to let them slip and disappoint him.

At lunch, I grabbed a Dew and a bag of chips and sat alone at my usual table. I hated it. I guess I took for granted that Brittany would always be there, wrinkling her nose and laughing her mischievous fairy laugh.

"Hey," Eff said, interrupting my musings. He held a tray of food.

"Hey." I motioned to the chair across from me.

He sat down. "Don't eat much, eh?"

"I see you do."

"Coach made us study nutrition." Two sandwiches, a banana, and a piece of cherry pie filled his tray. He unwrapped the sandwiches and put them together, sort of a double-decker. "You work out?"

"No. Why?"

"You look like you do." He took a large bite of sandwich and washed it down with milk. "I have a nice workout room set up in my garage. You should come over sometime."

"In your garage?" I chuckled. "Where do you put

your truck to bed?"

He grinned. "Yeah, she's sweet, isn't she? I wash and wax her every weekend. Make sure her tire pressure is just so."

"You pay for her yourself?"

"Yep. I work nights and weekends at my dad's hardware store. I've got plenty of time now that I'm off the team."

I finished my Dew and crunched the can.

Eff leaned back, eyes narrow. "Man, why are you even talking to me? Is this one of those keep your friends close and keep your enemies closer things?"

"Nah." I chuckled. "If I were thinking that way, it'd be about someone else."

He raised his brows, prodding me to spill.

"Just some kid I know," I said. "Homely. Kind of slow. Won't listen to reason."

"Sounds like a real bear."

I laughed. "You could say that."

His words stayed with me the rest of the day. By the time I got home, I was convinced I should pay William a visit. I left a note beneath Uncle Bob's coffee cup saying I was running through the woods to blow off steam. Then I took off.

The sky was blue, and the air was warm. Fallen leaves rustled beneath my Nikes as I pushed through bushes and scrub palmetto. I didn't shift into my wolf form. Showing up naked at the old fishing shack wasn't cool. But even as a human, my senses were ramped. I smelled the sea of sawgrass from miles away. And I could run faster than most anybody. It didn't take long to reach the cabin.

William sat with his legs dangling over the dock. If the pond hadn't dried up, he would've been in danger of losing a foot to a passing alligator. I approached from the side, rehearsing my excuse for seeing him. But as his eyes turned toward me, my flimsy apology for leading Uncle Bob to William the Bear fled my mind.

"What's up?" I said.

He looked surprised and then suspicious. "Something I can do for you?"

"Got a minute?"

"Want some water?"

"Thanks." I climbed the boulder that served as steps and snagged a bottle of Zephyrhills. I sat beside him. "Surprised you're still here."

"I like it here. It's quiet."

"Don't you miss being around people?"

"I see them often enough."

"Where?" I scoffed. "When you're a bear?"

"That reminds me. Did you know there are other werewolves around?"

"There are?"

"At least two. They were black."

I frowned. Had he run into two wolves other than my uncle and me? Then it struck me–we'd been wrestling in the muck. No wonder we looked black. "Thanks for the heads up."

"Can't be too careful. They reeked of blood.

Must've made a kill."

I took a swig of warm water. "So how do you turn into a bear, anyhow? Just put on your belt and say a magic word?"

"There is a chant, but it's mostly for focus. I wouldn't want my attention to wander. I wear the belt to draw the spirit of the bear into me."

"So if you want to turn into a different animal, you just switch belts?"

"Animals. Birds. I mean, I haven't yet, but that's the idea."

"Man." I smiled, looking up. "It would be cool to be a hawk or an eagle. See the world the way the wind sees it."

"Most people are afraid to become anything but what they are. Not you." He regarded me. "That's why I don't get it. Being a wolf is an honor and a gift. Why would you even consider making a potion to stop it? The wolf is inside you, part of you. Without it, you wouldn't be whole."

"I wanted to stay in Brittany's life. Becoming a regular kid seemed the only way to do that."

"A bit extreme."

"She's my mate. I would do anything for her. Even give up the wolf."

"I hope she appreciates how strongly you feel."

"She doesn't." I shrugged. "Right now, she won't even speak to me."

Before I could stop myself, I told him all about my fight with Brittany. I don't know why I told him, seeing's how I thought he was the enemy, but it felt kind of good to get it off my chest. William was an attentive listener, nodding and making noncommittal sounds in all the right places. As I spoke, the sun went down, setting the sky ablaze. It looked as if the Everglades were on fire.

"What should I do?" I asked.

"What does your wolf say?"

"I don't know." But, of course, I did. My wolf wanted me to storm into her house, bend her backward, and plant a wet one right on her lips.

"You should learn to trust your instincts, wolf boy."

"That's it? That's all you got?"

William stood and stripped off his shirt. "I'm going out for something to eat. Care to join me?"

I knew he didn't mean the nearest fast food restaurant. "Thanks, but I better get home." I held up the empty water bottle. "Do you want me to recycle these?"

"No need." He smiled. "I have a service."

The next morning, Uncle Bob greeted me by saying, "Don't forget the court hearing tomorrow. We're leaving at seven o'clock sharp." As if I didn't have enough stress. William. Dr. Saarsgard. My mother.

But of all the problems on my mind, the most

pressing was whether or not Brittany liked me. All day in school, I watched her from afar, thinking about what the wolf wanted. I couldn't stand being apart from her any longer. So after dinner, I hopped on my bike and peddled toward her place. I wasn't sure what I would say, so I brought the fairy ring in case words failed me.

The night was warm and clear, the waning moon a sliver past full. I rode along the private dirt road that led to her driveway. As I neared the yard, Brittany came down the front steps. The hem of a white robe flapped around her ankles. It flowed like silk. That surprised me. Usually she wore a black or purple t-shirt. She carried a canvas tote bag with a recycle symbol on one side. It looked heavy.

I pulled off, thinking I would catch her before she drove away–but she didn't go to her car. Instead, she walked swiftly across the lawn and into the surrounding trees. I frowned, ditched my bike, and followed.

Brittany moved through the forest like a ghost. Her skin smelled spicy, and her hair was damp. She hiked up her robe in front to keep it out of the clutching brambles. Her bare legs lit with starlight. She wore flip-flops. After a while, she reached a path, and I realized we were on one of the Sunspot's nature trails. The path held a layer of cedar chips. I had to step carefully so I didn't scuff my feet and give myself away. Eventually, the path veered right, and Brittany turned left. Back into the trees. I sighed. What was she doing out here?

Then she entered a clearing. Her friend, Eileen, turned to greet her. It appeared that Eileen wore only her smile, although I couldn't see her fully peering through the bushes as I was. I inched forward for a closer look.

"Hi," Brittany said in barely a whisper.

"Hi," said Eileen. "Did you take your purifying bath?"

Brittany nodded. "All those herbs left a ring in the tub. My mom will freak. I have to get home before she does so I can clean it."

"Let me see what you brought."

Brittany knelt and pulled out items from the canvas bag. There was a box of wooden fireplace matches, a cardboard canister of salt, and several chunky white candles. I thought of the *Awakening*, the metaphysical shop Brittany frequented for her candles and crystals.

Then she took out a black, pillar-shaped candle. Eileen sat beside her. She lit a white candle and dribbled wax onto the side of the black one. Brittany removed a photograph from the bag. Even in the dark, I could see it was a picture of her father.

Eileen affixed the photo to the side of the black candle, dripping more wax onto the edges to make it lay smooth. She blew out the flame.

At the sight of the old photograph, I realized whatever they were doing was personal. I felt like a voyeur, like Brittany's little brother hiding in the bushes to watch nudie volleyball. Shame heated my cheeks. I leaned back, intending to creep away.

Then Brittany untied her silken robe and let it slip from her shoulders. Moonbeams set her naked body aglow. My eyes widened, and my heart rate tripled. I shuffled forward, trying to see past the many branches in my way. She picked up the fallen robe and brushed off a smudge of dirt. Then she looked directly at me.

Panic seized my throat. She knew I was there! My body froze in a state of alarm. Brittany walked to the bush where I hid. I fixed my eyes on her small, perfect breasts. If I died here, let those be the last thing I saw.

Instead of calling me out, however, she tossed her robe onto the bush. She hadn't seen me, after all. I closed my eyes, sagging, blowing out a silent breath. Then I waddled to the side so I could peer around the robe.

Eileen had brought her own canvas bag. From it, she carefully removed something wrapped in dark velvet. She also took out an old-fashioned bell with a handle, like the kind schoolmarms used in the pioneer days. She carried the velvet, the bell, and the black candle to a rock in the middle of the clearing. On her knees, she unfolded the cloth and lifted an object high with her arms in an X shape over her head. It was a dagger with an ornate hilt. She set it with the other items on the rock.

Standing, she picked up the salt. "I'll make the circle. You light the candles and place them the way we did before. Light the black one first."

Eileen walked in a slow circle, pouring a stream of gleaming salt onto the dark grass. Brittany lit the black candle with a long match, then lit five smaller white candles from its flame. She spaced the small candles evenly around the circle that Eileen was making. That left two unlit.

As they worked, they chanted, "Mother, please hear us, let our light shine. Mother, please hear us, let our love bind."

Eileen gave the salt a little flourish to close the circle. There came a snap, more felt than heard, and a buzz of energy filled my head. Brittany stood next to the rock, still chanting. Her back was to me. Through brush and leaves, I saw the moonlit mounds of her buttocks, the gentle curve of her waist. My legs ached from their cramped position. Other parts of me ached, too.

Brittany lit two fat cigars from the candle on the rock. The black candle was melting fast; her father's face was already half-obscured by dripping wax. She handed one cigar to Eileen, and they walked the circle in opposite directions, waving smoke around. It smelled like burning sage. They put down the cigars. Eileen rang the bell, then held her arms in a V above her head.

In a loud voice, she said, "Great Hecate, Queen of the Underworld, Protectress of all Wicca, it is our will on this night to overcome the shadows and bring about change. We invite you to our circle to assist and protect us in our rite."

"Mother, please hear us," Brittany chanted.

Eileen set down the bell and picked up the knife. She crossed her arms in an X over her chest. "Great Anubis, God of Protection, it is our will on this night to overcome the shadows and bring about change. We invite you to our circle to assist and protect us in our rite."

She passed the knife to Brittany who held it the same way. Together they said, "Dark is the night as we reach this turning point. Here is a time of death, yet a time of rebirth. Endings and beginnings. Ebbings and flowings."

Death? I gasped. Every hair on my body stood in alarm. Was this a suicide pact? Was Brittany so distraught she would harm herself? I tensed, ready to rush into the clearing; but before I could move, Brittany set the dagger on the rock. I settled back, but my senses were still on alert.

Each girl picked up one of the remaining candles. They lit them from the central flame. The black candle had burned to half its height. Cords of wax hid the photograph of Brittany's father.

They held their white candles overhead and cried, "In darkness, there is light. I feel energy and life. I feel my heartbeat strong. I feel the power of the universe and the love of Mother Earth."

Then they passed the candles over their bodies so close I was afraid they would burn themselves.

"Let the light cast out all darkness," they chanted.

"Let the light cast out all darkness."

After several minutes of this, they set their candles in the grass. Eileen got out a bottle of water and a mini-loaf of bread. She cut the bread in half with the dagger and gave a piece to Brittany. They knelt together, eating and drinking, watching the black candle melt.

When it finally guttered, Eileen held out the dagger. "You have to do this part yourself."

With the knife in hand, Brittany stood and stared down at the dark puddle. She looked angry. At first, I thought she was going to stab the encased picture of her father. Instead, she knelt and, using the dagger, dug a hole. She pried the still-warm wax from the smooth stone and laid it inside. It looked like a black disk. With gasps and sobs, she pulled dirt over it until the hole filled.

Eileen stood, arms in a V. "We thank the God and Goddess for their presence." With a swipe of her foot, she broke the circle of salt. There was a slight pop, and the faint buzzing sound stopped. "There. As long as no one digs that up, your father can't touch you."

Brittany's face streamed with tears. "I want to move the rock over it."

Eileen nodded. "All right."

I'd seen enough. I backed away and returned to the nature trail. I felt like a jerk. I been spying on my girlfriend. More than that, I never realize how totally petrified she was of her father.

Brittany was the brave one. She didn't lose her head even when a serial killer werewolf was chasing her. So when her father said he was moving to Florida and she told me she was scared, I thought she meant frightened. I didn't listen. How could I? I'd never seen her truly scared before.

All I had to do was tell her I understood. But no. I had to say her fears were bogus. Now, here she was doing magic rites in the nude. If only I had supported her, she wouldn't have turned to Eileen for help. Double jerk.

I reached my bike and headed home. My head was filled with the ritual I'd witnessed. Brittany had mentioned that she had Wiccan friends. I should have guessed Eileen was one of them. I knew next to nothing about the Wiccan religion, but I couldn't deny the power I felt as the girls drew their circle.

At least it hadn't been a photograph of me on that black candle.

TWELVE

Seven o'clock Thursday morning found me showered and dressed in my new suit, anxious to leave for the custody hearing. I was too nervous to eat, even though Uncle Bob warned me that it might be a long day. He kept saying there was nothing to worry about, but I noticed he didn't eat, either.

The West Palm Beach Courthouse was actually two buildings connected by an archway. To one side, a big white clock on a tower showed that we were ten minutes late. I winced and shook my head, silently cursing the traffic in South Florida. We parked the truck and followed the sidewalk. People scurried by–women in high heels lugging overstuffed briefcases, men in suits with Starbucks in hand. There was a Lincoln Memorial out front–two concrete semicircles about waist high with part of the Gettysburg Address on them. We walked in between as we approached the stairs. The morning was cool, but I was sweating.

"It's in the building on the right," Uncle Bob said. "The family side."

I nodded, my eyes running up the ten-story

building. Gold plating encased a bank of revolving doors. We pushed inside. Several security lines greeted us. People jockeyed about, clattering their cell phones and beepers into bins to be X-rayed. A low murmur of conversation echoed through the huge room, punctuated by dings from the elevators. The black-and-white tiled floor amplified the scuff of every shoe.

My wolf cringed at the noise. I wanted to cover my ears and run. But my uncle gave me a bracing smile and led me into line. All he had to declare was his keys and a handful of change–we'd both left our phones at home–so we moved through quickly.

Once past security, he pulled the creased and crumpled paperwork from his pocket. "We want room 9E. Ninth floor. The sign says that these escalators only go to five."

"Over here." I motioned to the side where a group of people queued for an elevator.

We got there just as the doors opened. Everyone piled inside. Our group packed the car to capacity. The clashing odors of perfume, hair gels, bagels, and coffee struck my nose. I sneezed, then smiled to myself as the woman crowding me edged away.

By the time Uncle Bob and I reached the ninth floor, the elevator was empty, and we were a half-hour late. We stepped into a gray and white hallway. Onyx tile surrounded each doorway, and gold lettering labeled the doors: 9A, 9B. The whole outside wall was floor-to-ceiling windows looking out on downtown West Palm Beach. Wooden benches clustered here and there.

My parents sat on the benches ahead. They didn't stand when they saw us. But a man and a woman hustled our way. I recognized the man–he was head of the law firm my parents employed. I felt a sinking sensation. I was toast.

Steeling myself, I said, "Hello, Mister Meadle."

His bald head shone in the fluorescent light. "Hello, Cody. This is Doctor Landstar. She's a psychiatrist. She's been waiting to speak with you."

Dr. Landstar stepped forward, her smile taking in both my uncle and me. Her skin was the color of chocolate milk, her hair dark as devil's food cake. My stomach growled, and I regretted skipping breakfast.

She said, "Cody, I'd like to take you somewhere private so we can have a little chat. It won't take long."

Uncle Bob said, "Well, I suppose–"

"No!" My voice rang in the still hallway. "I won't be shut in a room with you."

Her smile never faltered. "Then how about we sit over here? Would that be all right?"

I nodded and followed her to a group of benches a short distance away. As we sat, she took a file folder and a steno pad from her briefcase.

"Do you have something against psychiatrists?" she asked.

"I just don't trust anyone involved with my parents right now."

"In that case, you'll be happy to know that I work for the State of Florida, not your parents. Judge Barker asked me to speak with you." She wrote on her pad. "Normally, custody cases are seen by magistrates, not judges. Your parents must have some clout."

"They like to push their weight around."

"You sound angry."

"I am."

"Do you hate your parents?"

"No," I blurted. "I love them."

"Why don't you think they deserve custody?"

"I like living with my uncle. I've settled into school. If my parents truly wanted me back, I guess I'd come to some kind of arrangement." I fought to keep my voice level. "But that's not the case, is it? They don't want me with them at all. They want to send me halfway around the world. With Doctor Saarsgard."

Her eyes flickered, and I smelled a jolt of adrenalin shoot through her. She was shocked. Alarmed.

"You don't know the whole story, do you?" I asked.

"I'm just here to ascertain if you can make your own decisions."

"Better than my parents."

"Why do you say that?"

I shrugged. "They're confused. Brainwashed."

"That sounds a little paranoid."

"You haven't met Doctor Saarsgard."

"Actually, I have." She flipped through the file. "She's the psychiatrist speaking on your parent's behalf."

My stomach twisted. "She's here?"

I gazed down the hallway to where my parents sat on their bench. Uncle Bob and Mr. Meadle stood nearby. And there was Dr. Saarsgard. She must've crawled out from under a rock somewhere. I clenched my fists, trying to control a flare of anger. It would be so uncool to turn into a wolf in the courthouse.

"Let's get back to you," Dr. Landstar said. "Do you have many friends here in South Florida?"

"A few."

"Girlfriend?"

I thought of Brittany. "I wish."

She nodded and wrote some more.

The elevator dinged, and out stepped Vice Principal Overhill and Coach Murgott, each carrying a coffee-to-go. What were they doing here? I was in for it now. Overhill hated me from the start. And I'd ticked Coach off because I wouldn't join the football team. He'd been badgering me about it ever since I outran everyone on the track.

I hunkered down in my suit coat, hoping they wouldn't notice me as they passed. I was doomed. First, I come off like a paranoid loser to the State psychiatrist. Now Overhill and Coach were here to testify. Things couldn't get worse. Why did everything always happen to me?

“One more question,” Dr. Landstar said. “What plans do you have for the future? What do you want to be?”

“I honestly don’t know. I mean, when I lived in Massachusetts, I was going to be a doctor. Like my parents, you know? I never questioned it. But now. So many things are opening up. I found out I like building stuff. Maybe I could become a carpenter. Or an athlete. Coach says I’m pretty good.” I broke off, thinking about Coach and Overhill.

She motioned down the hall. “I see they’re letting us in.”

I looked to where she pointed. My father put his arm around my mother as if they were at a funeral. They disappeared into room 9E, followed by Mr. Meadle and Dr. Saarsgard. Coach and Overhill filed in after. Uncle Bob stood outside the double doors looking at me.

Dr. Landstar and I got to our feet.

“Nervous?” she asked.

“Absolutely.”

“Why?”

I glanced at her as if she were joking. “For one thing, I don’t know what to expect, how to respond. I’m afraid anything I say will make matters worse. And if I lose, I’m afraid I’ll be shipped off again. Institutionalized.”

She nodded as we walked. “My advice is to be yourself. Don’t overthink the situation. Be open and forthcoming.”

I wanted to yell that it was easy for her to say. Instead, I murmured, "Thank you for your advice."

She smiled at me and went into the room. I looked at my uncle. My stomach somersaulted in my chest. He clapped me on the shoulder, and we went inside together. A beefy man in a uniform checked our identities. With a sound like a gunshot, the door closed behind us.

I expected a large courtroom similar to what you see on TV with a jury box and lawyer tables and a desk on a pedestal for the judge. This was nothing like that. There was a single long table. My parents and their two advisors sat on the far side. My mother looked pitiful and frail–going for the sympathy vote. Vice Principal Overhill and Coach Murgott sat on the closer side, leaving two seats open. Dr. Landstar sat at the end.

The head of the table held the elevated judge's desk. Spotlights lit the desk and made the polished wood gleam. A court reporter sat to one side already typing. I was surprised at how much noise her fingers made on the keys.

I sat reluctantly next to Vice Principal Overhill. "Hello, sir," I said, because it would be too rude not to acknowledge him.

He nodded to me. "Cody."

"Cody." Coach nodded as well.

A door opened, and a bailiff stepped out of the judge's chambers. "All rise."

We stood. Judge Barker entered. She was short

and stout, like a beach ball dressed in a black robe. The bailiff helped her up the step to her desk. She surveyed our group, looking like she'd been gnawing lemons.

"We are here in the matter of proper supervision for Cody Forester, a minor." She read from a paper. "Case 08-33470-AIFOR. In attendance are Doctor Torhild Saarsgard, Doctor Marie Nowak-Forester, Doctor David Forester, Frederick Meadle Esquire, Doctor Sylvia Landstar, Robert Nowak, Cody Forester, Lance Overhill, and Otis Murgott. Bailiff, swear everyone in."

The bailiff held out a Bible. "Do you swear to tell the truth, the whole truth, and nothing but the truth, so help you God?"

We murmured, "I do."

"Be seated."

There was a scraping of chairs.

Judge Barker said, "This is an informal hearing. You do not need to stand when spoken to. You will refer to me as Your Honor."

"Yes, Your Honor," both Mr. Meadle and Dr. Landstar intoned.

"These proceedings are to determine the rightful guardian of Cody Forester." The judge looked at me. "Are you Cody Forester?"

"Yes, Your Honor."

"And you are Robert Nowak, the boy's current guardian?"

"Yes, Your Honor."

"And you are the parents who want to terminate the guardianship of Mister Nowak and award it instead to Doctor Saarsgard. Is that correct?"

"Yes, Your Honor," my mother said. She dabbed at her eyes with a tissue.

"Why did you make Mister Nowak the legal guardian of your son in the first place?"

"It was a temporary measure. Until we found a more suitable home."

"Isn't your home suitable?"

She blushed. "My son is a handful. He needs constant supervision."

"Is that your professional opinion as well?" the judge asked Dr. Saarsgard.

"It is, Your Honor."

"Doctor Landstar, do you concur?"

"I do not, Your Honor."

"How do you find the boy?" asked the judge.

"He is amiable and articulate."

"Your Honor," Saarsgard said. "We do not contest the boy's intelligence. He is more than capable of manipulation."

"And no one can see through his manipulations as well as you?" Judge Barker turned her sour gaze to Saarsgard. When the good doctor failed to answer, she continued. "As far as his intelligence is concerned, the boy's grades have improved since coming to Florida. He appears to be an excellent student."

"He is, Your Honor," Overhill said.

"And you are?"

"Vice Principal Overhill from Seminole Bluffs High School. This is Coach Murgott. You have our affidavits."

"I do indeed." Judge Barker thumbed through papers on her desk. "Along with several others. Neighbors. Most of his teachers. Sheriff Brad."

I groaned and clutched my stomach.

"It was not necessary to come in person," the judge said.

"We wanted to show our support for Cody," Overhill said, "and to answer any questions that may arise."

My mouth opened. They were on my side? I'd thought Mr. Meadle had subpoenaed them. Had my uncle asked them to come?

"Very well," Judge Barker said. "You both work all day with teenagers. What are your impressions of the boy?"

"Bright. Opinionated."

"A born leader," Coach cut in.

"He sees himself as a bit of a superhero," Overhill said. "Standing up for the weak, that sort of thing."

"I have a report about an altercation with..." The judge checked the file. "Efrem Higgins. Cody, what can you tell me about that?"

I cleared my throat and looked at my hands. "Not much to say. We shoved each other is all."

"The sheriff was called?"

"Yes, Your Honor." I glanced up. "Eff and I are

friends now. He was at my house a couple of days ago. My uncle can verify that."

"What was the scuffle about?"

"A girl. Neither of us got her." My face grew warm. Of course, she said she loved me, but I screwed that up fast enough.

"Your Honor," Meadle said. "If the boy truly thinks himself to be a superhero, he may pose a danger to himself and others. He needs unceasing supervision."

Judge Barker glared. "On one hand, I have amiable. On the other, manipulative. On one hand, a leader, and on the other, a danger. What is your opinion on this matter, Mister Nowak?"

"I love my nephew," Uncle Bob said. "I would protect him with my life."

"No one's asking you to go that far. Cody, where do you want to live?"

"With my uncle. I don't want to be uprooted again. It was hard enough the first time. Besides, Uncle Bob is a great guy."

"Because he lets you do whatever you want when you want?"

I scoffed. "Hardly. But he listens to me, you know? He spends time with me. I didn't get a lot of that with my parents. They're pretty busy."

"That's a lie," my mother cried. "What about all the trips we made to Paris and London?"

"This is not a yelling match," the judge said. "One more outburst and I will hold you in contempt."

My mother sagged. “Yes, Your Honor.”

“Cody, a pair of county workers stopped by your house last week.”

I stiffened and glanced at my uncle. “They did?”

“They found your home to be clean,” the judge said, “but without the amenities many teenagers might expect. A television? An Xbox? How does this impact your lifestyle?”

“It doesn’t.” I shrugged, realizing it was true. The only thing I missed was being with Brittany.

“Very well. Does anyone else have something to add? Then, it is the opinion of the court that Cody Forester is a normal teenager of sound mind. His excellent grades in school prove that he is responsible and capable of making good life choices. There is no evidence of a mental condition that would remand him to an institution. Therefore, Cody Forester will remain under the guardianship of his uncle, Robert Nowak, until he is eighteen years of age, at which time he will take custody of himself.” She smacked her gavel down.

“That’s ridiculous,” my mother cried, jabbing her finger at me. “He ran away on Christmas Eve. In France, no less. And do you know what he said when the police found him? He thought he was a dog.”

“It was a metaphor.” I certainly was not a dog.

Judge Barker speared me with a beady eye. “Have you run away since?”

“No, Your Honor. That was my one and only time.”

"Mister Nowak?"

My uncle looked surprised. "He's never run away from me, Your Honor."

"Stop it!" said my mother. "Cody, you need help."

"I have help, Mom. I have Uncle Bob."

"Enough." The judge smacked her gavel again. "My decision stands. Mister Nowak, expect follow-up visits from Social Services for a period of one year."

He nodded. "Thank you, Your Honor."

My mother looked flabbergasted. "But... But..."

"You may appeal," the judge told her, "but I suggest you strengthen your case. Here in Florida, the courts side with the child. And at sixteen, Cody is old enough to choose where he wants to live."

"How dare you? I'm his mother."

Judge Barker's dangerous eyes flared. "On a side note, it is my opinion that you could not handle being a mother in addition to being a brain surgeon. You didn't like having a teenager underfoot, so you tore up roots and sent your son here. However, your actions garnered a negative response. It didn't make you look good. Now, you want to have your only son incarcerated in an institution. That way you can appear to be a kind and loving mother to an emotionally damaged boy. Only Cody isn't emotionally damaged, is he? At least, not yet."

Mom gasped as if she'd swallowed her tongue.

"I'm putting a recommendation in the file that you never regain custody of your son. I could make a case for child abuse. Count your blessings." Judge

Barker got to her feet.

"All rise," the bailiff bellowed.

We stood. My head swam. Was it over? Was that it? The judge returned to her chambers.

Suddenly, my uncle smothered me in a bear hug. He laughed.

I felt weak and might have collapsed if he hadn't been holding me up. "We won?"

"I told you there was nothing to worry about."

A grin spread over my face. I leaned back to look at him. He had tears in his eyes.

"Congratulations, Cody," Vice Principal Overhill said.

I shook his hand. "Thank you. Thank you both." I reached to shake with Coach.

"Glad you're staying, son," Coach said.

Overhill said, "I expect to see you in school tomorrow morning."

He and Coach Murgott left the room.

I gazed across the table. My mother picked up her purse and stormed out without a glance in my direction.

Dad walked over and hugged me. "No hard feelings, son. Your mother just wants the best for you."

"Are you sure about that?"

He held me at arm's length. "All I'm sure about is that I love you."

"I love you, too, Dad."

He shook hands with Uncle Bob. "About the television and such, I never sent all of Cody's things because in my heart I always hoped he would come back home to live. Now that he'll be down here permanently, there's no reason for me to keep them. I'll make arrangements to ship everything."

"That's very gracious of you, David," Uncle Bob said. "I hope you'll visit more often, as well."

Their banter faded into the background. I glanced across the table to find Dr. Saarsgard still seated there. She stared at me, her eyes narrowed into slivers of gray ice.

THIRTEEN

By the time we left the courthouse, my head was reeling. All I could think of was to find Brittany and tell her what happened. It didn't matter that she wasn't speaking to me. I just needed her to listen.

When I suggested that Uncle Bob drop me off at school, however, he completely misunderstood my reasons. He countered with the *Coffee Café*, his all-time favorite restaurant, and as hunger pangs were turning my stomach inside out, I agreed.

About a half-hour later, we pulled into the café parking lot. Foot-high grass sprouted from fissures in the asphalt, and the truck bounced like we were crossing railroad tracks. There were quite a few cars in the lot. My uncle tucked us into a spot, and I hopped from the cab. The sun beat down like it was July instead of April. I loosened my tie, scowling at the crystal blue sky.

We hurried into the welcomed coolness of the café. The place smelled like pancakes and coffee. It was busy, about half full, even though it was mid-morning. The din of conversation fell eerily as we stepped inside. Several people turned to stare, making me self-conscious.

Anne, the waitress, set her coffee pot on the counter and wrung her hands on her apron. "Well?"

Uncle Bob laughed, spreading his arms wide. "We want the big breakfast."

And I swear, the café erupted with "Atta boy," and "Good job." There was even a smattering of applause. My mouth dropped as I gazed over the many upturned faces. Were they clapping for me?

"Wonderful!" Anne cried, bustling over to give each of us a hug. "Breakfast is on the house. You go ahead and sit. I saved your favorite spot."

We crossed the room, zigzagging through the tables. People congratulated me and patted my shoulder. I recognized Mr. Archer; I helped re-roof his stable. Old Mrs. Binkley waved teary-eyed; her dog hated me. Uncle Bob knew everyone by name, of course, and thanked each for their well-wishes. Men stood to shake his hand or to give him manly hugs. He could've been running for office.

As we sat at the table, I whispered, "I don't even know most of these people. Why would they care about what happened to me?"

"You might not remember them, but they sure remember you." Uncle Bob grinned and gave me a wink. "That first week you helped me on the job? You made quite an impression."

"You went door-to-door asking for affidavits?"

"Nope." He motioned behind me. "Anne picked up the ball."

She placed a tall glass of chocolate milk and a coffee cup on the table. As she filled the cup, she said, “It’s a small town. Everyone knows everyone’s business. And they all wind up here at one time or another.”

“You did this for me?”

“No one wanted you to go when you wanted to stay. Scrambled eggs okay?”

I felt my face turn red. “I don’t know how to thank you.”

“You just keep being your own sweet self.” She pinched my cheek and walked away.

“I can’t believe it.” I shook my head. “The whole town gave me a character reference?”

“A lot of them,” he said. “When I went to your school to ask for help, your teachers jumped at the chance. Although I was surprised that the coach and the vice principal showed in person.”

“I was certain they were there for the other side.”

“Then I asked Anne, as I said. And then Earle Meyer.”

I perked. “Brittany’s grandfather? Does Brittany know, too?”

“I assume so. Didn’t she say anything about it?”

“No.” I wondered if she secretly worried that I would be taken away, or if she would be disappointed that I won in court. The idea made me squirm. I glanced around the room. A few diners still gazed in my direction, and they smiled and nodded as I met their eye. It was so weird. I never had so many virtual strangers care about me.

"Here we are, boys," Anne said. "Hope you're hungry."

"Starved." I beamed as she placed a platter of scrambled eggs, bacon, sausage, and home fries before me. Someone else carried the toast and grits.

"More coffee?" Anne asked. "Anything else?"

"Ketchup," said Uncle Bob.

She pulled a ketchup bottle magically from her pocket. "Then I'll leave you to it."

"She always makes me ask." Uncle Bob chuckled as he doused everything on his plate with ketchup.

I dug in, rolling my eyes in appreciation. It was the best breakfast ever. When I came up for air, I said, "Look who's here."

Sheriff Brad walked through the door. The sheriff hated my uncle ever since he was found innocent of a burglary, making the sheriff look bad. He hated me by extension. Now he crossed the room toward us, his face half-hidden by his sunglasses and hat, his pockets jingling.

"Heard what happened," he said. "Glad you're staying with us, son."

My eyes widened, and I stammered, "Th-thank you, sir."

Uncle Bob said, "And I want to thank you for your support, Sheriff. Your words went a long way."

"Just telling the truth." Sheriff Brad tipped his hat, then chose a seat at a distant table.

I blew out my breath. "This day is going down as the strangest day on record."

Uncle Bob said, "I'm just glad things can go back to normal."

The next day, I went to school still buoyed by the town's patronage. I felt certain that Brittany would want to congratulate me, too. So I tried to corner her in the hallway between classes.

She wouldn't meet my eyes. "Get out of the way, Cody."

"But, I want to talk to you. I want to tell you what happened."

"I know what happened. Everyone knows. Now, move."

My smile fell. The clamor of the crowd crashed over me. "I'm sorry, okay? For everything. Can't we just start over?"

"Start over?" she cried. "So you can take his side again? So you can tell me that I'm crazy, that I have no right–"

"I didn't say that. I didn't mean–"

"Sure." She pushed around me and disappeared in traffic.

I don't know how I got through the rest of the day. Finally I made it to my last class.

"You could try flowers," Maxwell told me after listening to my tale of woe. "Or chocolate. I never met a girl who didn't like chocolate."

"Chocolate won't work," Lonnie said. "It's too general. You need something that's just for her."

I thought of the fairy ring in the little box at home.

"All three, then," Maxwell said. "I'm telling you, the only way to get them to stop screaming at you is to stun them."

I knew he was right. I also knew it was worthless advice. Brittany wouldn't let me near her. I could get her the world, and she'd tell me to get out of her way.

I rode my bike home from school. By the time I reached my yard, I was drenched in sweat. I didn't think I could get more miserable. It was hard to believe that twenty-four hours earlier I was happy. I dumped my bike in its usual place and stared at the door. I did not want to go into an empty house. Instead, I walked across the yard into the woods.

Immediately, the sunlight cut off. The air felt ten degrees cooler. Leaves rustled, and birds sang. I started off at a trot, and before I knew it, I was streaking through the trees. I didn't know where I was going until I smelled sawgrass.

My subconscious had taken me to William. Was I seeking his advice because he was an older shapeshifter or because Brittany had obviously found him good looking? I shook my head, rejecting both ideas. I just didn't want to be alone. But as I neared the cabin, I heard voices. A familiar scent ran with the breeze.

Brittany.

Heart racing, I crept forward through the brush and sawgrass. Brittany and William sat together, legs dangling over the dock. They spoke quietly and laughed loudly.

Rage turned my vision crimson. Had she been seeing him all along? Had he scoffed behind my back the time I told him how much I loved her? A growl rumbled in my chest. I clenched my fists so hard, my nails bit into my palms. I would make them pay. She was my mate. She betrayed me. I imagined their blood dripping from my jaws.

What was I thinking? I couldn't hurt Brittany. It was the wolf that wanted revenge. The wolf was coming.

A spasm wracked my back, and I arched painfully. I shredded my shirt, my claws drawing blood. *Brittany. Run! I can't control...* Muscles bunched and rearranged. Fur swept my body. My senses sharpened; I smelled William's musky body, Brittany's hair gel. An apple she'd eaten was fresh on her lips. The lips I would never taste again.

Shoulders hunched, I stalked to the building.

FOURTEEN

I growled as I approached the wooden hut where William sat with Brittany. A ruff of fur stood straight out on my neck, making me look bigger, meaner. As if a hundred-and-fifty pound wolf needed help with intimidation.

William saw me first. All laughter drained from his face. He placed his hand on Brittany's arm.

Wrong move. I bared my teeth.

Brittany's eyes bulged. "Cody," she whispered. She scrambled to her knees as I stepped from the sawgrass. "Cody. Wait."

William urged her to her feet, his eyes never leaving mine. I imagined the taste of his blood, the crunch of his pretty-boy face in my jaws.

"Cody, stop!" Brittany cried.

William pulled her backwards. I gathered my haunches beneath me and bounded forward, leaping onto the porch. I struck the door just as it closed, nearly knocking it off its hinges. Brittany screamed. Her terror was like music.

I rammed my shoulder against the frame. Dust and debris rained over me. I hit again. The walls were solid, but they wouldn't keep me out. I barked. *Little Pig, Little Pig.*

The door burst in an explosion of splintered wood. A bear sailed over my head. He skidded and rolled on the dry lakebed then stood on two legs.

With a roar of rage, I leaped from the porch and fastened my jaws around William the Bear's throat. Hot, sweet blood filled my mouth. He grunted, and a frying-pan-sized paw caught my gut, knocking me free. By the time I gained my feet, he was running on all fours through the sawgrass. I flattened my ears and gave chase.

We zigzagged through clumps of rough-edged sawgrass. The bear took the brunt of it, forging a path and marking it with lost swatches of fur. It was impossible to lose him in the vegetation, although he obviously hoped I would.

With a burst of speed, I closed and dove onto his back, biting his shoulder. The heavy fur was like armor. He reared back, spilling me into the dirt. Then he took off in yet another direction.

A copse loomed ahead. Without warning, we splashed into a shallow pond. The clumsy bear lost his footing and fell on his face. I circled him and bit anything I could sink my fangs into. The bear spun, snapping at me. I avoided his teeth easily

His claws were the real weapon, however. He raked my face, bowling me over, then clawed my flank. I yelped and scrabbled to get out of reach.

He rose onto his hind legs, swamp water cresting

his thighs. Blood streamed down his neck, staining a white patch of fur on his chest. I bared my fangs and rushed him, aiming for that patch, but he back-handed me with unexpected force, sending me flying out of the pond.

I hit the bank hard. The blow left me dazed. By the time I staggered to my feet and shook the moisture from my fur, he was running for the trees. I streaked after him. He wouldn't get away.

I darted through the forest, skunk scrub and palmetto slapping my face. The gashes on my back burned. Ignoring the pain, I lengthened my stride.

I caught him as he entered a small clearing, latched onto his leg and wouldn't let go. He roared, rearing up, trying to swat me, but I buried my teeth further, ducking behind him to keep out of reach. His leg wobbled, and I knew I'd scored some major damage.

Then he sat on me. Air left in a whoosh. My vision went black with bear butt. I kicked and squirmed, trying to pull free, but he had me pinned. Stars encroached upon the darkness. My ribs felt crushed.

Struggling, I gathered my hind legs beneath me and levered the weight off. When I could breathe again, I coughed and wheezed.

He rolled over. As he lumbered to his feet, I went for his throat. He caught me in his massive arms. We stood together, jaws snapping, each trying for an opening. As a wolf I was taller, but he had me on weight, which gave him the edge in stability. Giving up, I spun from his grasp.

Then I went for his gut. Rooting with my muzzle, I found his magic bear hide belt and wrenched it from his body.

He melted at once, his bulk disappearing, leaving the pale, hairless shape of William. His face contorted with varying degrees of alarm. He backed away, limping as he did so, eyes darting as if searching for an escape.

There was no escape. I lowered my head, my lips curled. A growl rumbled deep in my chest. *You stole my mate, betrayed my friendship.* I paced to the side, my eyes on his.

"You're making a mistake." His voice cracked. Blood streamed from cuts upon his body. He picked up a fist-sized rock.

As if that would save him. I paced the other way, snarling.

"She loves you. All she talks about is you." He shook his head. "Why do you think she comes to see me?"

Liar, my wolf raged. But the human side of me jumped at his words. She loved me? There was still a chance?

"I'd just about had her convinced that you cared about her. Then you pull a stunt like this. What will she think now, huh? You tell me."

I pulled up short, staring at him. What had I done? Was I a monster? Out of control?

A liquid sensation spread from my stomach,

sending prickling waves over my flesh. Then the change hit. Muscles knotted and rearranged. Joints popped. I clenched my teeth against a howl of pain. My paws lengthened into fingers, and I buried them in the grass. Tears coursed down my cheeks. I wanted to cover my head and bawl.

But I felt William's eyes upon me.

"Leave," I said gruffly. "Go on. Get out."

His shadow fell over me. I looked up, filled with remorse and shame, and hating him even more.

He said, "I can't make it back without your help. My leg is mangled." He motioned to the dark wounds covering his calf.

That's how two naked and bloodied enemies ended up walking arm-in-arm through the Everglades. By the time we got to the cabin, night had fallen. I was exhausted, and William was writhing in pain. I dropped him at the dock, looking frantically for Brittany. Her car was gone. I didn't know whether to be relieved or disappointed. I settled on relief.

Hobbling across the dry lakebed, I searched for my clothes. I put on my Levis and checked the pockets to be sure I had my belongings. Then I slipped my battered feet into my shoes. My shirt was shredded, but I put it on anyway, wincing as it covered the claw marks. I walked back to William. He hadn't moved.

"I have a phone," I told him. "Do you want me to call 911?"

"I'll be all right," he said, panting.

“Fine.” Turning my back on him, I headed home.

I was so tired, I couldn’t even think of what to tell my uncle. When I saw his truck in the driveway, I considered sleeping in the yard and not facing him at all. But the lure of my bed won out.

I staggered up the steps to the porch and opened the door with difficulty.

Uncle Bob called from the kitchen. “You’re late. Dinner’s on the table.”

“Thanks, but I think I’ll pass.”

There was a pause, and then he shouted, “You’re bleeding.” He burst out of the kitchen and ran to me so fast I thought he would bowl me over. “What happened?”

I waved a hand, trying to limp away. “Something stupid.”

“Tell me.”

“You’re going to laugh.” I sighed. “Brittany wouldn’t speak to me in school today, and I was... upset. So when I got home, I decided to hike through the woods for a while. You know, blow off steam. And I ran into that bear that’s been spotted around town.”

His shoulders dropped, and he smirked. “Kill it?”

“No. But I think he’ll keep his distance from now on.”

“Let me have your shirt.”

I gave it to him. It was little more than a rag.

He shook it. “This is why I always–”

“Shop at Howard’s.” I chuckled. “I’m going to

shower and go to bed."

"All right. I'll put your dinner in the fridge in case you get hungry during the night."

I nodded and made my way to the bathroom. I looked in the mirror. Blood crusted my face and three long gashes crossed from forehead to jaw. Bite marks scored my shoulder. The deepest wounds, however, traveled over my hips and down the back of my thighs. Sitting down might be a problem for a while.

I turned on the water and stepped under the spray. It stung like vinegar on every cut. I washed my hair, but couldn't bear to put soap on the rest of me. I toweled off and went to my room.

Gingerly, I laid face down on my bed. I expected to fall instantly asleep. Instead, I wept. Great wracking sobs that made me feel worse. I squeezed my eyes tight, but I could still see Brittany's face, still hear her terrified screams. In fear of me. Oh, my God.

What have I done?

FIFTEEN

I awoke with a start, thinking I was late for school. It took a few moments to remember there was no school on Saturday. I wasn't going anywhere anyway. I felt like I'd been flogged, like any movement would crack my skin wide open.

I lay in bed on my stomach wearing only a bath towel. My room was bright and cheerful. I scowled and pulled my pillow over my head.

I was just nodding off again when Mr. Sunshine himself came in. He dragged a kitchen chair noisily behind him.

"Good morning," said Uncle Bob. "How's my young bear tracker today?"

I groaned and pulled the pillow tighter.

"You know, they say Davy Crockett killed a bear when he was three years old."

I groaned again.

He chuckled. "I brought you a cup of Howard's special tea. Can you sit up?"

"No," I said, my voice muffled.

"What was that?"

"No, I can't sit up. A bear bit my ass." I lifted onto

my elbows. "And whose big idea was it to make eastward facing windows? Whoever built this house was a total jerk."

"Grumpy is good," he said. "I can work with grumpy."

I buried my face in my pillow. To my relief, he left the room. I heard him moving around in the kitchen. Probably tossing the tea down the drain. That was fine. I didn't deserve it. If anyone was a total jerk, I was.

I rolled to my side, tugging the crumpled towel from beneath me and draping it over my middle. I reached to my backside. Damp claw marks ran from my tailbone to my knees. My butt cheeks felt like corduroy.

Memories rose like snapshots: Brittany sitting next to a shirtless William, her eyes alight, her nose crinkled in that way I thought was only for me. Then I saw her on her feet, her face stark with fear. She pleaded with me to stop, but I couldn't.

No way was I getting her back now.

Uncle Bob burst into the room with a grin and a purpose. "Success. I found a straw."

Actually, it was a *Bic* pen with the ink cartridge torn out. He set the mug of tea before me, the pen sticking out the top. Steam wafted into my face.

I eyed the mug warily. Howard made several types of tea. One had powdered snake blood in it. Another was as thick as mud. This one was as sweet and light as flower petals.

I sipped slowly, feeling warmth spread over my tongue and down my throat. The sensation was soothing. I imagined filling a bathtub with the stuff and crawling in.

Abruptly, I remembered Brittany talking about an herbal bath the night I watched her from the bushes. I shouldn't have spied on her. Everything I did was wrong. Now she was gone.

"You okay?" my uncle asked.

"Burned my mouth," I lied, blinking back tears. "Uncle Bob, when I took that walk in the woods yesterday afternoon, I never intended to be a wolf. But when I saw that bear, I just shifted. You know? Like I had no choice."

"That must've been scary." He sat on the kitchen chair and leaned his forearms on his knees, his brow furrowed. "I can only imagine how difficult it is to have the wolf with you all the time. You don't have an on-off switch like I do. I only change with the full moon. But it seems to me it was a lucky thing your subconscious took over when it did. A boy against a bear." He spread his hands. "You might have been hurt a lot worse."

"Still. I should be able to control myself."

"It will come. In the meantime, you could try keeping a journal. Mark down what you're doing when you feel the urge to shift. Maybe you'll see a pattern. Something you can avoid."

"But what if I get really angry at someone and shift right there in front of them? And they like run into a house or something, and I'm like leaping against the door and–"

"Never happen. I know you. You'd stop yourself before you hurt another human being." He stood, picking up my empty mug. "Get some rest. You'll heal faster. I'll check in on you later." With a pat to my shoulder, he left the room.

I stared at the empty doorway. He didn't know me as well as he thought. I *hadn't* stopped myself. Now William was hurt, and I couldn't even tell anyone where he was.

I grimaced and punched my pillow. Uncle Bob didn't understand. No one did. I should be locked up far away before I hurt someone else.

Suddenly, I thought of the werewolf asylum in the Fjallen Mountains.

I slept throughout the morning. My uncle woke me twice to give me tea.

Late that afternoon, Howard arrived. I didn't want to see him. When he entered my room, I kept my eyes shut.

"Howdy," he said quietly.

I said nothing.

"You asleep?" he asked.

I paused. "Yes."

With a grunt, he sat on the chair. "Bob told me you're concerned about being out of control. I brought this."

I opened my eyes. He held up a parchment envelope with something green inside.

"Bugleweed leaves," he said. "They'll keep you calm, stop the shakes. Just lay one in your cheek like this." He took a leaf out of the envelope and put it in his mouth. "If you feel like you might shift, bite it. Chew it like gum. They taste all right, and the effect is immediate."

I took the envelope. "That sounds easy enough."

"Might stain your teeth a little green."

I groaned. "Man."

"Which do you want, green teeth or fangs?"

I nodded and slipped a leaf inside my cheek. It tasted like freshly mown grass. "Like kissing a cow."

He said, "I'll bring more periodically."

"Thank you."

"Mind if I check out your ass?"

I sighed. "Suit yourself."

He lifted the towel. The terrycloth stuck to the dried blood of my wounds, and I hissed.

"Are you in pain?"

"A bit," I said.

"I'd better swab it out."

"No," I blurted, leaning away. "I can do it. Just bring me a basin or something."

Howard grunted and left the room. I was sorry to offend him by refusing his help, but it was too weird. I doubted he'd offer to swab my backside if he knew I'd tried to kill his son.

A short time later, my uncle came in carrying a stack of towels and a large bowl filled with a sour-smelling tonic. Howard followed on his heels. He held a steaming mug near my nose.

I propped up on my elbows, breathing it in. "That's not tea."

"Chicken soup. Old Indian remedy."

Uncle Bob set the bowl and the towels on the chair. "We'll give you some privacy."

They went out, closing the door behind them.

My stomach growled. Moving slowly so as not to spill the mug, I levered myself up into a sitting position. I leaned on one hip as I slurped the soup. There were chips of carrot and potato and chunks of diced chicken. It was the best thing I ever tasted.

After I finished, I washed myself with the tonic. It stung in places, but for the most part, it made me feel better. At least I was clean. I thought I was healing pretty well. The effort exhausted me, however. I plopped back in bed and was asleep almost instantly.

I woke once in the middle of the night. Someone had draped a sheet over me and cleared away the bowl and mug. My skin felt tight, but I could move without difficulty. I considered going to the kitchen for something to eat, but fell back to sleep before coming to a decision.

In the morning, I heard voices. They came from the living room. I relaxed. Only Howard would dare to show up so early. I squinted and rubbed my face. Sunlight streamed through the window, and birds sang cheerfully.

I kicked my way free from the sheet, then sat on

the edge of the bed. No pain. Stretching my arms overhead, I gave a loud yawn.

"Feeling better?" Uncle Bob asked from the doorway.

"Yeah." I grinned. "Hungry, though."

"You need protein." He stepped into the room. "I bought bacon and eggs, and there's still some cheese in there. Are you up to cooking for yourself? Howard has a fresh lead on William. We're going to follow it up."

My heart skipped, and I wondered if his wolf sense could hear it. I rubbed my face and tried to look nonchalant. "Really? What's happened?"

"A contact of his said William checked into one of those twenty-four hour emergency clinics in South Bay. Dog bite or something. Apparently somebody drove him to the clinic, but Howard's friend didn't catch the color or make of the car."

I scowled. It was probably a lime green Volkswagen. Brittany's car. She must've gone back to the cabin to be sure he was okay. I pictured her face as she saw him lying on the porch. Did she run to him? Did she kiss him?

"You okay?" Uncle Bob asked.

"Why? What do you mean?"

"Well, your face just went through about twenty different expressions at once."

"No, it didn't."

"It did. I just saw it."

"Saw what?"

"Boy, sometimes talking to you is like nailing Jello to a tree. Is something wrong or not?"

I almost told him all of it–where William was staying, his involvement with Brittany. Oh, and surprise–William can turn into a bear.

But then Howard appeared, and I looked away in shame.

"How's our young Mai Coh this morning?" Howard asked.

"Fine. Forget about me. Go get your son."

"We haven't found him yet," Uncle Bob said, "but the clinic's a good starting point. I'll see if I can sniff him out."

He slapped my back and grinned. Then they clomped down the hallway and out the front door. There came a shriek of door hinges as they climbed into Howard's beat-up old truck, then the deep roar of its eight cylinders as he started the engine.

I balled my sheet and tossed it behind me as I got out of bed. Rummaging through the pile of dirty clothes on my closet floor, I found the pair of jogging pants my father bought me. Didn't smell too bad. I slipped them on and headed toward the kitchen.

Before I got there, I heard tires crackling on the gravel driveway. At first, I thought my uncle was back–but that didn't feel right. Apprehension clenched my stomach, and my muscles tensed. I opened the door and stepped onto the porch.

Dr. Saarsgard's limousine rolled to a stop behind my uncle's truck. The windows were tinted, and I couldn't see inside, but I knew she was there.

Only, *why* was she there? I won the court case. Didn't that mean she had to leave me alone?

In the back of my head, a voice babbled–I knew it was too easy. I knew she wouldn't give up. It isn't over. She's just begun.

For several moments, nothing happened. Perhaps she was testing me to see what I would do. Would I take off running? Would I get a shotgun? When I did nothing, the driver got out, walked around the long car, and opened the door.

Dr. Saarsgard stepped from the vehicle. She wore an ice-white pantsuit, and her hair encircled her head in silver braids. "Good morning, Cody."

I tried out several responses in my head: What are you doing here? Get off my property. Nice day, isn't it? I settled on, "Have you come to say good-bye?"

She shook her head and mouthed the word *no*. "Your parents left. I tried to stop them. But there's something about me they never understood. I always get what I reach for. Always."

I gulped, trying to keep down the coldness creeping from my stomach. "I'll call my uncle."

She smiled. "He just left."

Was she watching the house? My wolf sense prickled. Suddenly, I realized there was someone else in the limo. Someone big. Like a bodyguard.

"I meant on my cell," I said flippantly, although, in truth, I didn't know where my cell was.

"There's no need to alarm him," she said. "I've merely come to reason with you."

"And you think it's reasonable for me to go with you quietly and allow you to conduct experiments on me."

She pressed a hand to her chest dramatically. "You speak as if I were a mad scientist. I assure you, I am not a villain. Yes, I take blood and occasional tissue samples from the lycans under my care. The rest of the time, they are free to walk the compound, play video games–"

"It's a mental asylum."

"They're safer there. No one will hunt them. Those they love are safer as well. I notice you have no girlfriend. Someday, however, you may fall in love. Wouldn't it be more prudent if you did so with one of your own kind in a controlled environment rather than here in society where anything could happen?"

I remembered Brittany's screams as I attacked the door, making the whole cabin shake.

"We don't need to be enemies, Cody. I have an agenda. We all do. But I like to think my retreat is mutually beneficial."

"What's your agenda?" I asked.

Her eyes lit. "To be immortal, of course. If I can isolate the hormonal inconsistencies in your body, I will make my vaccine. Children will be able to heal themselves. Disability will be conquered. Parents will praise my name forever." For a moment, she looked like a true mad scientist.

"Frau Saarsgard," I whispered, expecting to hear a crash of thunder and a horse whinny at her name.

She gave me a withering look. Without another word, she got back into her car. I caught a whiff of the man with her as the door opened. He had a musky scent, and I wondered if her bodyguard was a werewolf.

The limousine retreated and was soon out of sight. I sat on the porch swing. I doubted the good doctor had a chance of creating a werewolf vaccine and curing all children of their ills. But I understood what she meant about living in isolation. What if Brittany hadn't gotten into the cabin in time? What if the door hadn't held? She would be safer without me.

Maybe I should go.

I was still on the porch swing when Howard's truck rattled up the drive. He and my uncle got out and climbed to the porch. Howard carried a paper sack. He looked grim.

"Did you find him?" I asked.

"No," Uncle Bob said. "How are you doing? Did you eat?"

I shook my head. "Lost my appetite. The good doctor showed up."

A shadow crossed his face so fast I wasn't sure I'd seen it. He sat beside me. "What did she want?"

"She said my parents gave up too soon, and she always gets what she wants."

"Sorry to disappoint her." He slapped my knee and pushed to his feet. "How about a bacon and cheese omelet? Howard? You hungry? And we bought some fresh tomatoes from a roadside stand." He took the bag and disappeared into the house.

"That was abrupt," I said.

Howard growled. "Even a bear does not test the deep waters."

"Uh-huh. Do you realize that most of your proverbs have to do with animals?"

He looked at me. "Every animal knows more than you."

"Harsh much?"

He shrugged. "It applies to all of us."

I paused, and then asked, "Is it true that some medicine men can turn into animals?"

"A few."

"How long does it take to learn to do something like that?"

"Years of study, of cleansing the spirit."

"So how old would they be? Seventeen?"

He looked offended. "Certainly not. No boy has the stamina, the concentration."

"Never?"

"It would take a special child, a spirit child. Maybe there were such beings once, but..." He shook his head.

I avoided his eyes. William wasn't a spirit child.

He was just the jerk who stole my girl. Besides, if he was so special, how come I kicked his butt?

We ate our omelets on the porch. Mine was just the way I liked it: brown and crusty on the outside, slushy on the inside. Afterwards, I gathered the plates and carried them into the kitchen to wash. I was still bummed about William being referred to as a spirit child, angry that anyone should think he was special. If he was goodness and light, what did that make me? I was so deep in thought I didn't notice the commotion outside until my uncle called my name.

"Cody, would you come out here?" He met me at the door. "Have you been ordering things off that intro net?"

"No." Frowning, I stepped onto the porch.

A moving van was on the grass. Its back end was open and showing wall-to-wall boxes. The side of the van had *Thompson Air and Freight* printed in big blue letters. Two men stood near the cab. A third was at the porch steps.

"Cody Forester?" he asked. He had salt-and-pepper hair and about a day's worth of beard. Sunlight made the gray hair on his chin sparkle. "I need your signature here and here, and initial here."

I took the clipboard, glancing over the paperwork. "It's from my father."

Uncle Bob said, "He mentioned he was going to send your things."

"But I didn't think he meant a whole house worth."

I signed the papers, thinking Dad must've paid extra for a Sunday delivery. He wanted to be sure that we were home.

The man took back his clipboard, then called to the others, "Let's go, boys."

So began a progression of men and boxes up the steps and into the house.

"Just stack them against the wall in the dining room," Uncle Bob told them. "That's fine."

I stood to the side, my mouth hanging open. I never owned this much stuff, had I? But the boxes kept coming, stacked double high and three deep. Soon there was just a narrow aisle leading through to the kitchen.

Then they carried up a red couch wrapped in plastic.

"That's the old couch from our rec room," I said. "Mom always hated it."

"Guess it's ours now," Uncle Bob muttered.

I remembered him saying he didn't want many possessions in case he had to move fast.

"Anything that you don't want we can give to Howard." I said, then pointed to a large, flat box as it passed by. "Except that one. I'm pretty sure that's my forty-two inch plasma."

Uncle Bob gave me a strained smile. "We'll manage."

Howard stepped beside us. "Just know I'm here for you. Whatever you need to get rid of. What are friends for, right?"

By the time the moving van pulled away, the house was almost unlivable. A shrink-wrapped mattress and two dressers blocked the hallway. The couch and two armchairs filled the living room.

"I'm sure we can pitch most of this." I opened the nearest box. "Oh, look. My Blu-ray."

"We'll go through it slowly and make deliberate decisions," Uncle Bob said. "Let's not do anything rash."

So we went through it slowly. There was a box of textbooks that should have been turned in to school. A box of movies and x-box games, some of them borrowed from friends. Another box held my cds. I smiled at that–I'd missed my tunes. We came across a cache of Star Wars action figures and a clock shaped like C3P0's head. There were also some old Avengers comic books. Howard was happy to see them.

For a while, I forgot all about my troubles with Brittany and William.

SIXTEEN

Monday morning found me between silken sheets in a bed twice the size of my old one. The room felt crowded. I rolled over to see my desk with my old computer tucked beneath. On the wall above was a framed and signed poster of Angelina Jolie as Laura Croft. I was surprised my dad parted with that one.

Howard got the rest of the posters to sell at his perpetual garage sale. I also gave him the big dresser with the mirror. I kept the tall chest of drawers. It fit neatly into my closet and was now stocked with t-shirts and socks. My old suits and dress shirts went to Howard. There must've been a dozen. They didn't fit me, and where would I wear them anyway?

I dressed for school and padded barefoot into the living room. It looked like a different place. We had the red couch and a coffee table along one wall. Three lamps sat on the table–I guess my dad thought we needed more light. My uncle's worn-out recliner was still in the middle of the room smack in front of the flat screen. Having a real TV wasn't as cool as I hoped, however. We didn't have cable, so the reception was snowy.

Boxes filled the dining room. Most of them were empty–my uncle planned to take them to the recycling center. In the corner of the room was a full-sized pinball machine. Back home, my friends and I played it for hours. What would I do with it now that I didn't have any friends?

Shaking my head, I entered the kitchen. Even this room felt the onslaught of my possessions. My blender sat on the counter. I used to make smoothies in it. There was also a set of pots and pans–the kind you might get as a housewarming gift.

Uncle Bob stood at the sink making his cup of instant coffee.

I opened the refrigerator and pulled out a jug of milk. "I was thinking about staying home today."

"Nonsense," he said. "You've gone to school on much less sleep."

That wasn't the point, of course. I didn't want to face Brittany, didn't want to have her look at me like the monster I was. But if I told him the whole story, he'd know William was a bear and I was the *dog* that bit him. I wasn't sure how he'd react to that, so I ate my Lucky Charms in silence.

On the ride into school, I said, "I know you're not comfortable with all my junk in the house."

He chuckled. "I'm just used to having all my possessions fit in the back of this truck."

"That's what I mean. I don't mind if we get rid of it. Howard can sell the big stuff. And if we have to get out of town in a hurry, we can leave the rest."

"No," he said. "These are your things. Your roots. I want you to feel like you belong here."

"But if something should happen and we have to move–"

"Just make sure nothing happens." He glanced at me. "We'll live with everything as is for a while. See what we need and what we don't."

"One thing we don't need is a television that doesn't pick up any channels."

"Not so fast. Howard told me he could get us one of them satellite dishes."

I perked. "Really?"

Uncle Bob grinned. "We'll get one so big we can pick up the air traffic chatter from West Palm. Or the space shuttle launches from Canaveral."

"I don't think big is better in this case." I laughed, my head full of possibilities.

At school, we found the drop-off line backed up. We inched forward in the stink from the cars before us. I couldn't figure out the problem. Then I saw a silver limousine parked ahead.

My eyes widened. "Oh, crap."

Uncle Bob said nothing, but my wolf felt him fly into a rage. Heat radiated from his body, and his heart rate tripled. He pulled behind the limo and slammed out of the truck. Stomping to the driver's door, he rapped on the window so hard I thought he'd break it. "What are you doing here?" he yelled. "Where is she?"

I wondered if I should warn him about the big guy who'd been in the car before. I opened my door and slid out. A crowd formed, staring at my uncle.

"Answer me," he yelled. "Where did she go?"

Just then, Dr. Saarsgard stepped out of the main doors and crossed the courtyard toward us. Her hair seemed frozen in an intricate, upswept do that didn't budge as she walked. Uncle Bob strode over the pavement. Kids scattered out of his way. I trotted after him, trying to catch up. Part of me was embarrassed that he was making a scene. Part was grateful he wanted to protect me.

"What do you think you're doing?" he yelled. "How dare you show up at his school?"

She gave a tight smile, her expression icy. "If you must know, I had an appointment with the vice principal."

"You have no right."

"These are public grounds. I have as much right as you to be here."

"We'll see about that. I'll take out a restraining order. I'll have you arrested if you come within fifty miles of my boy."

"Do you truly think a minor writ will deter me?" She took a step forward. "Admit it, Mister Nowak. You are out of your league."

I heard a sound behind me and turned to see the

limo driver opening the passenger door. A man stepped out. He wore sunglasses and a suit like something out of *Men in Black*, but he was built like a pro wrestler. Even at a distance, I could smell the wolf in him. A warning cry died in my throat. Uncle Bob was no match for a three hundred pound werewolf.

"Did you expect them to give custody to *you*?" Uncle Bob yelled. "Who do you think you are? You lost the hearing. Go home!"

The big man stood beside the limo. His suit coat strained to contain his bulk. I turned to face him, my gaze even. I had Uncle Bob's back.

"Are you so naïve to believe that legal custody is the only venue?" The doctor laughed. "Keep your custody. I prefer possession."

"Is that a threat?"

"It's a declaration. The world is vast, Mister Nowak, and I own more of it than you."

She brushed past, and I caught a nauseating whiff of wolfsbane. She slid into the back of the stretch limo. The big man nodded slightly as if to say he'd see me again. He got into the car, and the driver closed the door. They drove away.

"Come on," my uncle growled, walking toward school.

I glanced around at the gathered crowd. Everyone stared. Eff stood among them, his eyes meeting mine. Ducking my head, I followed Uncle Bob.

At the office, a woman with glasses on her nose

smiled. “May I help you?”

Uncle Bob ignored her. He stormed into Vice Principal Overhill’s office. “I want to know what you told that woman about my nephew.”

Overhill didn’t look surprised or alarmed to see us. He nodded to me. “Cody, please close the door.”

I did, feeling bemused.

“I demand to know what she wanted,” Uncle Bob said.

Overhill spread his hands, elbows on his desk. “She asked about Cody’s grades, his friends, his absences. Oddly, she wanted to know if his absences corresponded with phases of the moon.”

“What did you tell her?”

“Nothing,” Overhill said. “Emphatically and repeatedly. I will not give anyone such information. Not without your expressed consent.”

I grinned. “Way to go, Mister O.”

“That woman is dangerous,” Uncle Bob said. “She may be mentally unbalanced. It’s possible she may try to take Cody against his will.”

“You mean kidnap him?” Overhill frowned and got to his feet.

“She told me as much just now.”

I stared at my uncle. I’d had the same fear the first time she showed up at the house, but hearing it spoken aloud made it that much more real.

“A serious charge,” Overhill said. “You should take your suspicions to the sheriff. As for security around the school, be assured that Cody is safe here. As long as he is on school grounds, nothing will happen to him."

"Thank you." Uncle Bob left the vice principal's office and led me to the main doors. "I'll pick you up at the office. Don't leave the building without me."

"I'll be all right."

"I mean it," he said.

With a curt nod, I went to class. I felt dazed, like in a dream. Or a nightmare. I kept thinking I saw the doctor lurking in doorways and around corners. My nerves jangled.

Brittany wasn't in history class. I worried that she was ill, worried more that she hated me. At least she missed the spectacle with Dr. Saarsgard and my uncle, although she was certain to hear about it later.

By lunchtime, my stomach was in so many knots, I couldn't eat. I grabbed a Dew and a bag of chips and sat at my usual table in the back of the room.

After a few moments, Eff set his tray across from me and sat. "Ever hear of a balanced meal?"

I sighed. "Not hungry."

"So what was that about with the ice queen?"

I looked at him, thinking I should clam up. But I couldn't stop myself. "Doctor Saarsgard. She's like this mad scientist or something. She wants to take me to an asylum and run experiments on me."

"Why? Because you're... different?"

I looked down at my hands. That was as good an explanation as any.

Eff took a big bite of sandwich. "How'd she find

out about your... special abilities?"

"She knows my parents. I guess they told her. And get this. They wanted to give her custody, take me away from Uncle Bob. There was this big court battle and everything." I shook my head.

"That sucks. So why was she here?"

"Trying to find something she could use against me. My parents gave up, but she's determined. My uncle thinks she might try to snatch me."

Eff looked at me for a long moment. "Let me get this straight. An evil scientist found out about your healing capabilities. Now, she wants to kidnap you so she can run mad experiments. She isn't afraid of your uncle, doesn't care about the law, and she's rich so she has resources. You've set yourself up with a heck of an adversary."

"You don't believe me."

"Oh, this isn't disbelief. Disbelief is when you beat a guy within an inch of his life and he shows up two days later without a freaking bruise. But that happened, so..." He crunched into an apple. "You say she's looking for something she can use against you?"

"Looks like it."

"Maybe we need something to use against her. Where's she staying?"

"How would I know?"

"Shouldn't be hard to find out. All the major chains keep an online roster."

I nearly choked on my drink. "They do?"

"If you know where to look." He frowned. "We'll break into her room and get some intel. I have the tools."

My wolf leaped in agreement but I pushed it down. "Too risky."

"Suit yourself." He took a swig of milk. "But I'd watch my back if I were you."

That didn't make me feel very good.

Uncle Bob picked me up after school. He hovered over me all evening, barely giving me a moment to myself. He even locked the front door–that alone proved how rattled he was.

Saarsgard didn't show. I knew in my gut she was out there somewhere waiting to spring on me, but I couldn't let on to Uncle Bob. So we ate pizza and watched the Stanley Cup playoffs. We could barely see the hockey puck for all the snow.

The next day went off without a hitch. I even finished my shop project early–a nice little spice rack with scrollwork on top. It was good enough to give to Brittany, if she ever let me. After school, I went to the office to find Uncle Bob waiting. He gave a grunt in greeting. As we walked to his truck, his head swiveled about like he was my bodyguard. All he needed was some dark sunglasses and a dangle coming out of his ear.

When we were safely seated, he started the

engine and pulled out of the lot. "I'll have to ask Howard to drive you the next couple of days. I have a big job coming up, and it's all the way on the other side of town."

I shook my head. "I'm not comfortable with that. I'd be pulling him away from his garage sale. That's how he makes a living," I added as if he didn't know.

Uncle Bob scowled. "Then I'll turn down the job."

"No! I'll take my bike like I normally would. I don't want her controlling my life."

"But what if she–"

"I'll outrun her. You know I can, especially on a bike. And I'll have my phone. I'll call 911."

He nodded. "I told the sheriff what's happening."

I gazed out the window, my thoughts whirling. Sheriff Brad and Grandpa Earle were best friends. If the sheriff knew I was in danger, it followed that Brittany knew because Grandpa Earle couldn't keep a secret if his life depended on it. Maybe Brittany would take pity on me and offer a ride home. We could start over.

"There's still time to tell them I can't take that job," Uncle Bob said. "It wouldn't be a problem. It's more important that you're safe."

I blinked from my daydream. "I'll be fine. Besides, I haven't caught a whiff of her all day. She probably went back to Sweden."

In the morning, Uncle Bob left before I got up. I heard him lock the door. The house was filled with sunshine and birdsong–and a bunch of furniture that didn't feel like it belonged. I showered and shaved, my thoughts on Brittany and the wild hope that she would speak to me again.

After breakfast, I grabbed my bike and headed for school. The morning was bright and sunny with a strong breeze that blew in scents from all over. I rode with my attention on my surroundings, aware of anyone coming up behind me. There was no sign of a silver limo.

I reached downtown in record time and pulled into traffic on Southern Blvd. I caught snatches of music from passing cars, mostly country tunes. I stopped for the light in front of the Crestwood Shopping Center and looked over at the Video Stop where Brittany worked.

That's where we met, where we'd had our first real kiss. I remembered how soft her lips were, the sweet taste of her lipstick, the curves of her body pressing against mine. The memory was so vivid, for a moment I forgot to breathe.

"May I offer you a ride?" asked Dr. Saarsgard.

I gasped, and a cloud of her wolfsbane perfume hit me in the face like she'd sprayed the stuff out the window.

My head spun. I had trouble staying on the bike.

How could I be so stupid? The limousine was right next to me, blocking traffic in the next lane. Saarsgard leaned back from the window, disappearing in shadow, and the goon across from her reached to open the door.

I had to get out of there. I gave my head a shake, trying to wake up. The traffic light was still red. Drivers around me sipped their morning coffee and stared forward like nothing was happening. The limo door opened.

I hopped the curb and took off down the sidewalk. Fresh air helped clear my thoughts. As I reached the corner, the light changed, and I zoomed across with no problem.

Of course, that meant that the limo could also move. I looked behind to see it weaving through traffic. Gaining on me. I lowered my head and pedaled for all I was worth.

At the next corner, the light turned red. I skidded into a right turn. The sidewalk ended with a thump. Instead, a well-worn horse trail ran along the blacktop. I sped down it, dust rising behind me.

Other than the gas station at the corner, there was nothing around. No place to hide. My side of the road had a flat field of scrub palm dotted with for-sale signs. The other side was thick with trees and vines. The road was straight. A stream of cars came at me, probably from a housing development, everyone trying to get to work.

I had no idea where I was, no clue how to get away. Panic made me see in all directions at once. My teeth ached. I knew my fangs showed, knew I traveled unnaturally fast.

Behind me, I heard a screech. A horn honked. The silver limo pulled into traffic against the red light.

I gripped the handlebars. My hands prickled with sprouting hair. Nails bit into my palms like claws.

Ahead, the horse trail ended. It continued on the other side of the road, cutting through the trees. I swerved across traffic, almost getting hit, and disappeared under cover of mangrove and pine.

The path wasn't wide enough for a car much less a stretch limo, but I knew I couldn't slow down. If that three-hundred pound werewolf gave chase, he might catch me on foot.

I concentrated on slowing my breathing, bringing my heart rate under control, and stopping the change. All I needed was for someone to snap a picture and sell it to the tabloids: Amazing Wolf Boy Rides Bicycle.

I burst out of the trees and made a sharp right, following the trail along another road. I expected to be lost, but familiarity whipped my head around. This street led to school.

Relief washed over me. My legs shook. I pedaled slower, pacing cars as they headed toward the student drop-off. Ahead, the school's concrete courtyard shone bright white in the morning sun. Groups of kids milled about. I coasted through them, garnering a few odd stares on my way to the bike rack. Self-conscious, I ran my tongue over my teeth. Everything fine there.

As I parked my bike, Maxwell and Lonnie waved me down.

"You kinda look like a ghost," Maxwell said.

Lonnie stared like I was sprouting horns. I combed my hair back with my fingers and found it dripping with sweat.

I forced a laugh, motioning with my thumb. “Just clocked my bike at fifty miles per hour.”

“That old thing? Yeah. Right.”

We walked along the front of the building. They talked about their garage band while I looked for a silver limo. No sign of it. I was safe.

As we entered the main doors, air conditioning hit me like a ton of ice. I was drenched through. By the time I got to Trig, I was shivering–which was a good thing because it kept me awake. I was exhausted, rebounding from an adrenalin overload.

Second hour was gym. It was volleyball day. As usual, I wasn’t picked for a team. Strangely enough, Eff wasn’t chosen either.

I sidled next to him. “You know the hotel room you wanted to visit? Let’s do that.”

“When?”

“As soon as possible.”

“Fine.” He nodded. “We’ll go after school.”

SEVENTEEN

I didn't see Eff again until lunch when he set his sandwich-laden tray on my table.

"You're late," I said. "I thought you weren't showing."

"I had to go to the little boys' room. You know, the one by the office?"

Everyone knew that the school's cell phone blocker didn't extend as far as the boys bathroom near the office. You could surf the Web on your Blackberry. I assumed that was what Eff was doing.

"What did you find out?"

He surveyed his tray as if deciding what to eat first. "Doctor Saarsgard is staying at The Breakers."

"Do you know that place?"

"As a matter of fact, I do. It happens that my dad's hardware store is one of their suppliers. I've made deliveries there."

"Great. So we'll just go and–"

"Not so fast," he said around a bite of baloney and pickle sandwich. "We have to arrange a little alone time. Wouldn't want anyone to walk in on us. That's your job."

"Why me?"

"Because you're the one she wants. You have to get her chasing you and make her think she's still chasing you while we go to the hotel." He wiped his mouth and balled up the napkin. "You do that, and I'll run home to pick up my equipment. Where do you want to meet?"

It felt a little surreal, like I was planning my own doom. My voice came out weak and whiny. "In the woods next to school, there's this horse trail–"

"Takes you to A Road. I know the spot." He stood, picking up his tray. "Just be sure to keep them busy."

I nodded. "I will."

But I had no idea how. It wasn't just Saarsgard that I had to worry about–I had to fool her werewolf goon, too. He could track me through the woods and out again. I had to make them think I was hiding–and the trick had to be convincing enough to keep them there.

I gnawed on it all afternoon. When last hour rolled around, I sat behind the worktable in Shop with my head in my hands. I was a dead man. Maxwell and Lonnie roughhoused around me. I didn't even look up.

Then Maxwell said, "Hey, Cody. You forgot to take your spice rack home yesterday."

I picked it up, staring at the perfect scrollwork, the lovingly lacquered grain, the eight glass bottles with cork stoppers.

Lonnie laughed. "You look like you found the Holy Grail."

"Pretty much." I grinned at him.

Mr. Conklin kept a stash of old Publix bags so students could carry their projects home. I put the spice rack in a bag and set it at my feet.

When school ended, I hurried to the bathroom by the office. I texted my uncle to let him know I was hanging with friends and would be home later. Then I smashed the spice rack into beautifully stained and varnished kindling.

I popped out all the corks, then broke one of the little bottles. With the jagged glass, I sliced my thumb deep enough to keep from healing up right away. I dribbled blood into the remaining bottles and swirled it around to coat the sides. Milking my thumb, I drizzled more blood into the bag of splintered wood. I touched each piece to be sure my scent was well distributed. Then I put the bottles and broken glass inside. I washed my hands after the bleeding had stopped, and tossed the wadded up paper towel into the bag with everything else.

Sack in hand, I walked outside. There were still plenty of students in the courtyard, so I wasn't conspicuous; I didn't want to look like bait. I walked slowly to the bike rack, acting as if I was enjoying the sunshine, all the while feeling that I was being watched.

When I reached my bike, I hung the bag from the handlebars and pedaled down the turnaround to the street. There was no sign of a silver limousine. What if they didn't make a run for me? What if they were in their room when we showed up?

That would put a stick in my wicket, as my mother used to say. For a moment, I saw her the way I had as a kid–driving her convertible, hair covered with a scarf, singing along with the radio. When did she start hating me?

I pulled onto the path that ran along the street. Like a surfacing shark, the silver limo appeared behind me. I glanced at it, standing on my pedals and picking up speed.

The horse path through the trees was nearly hidden on this end. I turned onto it sharply. As soon as I was out of sight from the street, I flung pieces of the bloody kindling to either side. A door slammed. I gasped, my eyes widening. I thought I'd have more time.

Leaving the path, I pedaled through the deep underbrush. Sweat poured down my body, and I knew I was leaving a trail a blind wolf could follow. A dozen yards in, I dumped the bike. I ran a distance farther, the bag clinking at my side. I came across a large mud puddle and tossed in a few corks. I put some broken glass inside a fallen log. With all my might, I threw the bottles, one by one, in different directions. They arced high into the air, and smashed on impact.

A breeze carried the scents of goon and wolfsbane–both my adversaries were in the woods. I walked as quietly as I could. Every few steps, I threw another stick through the trees, aiming for distance. I wrapped the last piece in the Publix bag and threw it straight up where it caught on a high branch. That should keep them busy.

When I reached A Road, Eff sat waiting. I climbed into his truck, almost giddy with relief. So far, I hadn't been caught. Maybe I would live through this insane quest.

The Breakers Hotel was on the ocean in Palm Beach, spread out along a stretch of pure white sand. It looked like the kind of place my parents would appreciate. I wondered if they'd gotten the good doctor her room.

Eff passed the main entrance and took a back way in. He parked behind a couple of semis. He pinned a nametag on his shirt, then handed me a blue ball cap with foam padding and Higgins Hardware stitched in white on the front.

"Put it on." He hopped out of the truck.

I put on the cap and followed him to the loading dock door. He also wore a Higgins hat, and he carried a cardboard box.

"That your equipment?" I asked.

"Yeah. I've been dying to try it out. I made it from instructions on the Internet. You can find anything on the Net."

We went inside. Down the hallway, a paunchy

security guard waved to us from a bank of vending machines. Eff waved back and kept walking.

"Internet, eh?" I stepped fast to keep pace. "You planning to become a terrorist or something?"

"Nah. Don't go spreading it around or anything, but... I like to read. Spy novels, mostly. I love the gizmos. The tech." He ducked into a stairwell and started climbing. "Put your hat on inside out and pull the brim over your eyes."

I did, but only after he did it first. Our hats were now white with green brims. "So you build things out of novels?"

"I started wondering if those things would really work. So one day I built one just to see. I must have a dozen now. Random stuff."

"You mean like pens that squirt acid and contact lenses with GPS microchips in them?"

"No. But that's a good idea." He kept turning corners and climbing higher. "I even started writing my own novel. This baby's in it." He patted the box.

I felt exasperated. Was this a game to him? "Do you have any idea where we're going?"

"Sure. Right here." He grinned, pulled his hat lower, and pushed into a long door-lined corridor.

"Phew. No one's around," I whispered.

"This is a good time of day," he said. "Everyone's out sight-seeing or beaching. But there are security cameras everywhere, so keep your head down." He rapped at a door, then pointed with his toe. "I need you to stand here facing me. Just look natural. That should do it." From the cardboard box, he took out a card with a magnetic strip attached by wires to a metal case. He slid the card into the door lock and pressed a button. A red light blinked.

I asked, "Where do you get the parts for all this?"

"Duh. My father owns a hardware store."

The light on the case turned green. Moments later, the lock also flashed green.

"Impressive," I said.

"Thank you." He opened the door. "Don't touch anything you don't have to. We don't want them to know we were snooping."

"Yeah. And we don't want to leave fingerprints."

He looked at me like I was slow-witted. "They won't dust for fingerprints if they don't suspect anyone was here."

I nodded and followed him inside.

The room was light blue with mahogany furnishings. The king-sized bed was neatly made. Curtains leading to a veranda were open, showing the sparkling ocean beyond.

"What should we look for?" I whispered.

"How about this?"

Eff stood before the dresser where a laptop sat open and running. The screen cycled through scenes as if from an overhead camera. I recognized some of the shots from the brochures–the lobby, the recreation room.

"She's tapped into someone's security camera," Eff said.

"Lindgren Institute," I told him, "where she wants to take me."

I saw a man watching television, two others playing cards. The scene blinked onto an empty hallway. Then to an Olympic sized pool enclosed in glass panes with a view of mountains beyond.

Suddenly the screen shifted to what appeared to be an operating room filled with figures in blue gowns. A creature neither human nor wolf lay strapped to a gurney.

"What?" Eff cried. "What is that thing?"

Of course, I knew. It was a werewolf frozen in the throes of transformation. His eyes were wide and terrified. A blue-gowned doctor rammed a syringe into his neck, and the wolfman screamed. His back arched. His limbs strained at the manacles. I felt his howls in the pit of my stomach, although the laptop made no sound.

"Like something from a Lon Chaney flick," Eff said. "Or Doctor Moreau." He motioned to the screen that now showed cages stacked one upon the other. Each held a wolfman in various stages of transformation. "It's a kennel. For weird dogs or something."

"They are people," I blurted. "Human beings. What is she doing to them?"

He looked at me. I couldn't tell if he thought I was being a sissy or if he only now understood why I was afraid.

"Let's get out of here," he said.

By the time Eff dropped me off at home, I was a basket case. No way would I end up like the guy on the gurney. I had to get Saarsgard off my back. I just didn't know how.

I paced the house, watching for Uncle Bob. He got home well after sunset. He stank of sweat and sawdust as he collapsed into his recliner. I couldn't imagine what his big project was–didn't really care. I just felt safer now that he was with me.

"Are you hungry?" I asked. "I left half a can of SpaghettiOs on the stove."

He nodded. "I'll get it in a moment."

"Stay there. I'll get it." I hurried to the kitchen. I put a spoon in the pot, a couple of pieces of bread on top, and carried it back.

He grunted his appreciation, then ate woodenly like he was only going through the motions to please me. I turned on TV, but he was asleep before the first commercial, so I turned it off again.

In the darkness, I listened to his soft snore. I wanted so much to tell him about what I'd seen on that laptop, but he'd go ballistic if he knew I broke into Saarsgard's hotel room.

I wished I could undo it, wished I could erase my memory–but it was burned there, eating at me. I needed someone to talk to, someone to bounce ideas around, to unburden myself.

Brittany always made me feel better, always put

things in perspective. She was the only one who understood me. I needed her.

Phone in hand, I rushed to my room. She had to take my call, had to listen to me. I punched in three numbers, then stopped.

What was I–crazy? Saarsgard didn't know about Brittany. What if she bugged my phone, or had access to my phone records? What if she kidnapped Brittany to get at me?

Dejected, I slipped the phone back in my pocket and stretched out on the bed. I wanted to sleep, but every time I closed my eyes, I saw the man on the gurney.

Somehow, Saarsgard had halted his transformation, trapping him between man and beast. I thought about how much it hurt to make the shift. Was the wolfman in constant pain? Were the other people in pain, the ones she kept in cages?

I imagined myself like Captain America, busting in and rescuing them from the good doctor's clutches. But in reality, there was no way to stop her. She owned more of the world than I did.

I tossed and turned for hours, trying to get the images out of my head. Suddenly, I bolted upright. Oh, crap. I'd left my bike in the woods. How would I explain its absence in the morning? I had no choice but to get it. But it was a long walk. The fastest way would be to turn into a wolf.

Moving as quietly as I could, I stripped off my clothes and tossed them into the closet. Then I put on a baggy pair of drawstring jogging shorts. I cinched the drawstring so tight I could barely breathe. Opening the window wide, I climbed outside.

I started the shift even before my bare feet touched the grass. I hadn't intended to do it so close to the house, but my overzealous wolf had other plans. I crouched in the shadows, clamping my teeth against the agony of having my joints and muscles reposition themselves.

When at last I became full wolf, I snapped and tugged at the jogging shorts still snug around my waist. My former self had to be joking. I couldn't wear these. But there was no getting them off, and I was wasting time. With an indignant growl, I padded forward.

Scents and sounds filled the night. I longed to chase a rabbit or raccoon–or even the armadillo that was waddling across the street. But I had a mission.

I streaked through the neighborhood, leaving the barks and whines of household dogs in my wake. It felt good to stretch my legs, in spite of the hindrance of the hated shorts, and I wondered why I didn't do it more often.

Houses became sporadic. I reveled in the trees and the underbrush, feeling at peace with the forest. I thought nothing could dampen my mood. Then I reached another housing development with buildings standing shoulder-to-shoulder. Ahead, light blazed in the night sky.

Southern Boulevard. I had no choice but to cross, although I risked discovery. The lingering stench of oil and exhaust made me sneeze. With my head lowered and my fur on end, I prepared to bolt across the multi-lane road.

But there were no cars moving, no people to be seen. *Of course, it's two o'clock in the morning*, my human side chided. I trotted across and slipped back into shadow. No one was aware of the wolf in shorts.

When I entered the woods with the horse trail, I smelled the doctor and her pet wolf–although he hadn't been a wolf at the time. He'd walked as a man back and forth throughout the area. I also smelled my human self. Sweat and blood. But the scents were old. Other than raccoon and armadillo, I was alone.

I found the bike as if a beacon led me to it. I pounced and snapped at the pedals. Mission complete. It was early yet–hours before daybreak. I should explore, maybe catch dinner.

Before I finished the thought, the change gripped me. I snarled, fighting for my life even as my fangs receded and my muzzle sank back into my sinus cavities. My ears slid down the sides of my head. No! It's too soon! I howled with rage–but it turned into a wheezing cough.

For a moment, I imagined that I was like the others–with hairy limbs and a deformed face. I patted myself all over, but I was fine.

The drawstring cut into my waist. With stiffened

fingers, I loosened it. Panting and shaking, I picked up the bike and walked it to the horse trail. Part of me was pleased that I had punched down the wolf–but it hadn't been easy. I had taken it by surprise. One day, maybe the wolf would win.

I wasn't in control.

When I reached the street, I hopped on the bike and raced home. Even in the coolness of night, I was sweating. I kept imagining a silver limo pulling behind me.

But I didn't see anyone the entire way–one of the advantages of living in a small town. I coasted up my driveway, cursing the crackle of my tires on gravel, and then tipped the bike onto its usual spot on the grass. On tiptoe, I circled the side of the house and climbed through my open window.

Uncle Bob sat on my bed.

EIGHTEEN

"Where have you been?" Uncle Bob's voice was low and gravelly coming from the darkness of my room.

I stammered. "I... I left my bike at school."

"So you thought it best to crawl out your window and get it in the middle of the night?" His voice rose with each syllable.

I spread my hands. "Well, yeah. I needed it."

"What if you'd been caught?"

"Don't worry. I'm sure Saarsgard is fast asleep."

"Forget Saarsgard," he bellowed. "What if you were caught by the sheriff?"

He stepped forward, and even though I was a few inches taller, I felt like he towered over me. I cringed. "I didn't–"

"After everything we went through to prove I was the better guardian, you pull a stunt like this? Did you consider how your conduct would reflect on me?"

Of course, I hadn't. "If you'll just listen," I said.

"They could still take you away. I have half a mind to let them."

"I'm sorry. I was wrong. It won't happen again."

"Don't talk to me like I'm stupid," he snarled. "It wouldn't have happened this time if you weren't hiding something."

I jerked with surprise. Silence fell between us. His eyes were like black wounds in his face.

"I didn't want you to know," I said quietly, "that I was hanging out with Eff."

"Higgins?" he roared. "I told you he couldn't be trusted."

"You can't pick my friends for me," I shouted back.

Uncle Bob threw his hands into the air and stomped out of my room. I heard him in the kitchen making a cup of coffee.

After a few moments, I followed.

"What happens now?" I asked. "Howard drives me to and from school?"

"He can't," Uncle Bob said. "He's in Tampa following a lead on his son."

I shook my head. That was a wild goose chase if I ever heard one. "Am I grounded?"

"What good would that do?"

He looked at me, and the disappointment on his face was worse than all his yelling. I wanted to tell him everything–the hotel room and the man on the gurney, William the Bear and Brittany. My mouth opened, but the words wouldn't come. If I told him now, I would just hurt him more.

His face fell further, and then hardened. He knew I had secrets. He turned his back.

"You should get some sleep," he said. "It will be light soon."

I went to my room and lay on the bed, my arms folded tight against my chest. Why did nothing go right? Days ago, my uncle and I bonded over a common cause. Now, the rift between us was a chasm.

My fault. Everything was my fault. My secrets were out of control. I should have come clean at the start.

I was worthless.

Sleep was the farthest thing from my mind, but I must have dozed anyway. The next thing I knew, sunlight streamed through the window, and my uncle was gone.

I rode my bike to school, keeping on the main streets, hoping that having people around would deter the doctor. It must've worked because I saw no sign of a limousine.

I went to class feeling washed out and grumpy. I spotted Brittany in the halls and didn't even try to say hi to her. By the time lunch rolled around, I was starving. I filled my tray with cafeteria-style ravioli and fries, then slumped in my chair at the back of the room.

Eff set his tray across from mine, singing, "He's mean, he's mean, you know what I mean."

"Didn't get much sleep," I told him. "I decided to get my bike in the middle of the night. My uncle caught me coming back in."

Eff whooped with laughter. "You really are as

dumb as you look, aren't you?"

I sighed. "I really am."

"I wouldn't mind driving you back and forth." He took a big bite of a salami and cheese sandwich. "But I get the impression your uncle doesn't like me much."

I shrugged, thinking *that* was an understatement.

"So, I brought you a present." He pulled a pack of folded paper from his back pocket.

I frowned. "It's a street map."

"If I learned anything from reading spy novels, it's that predictability is the enemy." He unfolded the map. Lines drawn with multi-colored highlighter pens sketched the streets. "You need to vary your routine. Leave school at odd times. Use different doors. Follow unexpected routes home. I took the liberty of plotting a few courses."

I considered his squiggly lines. "This one takes me out in the boondocks."

"There's no one and nothing out there, man. Who would think of looking for you there?"

I nodded as if agreeing with him, but in my head, my uncle was screaming *he can't be trusted.* What if Eff had given the same information to Saarsgard? What if this was all an ambush in the making?

"Thanks." I smiled and refolded the map.

"No problem." He smiled back.

After school, I hopped on my bike and, defying Eff's advice, stayed on the main roads right through the heart of town. I didn't see the limousine the whole way home. Maybe Saarsgard was waiting for me on one of Eff's alternative routes.

I could think of several reasons why Eff would deceive me, the biggest being revenge for getting him kicked off the football team. He'd probably also like me out of the way so he could have a better chance with Brittany. I knew he still liked her, in spite of his speech about me being the better man.

I sat in the living room as shadows gathered around me, taking apart every conversation I had with Eff. By the time Uncle Bob pulled up the driveway, I was convinced that Eff was a villain.

My uncle brought home a sack of hamburgers, and we ate in front of the TV. He spoke to me only when he had to, which was pretty much not at all. With dinner lying like rocks in my stomach, I went to my room.

Everyone was against me–my parents, Uncle Bob, Eff, Brittany. Howard still liked me, but he wouldn't after he found out I knew about William. I was on everyone's list.

The worst thing was I deserved it. Look at me. I turned into a wolf and attacked the girl I loved. Maybe it would be better for everyone if I gave up and went with Saarsgard.

Burying my head beneath the pillow, I slowly drifted to sleep.

The next morning, I overslept and ran out of the house without breakfast. I took my bike down the main roads, keeping up with traffic. As I turned onto Southern, a silver limousine edged beside me. A window opened.

I sighed. A dark cloud of resignation rolled over me. I looked over, intending to stop and talk.

But it wasn't Dr. Saarsgard who leaned out the window. It was her werewolf goon. He grabbed my arm, pulling as if to yank me through the window.

Any thought of surrender left me. I struggled to break his grasp. Cars honked. The limo traveled well below the speed limit, but fast enough to drag me.

The goon growled something in a language I didn't understand. His teeth had gaps between them, like he had a mouthful of yellow blocks. Behind him, Dr. Saarsgard leaned forward, watching. The driver looked over his shoulder, his attention on the altercation.

Then a huge crash shook the world. My bike and I went flying. The limo swerved over the curb and rocked to a stop.

Eff stepped out of his ruined truck, emerging red faced from a cloud of steam. "Jackass! You ran the light!" He shot me a glare that clearly said *What are you waiting for? Get out of here!*

I shook so hard, I could barely pick up my bike. The frame was bent, and the wheels wobbled as I tried to speed away. But I couldn't stop. I kept remembering Vice Principal Overhill saying that as long as I was on school grounds, I was safe.

When I got to the courtyard, I didn't bother with the rack–I just tossed my bike to the side of the main entrance. I rushed into the office. Behind the counter, the secretaries leaped to their feet, staring. I burst through Overhill's door.

"There's been an accident," I blurted, panting.

"Slow down." He stepped around his desk and sat me in a chair. "Start from the beginning."

"I was riding my bike," I said amazed at how my voice trembled. "That big limo. You know, that silver limo? It pulled up next to me. A man reached out. He grabbed my arm." I looked down. My wrist was twice its normal size. It looked like someone else's. "I couldn't get away. He started pulling me. Inside. Through the window. And then Eff... Eff..."

And wouldn't you know it, I started to cry. Big fat tears sliding down my face. It was like I was two people–one observing, the other falling apart.

"Efrem Higgins?" Overhill prodded.

I nodded.

"Is Efrem all right?" he asked.

I nodded again, not trusting my voice. Minutes ticked by. I guess he expected me to continue the story, but I couldn't. I kept seeing the blocky yellow teeth, hearing the crash.

Why would Eff do that? He loved his truck.

Was he my friend after all?

"Let's get you cleaned up." Overhill put his arm around my shoulders and helped me walk. When we reached the counter, he said, "Maureen, please call Sheriff Brad and tell him I need to see him right away. Then call Cody's uncle."

I tried to say *no, he's mad at me.* But my lips wouldn't work. Embarrassed, I hung my head. There was blood on my shirt. All over my shirt. I wondered how it got there.

Overhill took me to the clinic. The nurse leaped up from her desk, her shocked expression turning to one of concern. She slid a chair my way, and I collapsed onto it.

"Who's this?" she asked.

"Cody Forester. Car accident," Overhill told her.

She lifted my hair, looking at my forehead. Her fingers were cool and comforting. Then she shone a penlight into my eyes. "Cody, I'm going to help you. But first I need to take some photos."

I groaned. "You aren't going to post them on MySpace, are you?"

She chuckled. "Nothing like that."

I closed my eyes and leaned back. What I wouldn't give for a soft bed and a twelve-hour nap. But the camera kept flashing.

The nurse said, "It looks like he fell onto his right side and skidded on gravel. Lacerations from shoulder to elbow. Could you hold his sleeve up for me? That's fine." Flash. "A bump to the head. More scrapes along his face. Bloody nose." Flash.

"What's his condition?" said a new voice.

I opened my eyes to see Sheriff Brad standing in

the doorway.

"Possible concussion," said the nurse, "and I'm pretty sure his wrist is broken."

"Good," said the sheriff. "Let's hope it's a spiral fracture. You usually get those from having someone grab and twist. I can use that against his attacker."

"Attacker?" said the nurse. "I thought he was in a car accident."

"He was." Sheriff Brad nodded. "It seems Efrem Higgins t-boned a limousine after it ran a red light. Witnesses say the people in the limo were involved in an altercation with you, Mister Forester."

My voice sounded husky. "Is Eff hurt?"

"He's fine," said the sheriff. "Having his truck towed as we speak."

"What's going on here?" Uncle Bob burst into the clinic. Suddenly the room seemed crowded. "Cody, what happened?"

"Nothing," I said.

"You were right about a kidnapping attempt," Sheriff Brad told my uncle. "We have the Saarsgard woman under guard at the hospital. And her two accomplices are on their way to the station."

My ears perked. "You have them?"

Uncle Bob sagged as he blew out a breath.

Sheriff Brad said, "I want the boy here to go to the Emergency Room for a check-up."

"I'm all right," I said.

He pointed a finger at me. "What you *are* is evidence, boy. You *will* go to the hospital, and you *will* have your injuries documented."

"I'll take him." Uncle Bob motioned for me to stand up.

I would've rather kept sitting, but I hobbled over to him. "My bike's wrecked."

"That damned bike," he muttered.

We walked out of the school into bright sunlight. I was surprised it was still morning. Uncle Bob picked up my bike beside the door and carried it to the parking lot. It was in worse shape than I thought.

As we got into his truck, I said, "I can't go to the hospital. Even if my wrist is broken, it will heal in a few days."

"You'll just have to wear the cast and shut up about it." He started the truck and pulled away.

I wanted to tell him I was sorry–for climbing out my window, for wrecking my bike, for pulling him off an important job. Instead, I stared at my hands.

Then my phone beeped. It was a text from Eff.

Truck totaled. U O me.

NINETEEN

A miasma of blood and antiseptics hit my stomach as the automatic doors admitted my uncle and me into the Palms West Emergency Room. I cringed and held my breath. With the stench came the noise–people groaned, stretchers screeched. A woman tapped at a computer keyboard. Not typed, tapped. I wanted to strangle her until she stopped.

I think Uncle Bob sensed I was losing control. He put an arm around my shoulders and guided me to a reception desk.

"How can I help you?" a woman asked as if she didn't notice my bloody t-shirt.

I opened my mouth to answer when another woman said, "Cody?" It was Brittany's mother.

"Um, hi." I shuffled my feet. I forgot she worked at the hospital. How could I face her after all that had happened between Brittany and me?

Silence fell. I forced a smile. Belatedly, I wondered if I had blood in my teeth.

"Cody Forester," said the lady who was tapping the keyboard. "I have his file here. Sheriff faxed it in." She handed a clipboard to Brittany's mother.

"All right, Cody. Come with me." She walked briskly away.

"Me, too?" Uncle Bob asked as we followed.

"Of course." She threw a smile over her shoulder. "You're his guardian?"

"Bob Nowak."

"The Fix-It-Guy." She chuckled. Her laugh sounded remarkably like Brittany's. "I'm Dalia Meyer, Brittany's mother."

"A lovely girl."

"The light of my life."

We entered a large room. The stench of blood was overwhelming, and I gagged. Through watering eyes, I saw six beds, two of them curtained off. A doctor in a white lab coat stepped from one of the cubicles, sending the curtain flapping, and I glimpsed a small boy with a bandaged forehead and a lollipop.

"In here, Cody." Mrs. Meyer pulled a curtain around a bed. "Take off everything and put it all in this plastic bag. Here's a gown to wear. Let me have your hand." She snapped on my name band. Then she left, closing the curtain behind her.

I stared at the bed. "I don't want to do this."

In a low voice, Uncle Bob said, "We have to act normal, do what is asked of us. Let me help you with your shirt."

Getting undressed hurt worse than I expected, but with my uncle's help, I managed. I was getting into bed when the doctor came in.

"Good morning. I'm Doctor Abrams. Who might you be?"

Uncle Bob said, "Cody Forester. It's in his file."

Dr. Abrams gave him a tired smile. "I'm testing his memory." He shone a penlight into my eyes. "Cody, do you know what day this is?"

"It's Friday, May second, 2008."

"Uh-huh, and is that in summer or winter?"

"It's spring, although it feels like summer."

"Good." He moved my head from side to side. "Can you tell me how you got hurt?"

"Car hit me. I was on my bike."

"What did the car look like?"

"A silver limo."

He laughed. "Count your blessings. It could be worse. At least, it wasn't a cement truck."

I didn't find that as funny as he did.

"Do you remember what happened right before the limo hit you?"

"A man reached through the window and grabbed my arm." I showed him my bruises.

"Did you lose consciousness at all?"

As he spoke, his hands roved over my head and along my jaw. He searched my collarbones and my shoulders. I felt increasingly uncomfortable. Could he feel the difference in me? I squirmed from his touch, but he didn't take the hint.

"You have some old injuries here," he said as he examined my arm.

I closed my eyes, feeling like I'd been caught in

a lie. Eff had broken my arm the day he and his friends beat me up and tied me in a tree.

"Anything to worry about?" Uncle Bob asked.

"Just some calcification. I'll put it in my report to the sheriff."

"Can you leave it out?" my uncle asked. "This is a legal matter. I don't want to cloud the issue with something that might have happened when he was a little kid."

"That's fine. I'll only note it in the medical file." He probed my stomach. "Any nausea? Vomiting?" He didn't wait for a reply. "Sit up for me and raise your arms above your head."

Try as I might, I couldn't lift my right arm.

"You can relax." He turned his tired smile on me. "You have a concussion. I think it's mild, but I'm ordering a CT scan just to be sure. I also want X-rays of your wrist and shoulder. Someone will be in to see you." He left the cubicle.

Muffled conversation came from beyond the curtain, but my head hurt so bad I didn't even try to make out the words. I collapsed against the pillow.

Moments later, Brittany's mother wheeled in a cart. It held a basin of water and forceps. "I'm going to clean you up while we're waiting for X-ray to get you."

She wrung out a cloth and dabbed my face. Brittany did the same thing after she cut me down from the tree. So gentle. So caring. Tears burned in the back of my throat. I swallowed hard, my eyes squeezed tight. I wondered if *my* mother had ever sat at my bedside. I didn't think so.

"Your face is scraped, but nothing too awful," she said. "I think most of the blood came from your nose." With a squeal and a clatter, she pulled up a stool and sat beside me, examining my arm. "You have some embedded debris. I'm going to use a topical. It might sting for a second."

Using a wad of gauze, she swabbed my skin with a foul-smelling liquid. She picked out the gravel with the forceps.

I stared at the ceiling. "A woman was brought in a little while ago. White hair. Expensive clothes."

"Yes. The woman from the limousine."

"How bad was she hurt?"

"By law, I'm not allowed to discuss her case," she said. "I can say she was admitted in fair condition, she's on the third floor, and she has a 'round-the-clock guard."

"So, she won't be released anytime soon?"

"Look at me," she said firmly. "That woman is not going anywhere. You don't have to worry."

I felt tears again. I nodded, biting my lip.

She went back to work on my arm. "You haven't been to the house lately."

"Brittany's mad at me."

"Really?" She seemed genuinely surprised. "She can't be too angry. She was just telling her father about you. How smart you are. How you're such a gentleman."

"I am," I blurted. "A gentleman, I mean."

"You are also a good patient." She bandaged the scrape with gauze and tape, then moved her cart away. "Can I bring you anything, Cody? Are you chilly?"

"Yes, actually."

"I'll get you a blanket."

The blanket she brought was as warm as if she kept it in a toaster oven. She tucked it around me, making me feel safe and cared for. I smiled my thanks. I'd never seen this side of Brittany's mother. Did she really think I was a gentleman? My thoughts drifted to Brittany. Why had she told her parents I was still her boyfriend? Maybe there was hope for us yet.

Another nurse poked her head inside the cubicle. "They're here for him."

Two men wearing hospital scrubs opened the curtain. One tossed a clipboard on my legs and stood at the foot of the bed.

The other checked my wristband. "All right, Cody. We're going to take you to X-ray now."

"Should I come?" asked my uncle.

"Wait here. We'll bring him right back."

They rolled me out the room and down the hall. I watched light panels in the ceiling whiz by.

The CT scan was cool. I lay on a table that slid through a big doughnut-shaped machine. After that, the X-rays of my wrist and shoulder seemed dull. The men wheeled me back to my cubicle in the ER.

Uncle Bob greeted me. “Are you hungry? I can get you something from the cafeteria.”

I gauged my stomach. “No. You can go eat, though.”

“I’ll stay with you.”

The curtains burst open.

“Well, the CT confirmed a concussion,” said Dr. Abrams. “No broken bones. You’ve bruised your shoulder. It should feel better in a few days. However, your wrist is sprained. It takes a while for that to heal. I want you to ice it for twenty minutes eight times a day for forty-eight hours. If you need something for pain, take Tylenol only. Because of the concussion, anything else might cause bleeding of the brain. Any questions? No?” He shook my uncle’s hand and then mine. “Wait here for the nurse.”

I sat on the edge of the bed. The world was cold outside my blanket. Uncle Bob handed me my Levis, and I put them on.

Brittany’s mother came in. “I brought a clean shirt.” She popped my head through a t-shirt with *Palms West Hospital* and a big Band-Aid printed on the front. Then she put a brace on my wrist and strapped it tight. “Did he tell you to ice this?”

“Every four hours.”

“Use a slush bath. Fill a sink with water and crushed ice.”

“I will.”

“All right, then. You’re free to go.”

“Thank you,” I said, “for everything.”

She smiled. "Take care, Cody."

I left the ER feeling embarrassed, as if I'd made a fuss over nothing. To make matters worse, Uncle Bob was still mad at me. He didn't speak the entire way home.

As we pulled to the front of the house, I said, "I'm going to bed."

"Rather you stayed with me," he said. "I want to be sure there are no aftereffects of that concussion."

So, I sat on the porch steps while he took a sledge hammer to my bike, trying to straighten the frame. The way he pounded, I was glad he was aiming at the bicycle and not me. Just as he was giving it up as a lost cause, Sheriff Brad pulled up.

His pockets jingled as he stepped out of the cruiser and approached me. "The hospital sent in its report. I'm glad you'll be all right."

"Thank you, sir." I stood, but the movement made me woozy. It must have shown on my face.

"Sit!" Uncle Bob barked.

At the same time, Sheriff Brad said, "Take it easy, son."

I plopped down on the porch steps and leaned my forearms on my knees. "Did you arrest Doctor Saarsgard?"

"No hurry," he said. "She'll be in the hospital a while longer, and I have a man stationed outside her door."

A slow grin spread over my face. If Saarsgard was in jail, I could go to see Brittany without fear of endangering her. I could remind her I was still her boyfriend.

"Boy, you look like a drowning man who just found out he could float," the sheriff said.

"Yes, sir."

"Wait," said Uncle Bob. "You're saying we can relax? It's over?"

Sheriff Brad nodded. "The attempted kidnapping case against her is strong. I have several credible witnesses. I'd like to have a statement from each of you, if you wouldn't mind coming to the station. Ask for Deputy West."

"When?" asked Uncle Bob.

"Today or tomorrow. Like I said, she's not going anywhere." Pockets jingling, Sheriff Brad got into his cruiser.

I watched him drive away, still grinning.

Uncle Bob eyed me like I was trying to get away with something. "I have to work tomorrow to make up for lost time."

"We'll have to give our statements today, then."

"The station's in Royal Palm Beach. Are you up for a ride?"

"I can make it."

I almost didn't though–the rocking of the truck made me dizzy. The traffic smells of car exhaust, hot asphalt, and brake dust made me want to barf. When we got to the station, I actually groaned with vertigo when the elevator sped us to the third floor.

Fortunately, Deputy West saw us right away.

She took my uncle into a conference room and spoke to him alone for a while, then she interviewed me with my uncle present. I was beginning to think I could recite what happened even in my sleep. Less than an hour later, we were out of the building and on our way home.

I leaned back in my seat and silently rehearsed my apology to Brittany. I wanted to call her as soon as she got home from school, but no, apologies were better in person. I'd walk to her house in the morning–my uncle would be at work, Dr. Saarsgard was out of the picture. Brittany told her father I was a gentleman.

Everything was coming together.

TWENTY

Early the next morning, my uncle stepped into my room to check on me before leaving for work. I pretended to be asleep. I didn't want to risk having him give me a direct order to stay in the house while he was gone. I waited until the front door closed and the truck pulled away before getting out of bed.

Pulling my shirt over my head, I hurried into the bathroom to shower. When I looked in the mirror, I laughed. My image reminded me of my father's old joke–I feel like a million bucks, all green and wrinkled. My bruises had gone a grisly green–the side of my face, my forearm where the goon grabbed me, the opposite shoulder where I hit the ground and slid. Nothing hurt, though. In fact, I felt stronger than ever.

Hopefully, the same couldn't be said about Dr. Saarsgard. I thought of her lying in a hospital bed and wished her a long and painful stay. After that, I hoped they put her in jail for trying to snatch me. Maybe if she didn't return to the asylum, it would close down and set those werewolves free.

I showered and shaved, then ate a red Pop-Tart. My thoughts were light-years away, picturing scenarios with Brittany. Would she see me? Would she listen? Or would she just slam the door in my face?

After I caught myself wiping coffee rings off the countertop, I realized I was stalling. I slid the little box with the promise ring into my pocket. Rehearsing my intended speech, I started the long trek to Brittany's house.

An hour later, I stood on her driveway, licking my lips and shuffling my feet. Sweat dripped down my temples, although the morning was still cool. Maybe I was nervous.

I climbed the creaking, whitewashed steps and entered the screened-in porch. An aroma of bacon and pancake syrup reached me. My stomach growled, even though I didn't feel like eating. I wiped my palms on my pants and knocked on the door.

No answer. Was I disturbing their breakfast? My wolf hearing decided there were no sounds from the kitchen. Breakfast was over. I knocked again.

The deadbolt clicked, and the door jerked open, revealing a craggy, unshaven face.

"Uh-huh," said Grandpa Earle.

My mouth went dry. "Um, good morning, sir. I was hoping to speak with Brittany. Is she home?"

"Hang on. I'll get her." He closed the door to about an inch and yelled, "Brittany! Front 'n center!"

There was a moment of silence. Then footfalls thundered down the stairs. I gulped and eased back a step.

Brittany opened the door. Violet streaks shone in her hair, and she wore purple mascara. She looked so beautiful it made my heart ache.

"Oh!" She blinked.

I held out my hands. "Wait. Please. I only want to talk."

She considered me for a long moment, then folded her arms. "All right."

"I just want to say I'm sorry. I was totally out of line. I never should have told you how to feel about your dad. I shouldn't have had an opinion at all. I've never been abused or terrorized. I can't even imagine what you went through. All I know is that I never want you to be put in a bad situation again." I raised my chin. "So, if you want me to, I will. I'll rough up your dad and chase him back to Georgia where he belongs."

"Cody." She glanced around as if checking if anyone was listening.

She stepped outside, closing the door behind her. I smelled the fruity scent of her hair gel, mint toothpaste on her breath. My heart raced.

"I don't want you to hurt him," she said in a hushed tone. "I just wanted to complain about him, to call him names behind his back without feeling I was being judged. I wanted you to listen. To hear me."

And I did. I heard the pain behind her words. Pain her father put there. Pain because of me. "I'm sorry you didn't think... I'm sorry I let you down."

She nodded, then sat on the wicker loveseat. "That's not the only issue between us. We have to face it. You got mad and you almost killed me."

I closed my eyes. *Oh God.*

"I was so scared."

How could I explain? "It's just, when I saw you with William–"

"He's a friend, Cody," she snapped. "I talk to him. Mostly we talk about you."

"I wouldn't have hurt you. I could never hurt you," I said, although I wasn't sure that was true. "But at the time, I wanted to kill him."

"Well, fortunately, he'll be all right."

"You've seen him?"

"Sure. He couldn't fend for himself. But I couldn't stay with him all the time, so I brought in Eileen to watch him. They hit it off. He calls her his little naked healer." She shrugged. "They're kind of cute together."

I sat beside her and buried my face in my hands. "I don't know how to promise–"

"That it won't happen again? That's the problem, isn't it?" She huffed out a breath. "You have to be its boss. This isn't a partnership. You use the wolf when you need it and put it away when you don't."

I nodded.

Her voice rose. "Because I can't live my life in fear that anything I do might set you off."

"I know," I whispered.

Silence fell. Then she took my hand.

I couldn't bear to look at her. But I clung to her fingers as if I were drowning, as if she was the one stable thing left in my life.

The door opened, and her brother appeared. He carried two tinkling glasses of lemonade. "Here." He held them out to us.

Brittany giggled. "What are you doing?"

"Grandpa said." He shrugged. "I'm going over Wolcott's house."

"Wait. I thought you had homework."

Butt Crack flashed a smile. "That's what we're doing. Studying." He bounded outside, letting the screen door slam behind him.

"Probably magazines again," Brittany muttered.

I pressed the cold glass against my forehead.

She motioned at the bruises. "Mom said she saw you at the hospital. I was surprised you went."

"Sheriff Brad insisted on it." I sipped without tasting. "I was surprised your mother was there. I thought she worked afternoons."

"Her hours have been screwy. Seven to seven four days a week."

I nodded. "That's nice."

"The car crash was on the evening news," she said. "Was Eff involved?"

"Yeah. He saved my life."

"Eff? Hard to believe."

I took a long swig of lemonade, then motioned at a wicker rocking chair. "Is that new?"

She groaned. "Yes. Every time Dad comes over,

he brings something with him. I keep hoping the dog will barf on this rug." She scuffed the sisal rug beneath their feet. "And I refuse to water that stupid plant."

I looked over at a pot of wilted daisies. "Does he come over often?"

"Too often. But mostly he hangs out with Gramps, doing projects around the house."

I finished my lemonade, then dumped the ice onto the daisies. She raised a brow, and I shrugged. "It's not the plant's fault."

"Since when are you a tree hugger?"

"I'm not. At least, I never used to be. Maybe the wolf makes me look at things differently."

"Yeah. Well, if you like plants, you should go to that Japanese garden in Delray. It's really nice. I used to go all the time when I first got my car. Just sit there, you know, and commune with nature."

"Sounds great."

"Want to see it?"

"Now?" I perked. "Sure."

She took my empty glass. "Let me tell Gramps, and we'll go."

I got to my feet, frowning. Did that mean we were friends again? I'd give anything just to have her talk to me every day.

A few moments later, she bounced out of the house with her purse slung over her shoulder and her purple-streaked hair over her eyes.

I said, "So, are we good?"

"We'll see." With a slight smile, she bounded down the steps.

I followed, grinning. My head felt like a helium balloon, filled to burst and floating. If anything went wrong, the balloon would pop. I'd never recover.

We crossed the yard to her lime-green Volkswagen, and I climbed in shotgun. The familiar sag of the seat cupped my behind. With a sigh, I leaned back, gazing at the bumper-sticker-plastered dashboard. A teardrop crystal hanging from the rear-view mirror scattered tiny rainbows across the steering wheel.

Almost too shy to look, I glanced at Brittany as she put the car in gear and backed out of the driveway. Her pale skin made her violet lipstick look almost black.

I longed to kiss her, to part her sugary lips with my tongue and taste the syrup she had for breakfast. I felt the bulge of the promise ring box in my pocket. I folded my hands to hide another bulge.

We got onto I-95 and listened to Pink Spiders all the way to Delray Beach. Sunlight glinted off passing cars. The morning warmed quickly.

We pulled into the parking lot of the Japanese garden. I hung my head out the window, gazing at the manicured grounds. The bushes and trees hummed with energy, as if they strained to break free of their well-trimmed shapes. A lone gardener wearing a bamboo hat pushed a wheelbarrow among them. I was amazed at the power he held over the rampant growth. He reminded me of a lion tamer–only instead of a whip, he used a pair of ordinary scissors to keep his charges in line.

We parked, got out of the car, and walked toward a white building. The air filled with the roaring babble of rushing water. A koi pond came into view–but not the type of pond my uncle built for the neighbors. This one had towering boulders and four-foot waterfalls. Trees surrounded the display, all of them trimmed into precise shapes. They were taller on one end of the pond, shorter on the other.

Brittany said, "If you stand here, it's like you're looking through trees at mountains in the distance. Everything here is meant to be a miniature version of a huge vista."

"Like a painting," I said, "only alive."

"Yes." She glanced at me as if surprised I'd gotten the answer right.

I basked in her smile.

We climbed a series of wide steps and entered the building. The cool air was a welcomed break from the humid morning. I paid our admission and received two purple wristbands and a map in return.

The lobby was large and silent. Picture windows overlooked a pallet of gravel raked in wavy lines. I didn't see the point of it, but Brittany nodded and smiled as if showing me something wonderful. Taking my arm, she guided me out the back door into the garden.

My first thought was that you would never know

there was a drought in this place. I'd never seen so many different shades of green. Soft grass led to a green lake edged with reeds and lily pads. Bushes shaped like emerald globes rose from beds of ferns, and trees stood like sculptures with barely a leaf out of place.

We followed a gravel pathway that wound through the grounds.

I said, "I feel like I should keep my voice down. Like I'm in church."

"I guess we are, in a way. The Japanese people believe spirits inhabit everything. Rocks. Trees."

"Native Americans think that way, too."

She nodded. "They say when you are quiet, the spirits of the gardens speak to you. What you hear with your heart influences what you see with your eyes."

"So, everyone views all this differently?"

"If you're attuned to it," she said. "I like to describe each garden with one word. I've dubbed this area tranquility. What do you see?"

I looked at the growth held in check by a gardener's shears. "Restraint."

"Yes," she said. "I see how that might be true."

We crossed a wooden bridge to the first of two islands. Brittany held my hand. My heart skipped.

In this area, the trees and bushes were allowed to flower. We walked through dappled sunlight, surrounded by blooms of every shade and shape–pink spikes, purple trumpets.

"What word describes this?" she asked.

"Happiness." I smiled. "Redemption."

She laughed. "That's two words."

"Take your pick."

"To me, it says freedom. Non-conformity. But it doesn't always look like this. I've come through when the bushes aren't in bloom. Then it looks very solemn." She gave a pouty face as illustration.

I wanted to kiss her, wanted to dance with her through the blossoms. But she turned and led me to another bridge.

The next island was deeply shaded, and the drop in temperature was noticeable. I gazed up the rough trunks of Australian pines, their branches weighted by clusters of long green needles. Pinecones covered the ground, and rocks rose among them like monoliths.

Brittany said, "This place is all about contrasts."

"A tactile garden," I said. "Smooth and jagged, sharp and soft."

"Let's go this way." She deviated from the path, taking an offshoot that led along the water's edge. The ground was so ribbed with tree roots, it was almost like descending stairs.

We sat on a bench overlooking the green lake. The glassy surface reflected the trees and clouds.

Brittany sighed. "I always expect to see ducks."

"The fish would probably eat them. Nibble on their toes."

"I don't see any fish."

"Trust me," I said. "It's teeming with them. Some are three-feet long."

As if on cue, a huge orange carp broke the surface then disappeared beneath expanding ripples.

"Wow." She cast me a sideways smile.

We sat in silence. I tried to think of something to say. So much had happened while we were apart–my parents and the hearing, the doctor and her threats. The crash.

But before I could speak, Brittany leaned her head on my shoulder.

"I missed you," she said.

I squeezed my eyes shut. My throat choked. "I missed you, too."

I put my arm around her slowly. Gently. Afraid to frighten her away.

She snuggled closer. "Even when we're mad, I still think about you."

"Always," I whispered. Screwing up my courage, I fumbled in my pocket and pulled out the little box with the promise ring. The golden fairy glittered as I held it out.

Brittany gasped.

My thoughts snatched at my prepared speech as it fell apart–*even when I say stupid things, even when you think I don't care*–"I love you."

She met my gaze. Tears sparkled in her eyes, but she smiled. "And I love you."

With her fingertips soft upon my cheeks, she guided me into her kiss. Her lips parted as they met mine. I felt like I was falling and flying at the same time. When she pulled back, I could hardly breathe.

I took the ring from the box. "It's engraved."

She read aloud. "Always. Cody."

I slid the ring onto her finger. It fit perfectly.

We sat together, my arm around her. I felt the slight movements of her breathing. I heard the steady rhythm of her heart. Occasionally, she held her hand into the light. The topaz fairy wings shone. I sensed her happiness, and it filled me with joy.

After about twenty minutes, she stood, tugging me with her. "Come on. We had better see the rest of the park before the day gets too hot. I do *not* want a sunburn."

I would just as soon sit with her, but I smiled and said, "Let's go, then."

We crossed another bridge to a bamboo grove. The tall, green stalks clattered and creaked.

Brittany said, "I call this garden life's folly. The bamboo rushes to grow up and then what? It dries out and dies. It's kind of sad."

"No." I gazed upward. "They're dancing. Look at them. Constantly in motion. Arms spread toward the sun."

She chuckled. "You're in a good mood today."

I laughed and kissed the top of her head.

We came to a bunch of boulders piled on a hill of gravel. The sign said it was a rock garden.

"It's supposed to represent mountains and cliff sides," she said. "The gravel is frothing water. Notice how the taller rocks are lighter in color, as if the sun were touching them first."

"You're an artist."

"I want to be a graphic artist. Like my brother." She shrugged. "I never see him anymore. He lives in Jacksonville."

"So, you have a younger brother here with you in Loxahatchee, an older brother living in Jacksonville, and a sister who lives in Kissa– Kissa-what now?"

"Kissimmee." She smirked and nodded. "With my niece, Miley."

"You have a large family."

"I always wanted to be an only child."

"You can be. Just ignore everyone."

She nudged me. "Tried it. Doesn't work."

"Well, being an only child gets lonely. I had an imaginary friend when I was a kid."

"You did?"

"Yeah. Used to set a place for him at the table and everything. Had my parents worried."

"Why didn't your parents have more children?"

"I guess they didn't want to risk having another one like me."

Brittany squeezed my hand.

I wanted to tell her about my day in court, but suddenly the wound was too raw, the betrayal too deep. I couldn't talk about it.

We passed another rock garden, this one with gravel raked into wavy lines. There was no shade. I pushed my sweaty hair out of my eyes, wishing for a rain shower.

We walked on. Thick green bushes sculpted into neat mounds surrounded the next garden. Large, mossy rocks rose from a bed of gravel. Even I could see the gravel was raked to imitate waves around islands.

"The bushes signify rolling hills," Brittany said. "The stone pagoda is like a tall building in the distance, maybe a city barely seen. I always wondered if this were a real place recreated from memory."

I nodded. "Japan has a lot of rocks."

"I wish I could see it. Wish I could see anything. I've always wanted to travel. I envy your trips around the world."

"But never to Japan," I told her. In a quiet voice, I added, "Maybe we should go there on our honeymoon."

She gasped, eyes sparkling, nose crinkled in the way I loved. "It's a date."

I pulled her close and kissed her. Her lips tasted like grape lipstick with just a hint of maple syrup. I wanted to freeze time, to hold her forever. We could be like a statue–two lovers entwined.

Unfortunately, I had to breathe. I pulled back, cupping her face in my hands and gazing into her bright green eyes. Then I kissed her nose and smiled. I never felt so happy.

We climbed a series of steps that led to a wooden pavilion. An unseen waterfall roared. I looked out upon the surrounding treetops, feeling as if I were actually on a mountain.

Of course, I wasn't. South Florida is flat. Any hills are trucked in. It occurred to me that the garden was an illusion, all of it meant to look like something else. It was a trick.

We strolled down the *mountaintop*, crossing babbling streams, passing from shade to scorching sun. Brittany's phone beeped. She took it out, checked a text, then returned it to her purse. I wanted to ask who was texting her, but she steadfastly avoided my eyes.

A stone bridge took us to an island with bonsai and a museum filled with exhibits about daily life in Japan. The building consisted of several rooms. Each had a wide door opened to a central courtyard and yet another garden of raked gravel. There was no air conditioning.

Brittany said, "Whew. It's hot. I feel a little woozy."

"Here. Sit down." I led her to a bench in the shade, fanning her with the map. Her face was splotchy.

"Could you get me a Coke?" she asked. "There's a machine next to the restrooms. Just go back across the bridge."

"Sure." I checked the map, and there they were—restrooms off the beaten path. "Be right back."

I took off at a trot, hurrying from the island to the main walkway. A sign pointed me in the right direction. I jogged down an adjoining path out of sight from the museum.

The road to the bathrooms was on another planet. Gone were the meticulously trimmed bushes, the lush lawns. I now walked cracked asphalt amid drought-gray grass and untended pine. On one side, a chain-link fence barred a parking lot filled with utility vehicles and orange caution cones. On the other side, trees kept the gardens from view.

Just when I thought I'd gone the wrong way, I saw a small white building. The stench of garbage from an open can met my acute senses. I rushed to the Coke machine, took two singles from my pocket and fed them into the slot. A can clanked against the door. It was as cold as ice.

I bought another. As I reached to retrieve it, I caught a whiff of wolfsbane. I gasped and froze.

From inside the doorway, Dr. Saarsgard said, “So, you have a little girlfriend after all.”

TWENTY-ONE

The can of Coke exploded in my grip, spraying the vending machine and the restroom wall. I looked down at my hand. Thick, yellowed fingernails curled into claws. Crap! I had to get my wolf under control. I couldn't let Dr. Saarsgard know that I could shift in the middle of the day.

I dropped the foaming can in the garbage. As I shook Coke from my fingers, it occurred to me how isolated the restrooms were. I could be tasered or shot with a blowgun. Or simply hit on the back of the head.

I should run. I wouldn't, of course. But I should.

As if she hadn't freaked me out, I wiped my dripping fingers on my pants then pulled out two more dollars. My hand trembled as I fed them to the machine. I glanced to where I'd heard her voice.

She stood just inside the ladies room doorway. The shadows were dark in contrast with the bright sun. I could barely make her out. With all my might, I listened. Her heartbeat thrummed. Her breath rasped. She made no threatening moves. Why didn't she come out to confront me?

Maybe because she was alone.

"You're supposed to be in the hospital," I said. "I guess you weren't hurt as bad as they thought."

"My injuries were quite extensive," said Dr. Saarsgard, her accent a bit more pronounced. "Fortunately, I carried a vial of serum in my purse. The formula is almost complete."

That caused goose bumps to break out over my arms. I thought about the werewolf screaming on the operating table. Feigning nonchalance, I said, "Good. You don't need me, then." My Coke slid down the chute. I retrieved it and, with both cans in my possession, turned to walk away.

A hand shot from the darkness and grabbed my arm. It withdrew immediately, but not before I saw it–bone thin with yellowed claws and tufts of white fur.

I recoiled, then forced a chuckle. "Looks like your serum has a few side effects."

She blew out a breath as if exasperated. I peered into the open doorway. Saarsgard hid in shadow, but my wolf could see her. She wore a dark hoodie, concealing much of her body and face, but her eyes glowed yellow.

She said, "My wolfish attributes will fade in a few hours, but my bones will remain healed."

"And you're here to show me how well you're doing?"

"No, fool." She growled. "I'm here to prove how vulnerable you are. I could take you at any time."

"Then why don't you? Run out of cronies? Are all

your sycophants in jail?"

"My network is more extensive than you know. You can't win." She waved her arm. "Look how easy it was to lure you to this lonely location."

I blinked. What did she mean by that? I hadn't been lured. I'd gone there of my own accord to get Brittany and me a Coke. Hadn't I?

Sudden anger rushed through me. I shouted, "What is it with you? Do you think stalking me is going to change my mind? Just accept that I don't want to go to your party and leave me alone."

"Perhaps you believe that Lycans are common or that tracking them is simple."

I thought of all the werewolves I saw on her security cam–some in the rec room, some in cages. I lowered my voice. "What will it take to make you forget me?"

"Oh, I don't know. Maybe... stop being a werewolf." She erupted into peals of laughter as I stormed down the walkway. After a moment, she called, "Say hello to your little girlfriend for me."

I doubled my pace, barely aware of my surroundings. The woman was insane. I had to get Brittany out of there. She was too precious to be endangered by a raving mad scientist.

Somehow, I made my way back to the building on the island. Brittany still sat in the courtyard staring at the plot of raked gravel. I handed her a can of Coke and sat beside her without speaking.

She flashed a dazzling smile. "Everything okay?"

"Why do you ask?"

"You were gone a long time."

"I couldn't find the place." I opened my Coke. Foam boiled over my hand and onto the wooden floor.

Brittany laughed and opened her can. It didn't overflow. She took a sip. "Yum. Icy cold."

"You're right. It's too hot to stay out here. We should probably head home."

"Oh? Okay, then."

We left the building and crossed the stone bridge to the main walkway. Brittany was quiet. My thoughts knocked around so hard, I was surprised she couldn't hear them. How had Saarsgard known I was at a Japanese garden? What happened to the police guard outside her hospital room?

I walked protectively at Brittany's side, hyper alert and watching for ambush. She glanced at me as if puzzled. We passed another waterfall then at last climbed the steps to the entrance hall. Air conditioning chilled my sweaty skin. Brittany dawdled at the exhibits, but I kept walking. I needed to put some distance between us and the good doctor. Finally, Brittany followed me out the front door to the parking lot.

We climbed into her Beetle. She fiddled with the radio, searching for whatever struck her fancy. I stared outside, certain we were being watched. My shoulders were so tense I thought my head would pop off. It was a relief when she put the car in gear and pulled out of the parking lot onto the road. There were few houses and no traffic.

We took I-95 north. While Brittany sang with Slayer, I frowned, deep in thought. Who could have told Saarsgard where to find me? No one knew where we were going, and it wasn't like a Japanese garden was my usual haunt. Anxiety twisted my stomach. I glared at other drivers as they passed. Someone was trying to get me killed. But who?

We took the Belle Glade exit, heading toward Loxahatchee. I gazed out at familiar territory.

Over the blaring music, I asked, "Did Grandpa Earle know where we were?"

"Not specifically. I just said we were going out. You know, to talk. He knew I was mad at you."

Along with all your girlfriends and half the school.

She turned down the radio. "Is anything wrong?"

"Of course not. Why?"

"You're just acting a little... crabby."

"Well, I'm not."

"Okay." She shrugged. "Do you want me to drop you off at home?"

"That's fine."

"Where's your bike?"

"Wrecked."

"Oh." She glanced at me. "I'm happy to drive you anywhere. Brittany's Taxi Service. Just call."

She looked so cute, I had to smile. "Thanks."

She smiled back. "So when were you going to tell me about Doctor Saarsgard?"

I wheezed like something large and heavy slammed into my chest. "You know about her?"

"She's been to the house a couple of times. She seems really nice. You won't believe this, but I think Grandpa was hitting on her."

She laughed, sounding like a mischievous fairy. I stared with my mouth hanging open. Brittany was the one who set me up? Brittany betrayed me?

"The first time she came over, I didn't trust her," Brittany said. "She asked all these questions about you. When she said she knew your little secret, I thought yeah, right. But then she started throwing around words like lycanthropy and werewolves, and I realized she was on the level. And when she told me she could actually cure you–" She glanced at me, and her smile faded. "What's wrong?"

I saw her as if from a distance, as if I were in a different reality. In a hoarse voice, I asked, "Did you tell her we were at the garden?"

"Yeah. I called her when I went in for my purse. She wanted to talk to you face to face, and I thought the garden would be–"

"Stop the car."

"What?"

"Stop the car!" I bellowed. "Now!"

She veered onto the dusty shoulder. Someone honked as they passed. While Brittany was still braking, I opened the door and leaped out. I couldn't stand to be with her another moment. Fortunately, the car was moving slowly enough for me to keep my feet. I shoved my hands in my pockets and started walking.

Behind me, Brittany cried, “Cody, wait!”

I couldn’t look at her, couldn’t bear to hear her voice. I hurdled a wire fence and entered a line of trees. Once out of sight, I let the panic come. I paced and moaned, yanking my hair. How could this have happened? Brittany, the love of my life, had sold me out. Nothing was right anymore.

Then Brittany’s voice called my name, and I ran–ran as if I could leave everything behind, as if I could bury my heartache in dust. My muscles stretched and burned, and my breath hissed between my teeth as I sprinted through the trees. I knew I ran faster than humanly possible. I risked being seen. But all I could think of was getting somewhere safe.

It was late afternoon when I reached home. I was drenched in sweat and so exhausted I could barely make it up the steps. Uncle Bob wasn’t back from work yet, which was good. I didn’t want to answer any questions. I locked the door behind me, went into the kitchen, and pulled out a jug of chocolate milk. I just stood there at the sink, drinking and staring out the open window. Dazed, I guess–my thoughts too painful to think.

A vehicle crackled up the gravel driveway. Probably Uncle Bob. I put away the milk and headed for my room. The front doorknob rattled.

Then Brittany called, “Cody? Let me in. I want to talk to you.”

TWENTY-TWO

I staggered as if socked in the stomach. *Brittany was on my front porch.* Maybe if I held still, she'd go away. I couldn't talk to her. I knew I'd say something I would regret.

"Cody, are you there?" Brittany cried. "Please open the door."

I winced against a pang in my heart. Her footsteps scuffed the wooden porch as if pacing. I pictured her wringing her hands. My resolve weakened, and I almost stepped forward.

Then, hands cupping her face, she peered through the dining room window. I froze, hoping she couldn't see me in the hallway. A minute later, she clomped across the porch and down the steps. Her car door slammed, and the engine started. I blew out my breath and sagged against the wall.

Instead of backing down the driveway, however, the little car drove onto the grass. It made lurching sounds as it crossed the front lawn and pulled to the side of the house.

I tiptoed to the kitchen and stared in horror at the open window. Should I rush to slam it shut? Before I could decide, I heard Brittany get out of the car and climb onto its roof. She gazed through the window, her face pinched in concentration. Without warning, she leaped forward, catching the sill and scrambling over.

Like my privacy meant nothing. Anger flashed through me. I puffed up until I filled the kitchen doorway.

She landed in the sink with a muffled "oof." Untangling her arms and legs, she reached a foot toward the floor. It would have been comical if I wasn't so mad.

With a sigh, she stood and brushed herself off. Then she noticed me. Her face blanched, and she took a step back.

"Don't," she said. "I just want to talk."

I growled. "By breaking and entering?"

"I didn't break anything. Except maybe my tush. When you didn't answer the door, I figured you weren't home. I thought if you saw me sitting on your front porch, you wouldn't come up. So I pulled my car to the side of the house where you wouldn't see it and came in to wait for you."

I snuffled a derisive laugh.

"Cody, please. I only want to talk. Put your fangs away."

Only then did I realize how I appeared to her. I was menacing the girl I loved. With closed eyes, I willed the tension from my shoulders, down my arms, and out my fingertips. I actually felt like I was getting smaller. My mouth ached, and I realized I'd been showing my fangs without even realizing it. Didn't I have any control at all?

"All right," I said, my voice gravelly. "Talk."

"You're angry about Doctor Saarsgard. I get that. I just don't get why. How could you hate someone you never even met?"

"Oh, we met. Remember way back when? I told you my parents were trying to take custody away from Uncle Bob and give me to a mad scientist."

"She's the mad scientist? But you won the court case. Why is she still here?"

"She never gave up. I'm sure you heard about the yelling match she and Uncle Bob got into in front of the school."

"No. I didn't hear that one."

"Well, maybe you heard about this. Doctor Saarsgard was in the limo that ran into me. She was trying to kidnap me, snatch me right off my bike. Eff saw it and rammed them. On purpose."

"Oh my God. The news didn't say anything about that. I didn't know."

"You didn't know." I glared at her. "But that didn't stop you from discussing my personal business with a stranger."

She gasped, and her eyes filled with tears.

I went for the kill. "I thought I could trust you. I thought you were on my side. Do you even know what the word secret means?"

She collapsed onto a chair, sobbing, mascara

running all over her face.

I folded my arms. "So I just want to know why. How could you do that to me?"

She took a moment to compose herself, but when she spoke her voice still trembled. "You don't know what it's like to live in fear. Never knowing what's going to set him off. Not know if you would live through the night. I promised myself I'd never be in that situation again." Her face scrunched. "Then you turned into a snarling wolf and started battering the door trying to get to me. And I. Was. Terrified."

I frowned and leaned against the doorframe.

Brittany pulled a napkin from the holder and blew her nose. "When Doctor Saarsgard came around, I didn't welcome her with open arms. But she knew just what to say to gain my trust. I don't know. Maybe she saw the fear in me." She met my eyes. "She offered hope, Cody. Hope that you could be normal again. And I wouldn't have to be afraid."

My wolf riled at that. *Oh sure. Let's make this all my fault.*

A knock came at the door. I answered it, grateful for the diversion.

It was Sheriff Brad. "Is your uncle home?"

"No, sir. Can I help you?"

"I have some bad news, son. Somehow Doctor Saarsgard overpowered the guard and walked right out of the hospital."

A high-pitched keening came from the kitchen.

Sheriff Brad frowned. "What's that?"

I called, "Brittany, come out here so he can see I'm not torturing you."

She stepped into the dining room, her eyes red and her cheeks black with spoiled makeup. "Hello, Sheriff."

He said, "What's going on here?"

In a high, tight voice, she said, "I think we're breaking up."

I looked at her. Was that what I wanted? "No. We're just having words."

She sobbed and flew into my arms. I wrapped her tight. I could no sooner leave her than I could stop being a werewolf.

"All right," said the sheriff. "Cody, I suggest that you stay indoors. I have troopers stationed at both entrances to your neighborhood. We'll catch her."

"Thank you, Sheriff," I said.

He stomped down the steps, pockets jingling all the way. Before he reached his squad car, Uncle Bob pulled up in his truck. The two men stood outside and talked awhile.

I hugged Brittany to my chest and rested my cheek on the top of her head. It felt good. I thought about the things she said, about how Saarsgard had offered her hope. No doubt, the same hope she'd offered my parents.

And just like that, I forgave them all. Everyone but me.

Uncle Bob came inside and locked the door. He put his hand on Brittany's shoulder. "Don't worry.

We'll get through this together."

That just got her started again.

Over her muffled wail, he said, "Why don't you two sit down. I'll make some coffee."

I drew Brittany deeper into the living room and sat her on the red couch.

She looked startled. "You have furniture."

"My dad sent it down. My parents are probably remodeling. You know, turning my game room into a spa or something."

"Well, it looks nice."

"Just like home," I muttered, realizing that I resented seeing my old stuff every day.

Uncle Bob stepped into the room carrying two mugs of instant coffee in one hand and the container of napkins in the other. Brittany wiped her face.

After several silent minutes, my uncle said, "Nice ring."

She held out her hand, looking at the promise ring like she was going to start crying again.

"Well," said my uncle, "who's up for a game of Gin Rummy?"

We played cards on the coffee table until well into the evening. Then we ordered Chinese take-out. Brittany insisted on reading all our fortunes out loud. I had just relaxed enough to laugh without feeling self-conscious when she announced that she had to get home.

"You can't go alone," I blurted. "You know what might happen."

"Cody," Brittany said, then shot my uncle a guilty look.

At the same time, Uncle Bob said, "Why? What's up?"

"Saarsgard knows where Brittany lives."

"She's been to the house twice," Brittany said as if it was no big deal.

I said, "If Saarsgard gets Brittany, she gets me."

"Right." Uncle Bob stood. "Young lady, you have just earned yourself an official escort. Cody, why don't you ride with her, and I'll follow in the truck."

All my awkwardness flowed back. I followed Brittany out of the house like a puppy on a first date. We crossed the grass to where she'd left her car. I took the passenger seat. She started the car and pulled it around to the driveway. Uncle Bob gave us a little wave.

"Are you going to tell your uncle that I almost got you kidnapped?" she asked.

I shrugged. Was that what she worried about–what my uncle would think? "I didn't realize that you hated my wolf so much."

"Not hate. But it would be easier. Much easier."

Her words couldn't have hurt more if she had stabbed me. With newfound clarity, I realized that she didn't accept me as I was. She only liked parts of me.

"Don't you ever wonder what life would be like without your wolf?" she asked.

I folded my arms and gazed out the window. How

could I answer that? My wolf was ingrained. It wasn't like I could shave my head and change my clothes and–

"I'm sorry," she said. "I didn't mean to upset you."

My fingernails dug into my arms. I blew out a breath, releasing the tension. I tried to think of a witty way to change the subject. Lamely, I said, "How's William and Eileen? Are they going out?"

"They've gotten pretty close." She nodded. "She's trying to convince him that he can't live in an abandoned fishing cabin for the rest of his life."

"Maybe he should become a nudist."

"Naturist." She smiled. "That's a possibility, but I think she'd rather he went home."

"To the tribe? That would make a long-distance relationship."

"At least, it would be more stable."

Read: At least *he* can't turn into a bear without putting on a belt. I went back to digging my biceps with my claws.

When we reached her house, I walked her to the door. The headlights of my uncle's truck lit her like a spotlight. Without any makeup, her face was luminescent, her eyes bright green. She smiled, crinkling her nose. My mischievous fairy.

I said, "I love you, and I will always protect you."

Even if all I am to you is an unstable lapdog.

I didn't kiss her. It felt too much like I was kissing her goodbye. I just walked away and got into my uncle's truck.

I lay in bed that night with my head full and my heart heavy, reliving the day in the Everglades when I attacked William. Would I have hurt Brittany if I'd gotten inside that cabin? Was she right to be afraid of me?

She deserved better. I should get out of her life now before things got any more complicated. I could keep out of sight like a comic book super hero and make sure she was safe, follow her around for the rest of her life.

With no life of my own.

What if there *was* a treatment for lycanthropy? What if I had the doctor all wrong, and she really could cure me? Maybe I should go to the mountains with an open mind.

Would Brittany miss me?

The next morning, Howard came by early; I heard him and my uncle laughing. My head ached with lack of sleep, but I slipped on a pair of sweats and went out to say hello.

"Howdy." Howard grinned. "And goodbye. Bob, I'll wait for you by the truck."

"Be right out," my uncle called.

I went to the kitchen doorway to see him gulping

down a piece of toast. I hooked my thumb at where Howard disappeared. "He's in a good mood."

"Got another lead on Willie."

"Again?" I scoffed. "Where to this time?"

"A halfway house in Belle Glade."

"You'd be better off following leads on bear sightings," I muttered.

He looked at me. "What do you mean?"

"Well, you know. Howard can turn into a bear. Maybe his son can, too."

"Not likely. Howard is an accomplished medicine man. Willie is just a seventeen-year-old kid."

I bristled at that. Why did adults always think teenagers were inept?

"I've got to go." He rinsed his coffee cup. "Do you want to tag along? I'd feel better if you were with me."

"No, thanks. I've got homework to do after missing school on Friday."

"Okay. Stay in the house. We shouldn't be long." He left, locking the door behind him.

I felt like a prisoner. Would Saarsgard keep tracking me for the rest of my life? I remembered what she'd said about not being a werewolf. If I were cured, would she lose interest? Would she leave me in peace?

I ate a couple bowls of Fruity Pebbles. I only had chocolate milk, so they tasted a little weird. As I cleaned up, my cell rang.

It was Brittany. "Hi. I didn't wake you, did I?"

"No. I'm up. Why don't you come over?"

"I can't. I promised Grandpa Earle I'd take him to the Swap Shop over in Lake Worth. He's looking for a wheelbarrow."

I chuckled. "What are you going to do if you find one? Strap it onto the roof of the Beetle?"

She laughed. "I figured we could just tow it home, use it like a trailer."

"I can see it now."

"Do you want to come with?"

"Can't. I promised Uncle Bob I wouldn't leave the house."

"Oh. All right, then. See you tomorrow at school?"

"You bet."

"Bye."

I frowned and pocketed the phone. The house was suddenly too quiet. I went into the living room and watched the last ten minutes of the news. No rain in sight. No new bear sightings, either.

I wondered if William was okay. I didn't like the guy, but I didn't want to hurt him. Maybe one of his medicine man concoctions would magically heal his mangled leg.

When the news ended, I flipped through the channels for a while. Only three of them came in clear enough to watch. Two showed Sunday morning Mass, and the third had a documentary on the mating habits of wombats. I turned off the TV.

I went into the dining room to play pinball. That was fun for about two seconds–then a barrage of memories hit me. All the friends I left behind. I mostly thought about Mickey Martin, my once-and-only best friend. Could he become a doctor without me? Or did he find someone else's homework to copy?

Suddenly I felt old, like I'd lived two lifetimes. All I had left was a belly full of regret.

I took a shower, hoping to drown my gloom with a blast of hot water. I didn't realized how long I'd been standing there until the water turned cold.

Taking a cold shower made me think of Brittany. I lay in bed dripping wet and stared at the ceiling. There was no way I would ever stop loving her, but now I knew she didn't feel the same. The wolf stood between us. I had to choose.

And I chose Brittany, of course. Right?

My wolf stirred. My senses prickled. It took a moment to realize that it wasn't my thoughts about Brittany that had alerted me but something outside.

I bolted upright, eyes wide. The window was open about three inches. A breeze spun the crystal Brittany hung there. Rainbows danced on the walls.

I smelled wolfsbane.

Heart hammering, I slipped on my sweat pants and stood at the window.

Dr. Saarsgard stared at me from the forest just outside the yard. She'd lost any resemblance to a wolf; now she looked like a bag lady. Her gray hair was bushy and tangled. The hoodie she wore had holes.

Not her usual attire. It occurred to me that she

couldn't go back to her room at the Breakers–the sheriff would have it under surveillance. She lost everything–her money, her clothes, the laptop she had linked to the security cam at the Institute.

Had she killed that link, or did Sheriff Brad see what I saw?

And what had I seen, really? Maybe there were reasons for keeping those people in cages. Maybe they were a danger to themselves and others.

I put my hands on the window, actually intending to open it wide and climb out. I wanted to confront her, ask her if she could truly cure me.

But then I saw her eyes. They were cold and conniving. I remembered her saying she always got what she wanted. She was not the Good Samaritan Brittany thought she was. She was a monster.

And she would never stop as long as I was a werewolf.

I closed and latched the window. Backing away, I went into the living room. Should I call the sheriff? No. She would just disappear, and he'd think I was jumping at shadows. But what if she breaks into the house? I should shift into my wolf form just in case. Wait by the door so I can rip her to shreds.

But what if she's ready for me? What if she has a syringe full of animal tranquilizer? What if her wolfsbane turns me docile and obedient like her werewolf henchman?

I thought of the big man. Was he still in police custody? Or was he in the woods with her? I was no match for a three hundred pound goon.

Sweat broke out on my upper lip. I hugged my arms, senses on overload. Every fifteen minutes, I tiptoed back to my room to check if she was still outside. About an hour later, she disappeared. That freaked me out more. Where was she?

By the time Uncle Bob got home, I was a gibbering wreck. I met him at the door babbling about how Saarsgard and a dozen werewolves had the house surrounded. He and Howard rushed to secure the perimeter. They didn't find anyone. Uncle Bob said he scented Saarsgard and one other. He must've known I was spooked and exaggerating, but he never mentioned it.

Howard stayed with us the rest of the day. I was glad for the company. I think he was, too–he seemed really down. After a while, Uncle Bob went to pick up hamburgers, leaving Howard and me alone.

I asked, "Your son wasn't at the halfway house?"

"He was gone." He shook his head. "It was him, though. They recognized his photograph. Said he was limping."

"Oh?" I asked through a pang of guilt.

Howard sighed. "I hope he's all right."

I nodded. He might be limping, but at least he was moving about. Maybe Eileen would talk him into going home.

At school the next day, I decided to ask Brittany if William was still living in the cabin. I walked into the lunchroom half expecting her to be a no-show–and did a double take when I saw her at the back of the room sitting at our table. I grinned, feeling slightly drunk–like that time Mickey and I spent the night in his tree house, and I puked over the edge of the platform.

I followed the cafeteria conga line and picked up a couple of apples and yogurt. Just like old times. With my tray in hand, I floated down the aisle toward Brittany. She looked so beautiful. My mouth was dry, and I didn't think I could speak even if I knew what to say. Still grinning, I sat across from her.

"Hi," she said. "How was your day yesterday?"

"Great. You know. Just stayed in all day." My face grew warm, and I sputtered, "How were things at the Swap Shop?"

"I saw a lot of fun stuff. Bought a wind chime with little ceramic fairies hanging down. But sadly no wheelbarrows."

"Poor Grandpa Earle. What does he want it for?"

"Since Dad moved nearby, the two of them have been doing project after project. I wish Gramps would go back to napping in the afternoon. He's not a young man."

I nodded, imagining Grandpa Earle's wrinkled hands wrapped around a hammer or a shovel. Maybe I should take his place on weekends.

Clearing my throat, I said, "I wanted to talk to you

about William. Howard said he was spotted in Belle Glade."

"Who's William?" Eff said as he set his tray clattering next to mine.

Brittany cried, "None of your business."

"I kind of told you about him," I said. "He's the know-it-all who's a bear to get along with."

"Oh, yeah. How's he doing?"

"Hurt his leg."

"More power to him." Eff took a big bite of sandwich.

Brittany stared at him. "You two are certainly chummy all of a sudden."

"Yeah, that's us," he mumbled through a mouth full. "Best buds."

I glanced over, irritated at the implication. But I couldn't deny it. Eff had saved my life. "I want to thank you, by the way, for what you did. I'm sorry about your car. But if you hadn't come along, I would be–"

"In the hands of the ice queen," he said.

"Who?" asked Brittany.

"Doctor Saarsgard," I said.

She blinked and pointed at him. "Eff knows about Saarsgard?"

"Sure," he said. "Didn't Cody tell you how we broke into her hotel room?"

I waved my hands, choking out, "Nope... Not..."

"You won't believe what we saw in there," Eff said. "She had a security cam hooked into that asylum she runs. What she was doing to those poor people..." He shook his head. "They were like half human and half animal. She kept them in cages. And they had one poor devil strapped down–"

"Okay, okay," I said. "Trying to eat here, buddy."

"I hear you." He finished his sandwich and downed his milk. "Anyway, I've got a meeting to get to. I'm trying out for the school newspaper."

"You?" Brittany blurted. "A writer?"

"Yeah. Something wrong with that?"

"No. I just... didn't think you could read."

"Nice." He stood and picked up his tray. "Catch you later."

"Good luck," I said as he walked away.

Brittany stared at me. I squirmed.

"Tell me the truth," she whispered. "What did you see?"

I shrugged. "Like he said."

"She's not helping them? Curing them?"

"She's trying to create a vaccine so that everyone can enjoy super strength and super healing. She wants her name to be immortal."

"But cages?"

"From what I saw, cages were the least of their problems."

Brittany bowed her head. "I really messed things up."

I nearly blurted *Yes. Yes you did.* Instead, I took her hand. I felt my promise ring on her finger.

"It'll be all right," I lied.

TWENTY-THREE

Early the next morning, Uncle Bob hammered on my bedroom door. "Get dressed! Hurry!"

I fell out of bed half-asleep, but my wolf woke on high alert. As I staggered into the Levis I'd left on the floor, the wolf howled *forget the clothes. Run!*

Shoes in hand, I rushed to the living room. The TV was on, giving a fuzzy rendition of the news. My uncle wasn't there. The front door stood open, showing darkness beyond.

I smelled smoke.

Oh, crap. The house was on fire.

"Uncle Bob!" I burst out the door and leaped the stairs, turning in mid-stride to look at the roof.

There were no flames. The pre-dawn sky was brown and hazy. The horizon glowed with an orange sunrise–only in the wrong direction.

What was going on?

"Uncle Bob!" I coughed, nearly choking on a ball of panic. My skin prickled. The wolf clamored to get out. It wanted control, wanted to run. I knelt deliberately to tie my shoes.

Just then, the sprinklers came on, spraying the

drought-dry grass with fetid liquid. I jumped back. I didn't even know we had an irrigation system. The sprinkler heads gurgled. A few were missing, and water shot in three-foot geysers. Dodging the irregular spray, I moved to the side of the house. Relief washed over me as Uncle Bob stepped from the backyard. He carried a coiled garden hose in one arm and a ladder on the other.

I hurried to him. "What's happening?"

"Brushfire. The news said it was near State Road 80."

The cabin.

I jammed my fingers in my hair, spinning like a dog chasing its tail. Should I tell him William was out there? Was I risking William's life by not giving him up?

"Take the ladder," Uncle Bob said.

I turned from the glowing horizon. Ashes floated upon the breeze like snowflakes. Surreal. With clumsy fingers, I helped my uncle wrestle the ladder against the wall.

My thoughts warred with the promise I'd made to William. But he would know about the fire by now. He was a big boy; he could take care of himself. That decision made me feel like a coward.

Uncle Bob hooked one end of the hose to a faucet and the other end to a rotary lawn sprinkler. He plopped the heavy rubber coils on my shoulder. "Take this to the roof."

I climbed, unwinding the hose as I went. When I

reached the cedar shingles, I stood in awe. Smoke billowed on the horizon like an orange and gray thundercloud. Distant sirens wailed. A flock of birds flew overhead.

"You there?" my uncle called.

I blinked. "Yeah. Now what?"

"Put it in the middle, then wait while I turn it on."

I dragged the sprinkler to the center of the roof. "Okay."

Water gushed, and the sprinkler spun. Rusty-smelling streams arced into the air.

Uncle Bob appeared at the edge of the roof. "Is it hitting everywhere?"

"I need to move it to the right," I said.

He squeezed the hose until the sprinkler stopped spinning, and I repositioned it. Soon water struck all four corners of the house.

"That should help guard against flying embers," he said.

"Won't the fire department be miffed about us using all the water?"

"We have city water inside the house, but out here it's from a private well. They're probably flying it in from Lake Okeechobee anyway." He climbed down.

I gave a last glance to the burning Everglades and followed. Shadows deepened as I reached the ground. "Dark out here."

He carried the ladder toward the tool shed. "Yeah. Hard to believe it's after seven o'clock."

"What? I have to get ready for school."

"No classes today," he said. "They've already announced the high school as a designated evacuation point. Besides, I need you with me. We have a lot to do."

"But what about Brittany?" We were supposed to have lunch. Why did everything always go wrong?

A smile touched his voice. "I'm sure she's fine."

I splashed toward him. The parched ground was too hard and dry to accept our belated offering of water. I asked, "Are we evacuating?"

"I hope not. I want to get some of this dry brush out of here." He opened the tool shed and pulled out two machetes. "Do you know how to use this?"

I took the machete, holding it like it was a snake about to strike. "Um, we had a lawn company..."

"That's okay. Just use a downward chopping motion. And keep it away from your body." As an example, he stepped into the trees, hewed a woody vine in two, then pulled it into the yard. "We'll make a pile by the truck, then take the refuse to the dump."

"All right." I sounded unsure, even to me.

"Start on that side. Try to get at least twenty feet inward. Clear out as much as you can. But remember. Speed over quality. I'll work toward you. We'll meet in the middle."

"Speed over quality."

This was a nightmare. I walked to my area and waved my blade. The bush fought back. I swung again. The dry wood snapped. Branches clawed my bare skin in revenge. I pulled the debris into the yard, victorious. Only 999 more to go.

I kept at it, chopping and hacking, yanking and heaving. My pants became soaked to the knees as I dragged the dead brush across the puddled lawn. Falling ash turned my sweat gritty, making my eyes and throat burn. I tried not to notice, tried not to hear the sirens growing louder.

Slash. Hack. Slash. Hack.

The day brightened. The sun looked red. It had a sooty brown halo. The breeze picked up, carrying with it the stench of burning straw.

We should get out now while we still had the chance. Evacuate to the school. Maybe Brittany was there looking for me.

Slash. Hack. Slash. Hack.

I met my uncle in the middle, our two areas merging. We stepped back to admire the broad swath of forest floor we'd cleared. Only the trees remained. I hoped he didn't plan to take those down as well.

I turned to the whine of a dirt bike coming up the driveway. The rider stopped behind the truck and took off his helmet.

It was William.

My jaw dropped. I glanced at my uncle.

"Willie?" Uncle Bob said.

William looked at me. "Is my father here?"

"I haven't seen him," I said.

Uncle Bob stared. "You know each other?"

"Oh, man." William looked toward the forest.

"This is bad. This is real bad."

"You know each other?" Uncle Bob roared. He grabbed my arm.

I broke his grasp. "Look. We'll talk about this later, all right?" I crossed the lawn to William. "What's bad? What happened?"

"I went home," William said, "and as usual my stepfather blew up. He wasn't happy to see me. He only wanted to know where I was all this time. So I told him."

"About the cabin?" I blurted.

"What cabin?" said my uncle.

"An abandoned fishing cabin," I said.

Uncle Bob's face fell as if with sudden realization. He murmured, "Out by State Road 80."

Did everyone know the place?

"Joseph was enraged," William said. "He vowed I would never again sneak off to see my father. He called him and told him I was at the cabin. A while later, I heard about the fire. I think Joseph deliberately set it to kill my father."

"Joseph?" Uncle Bob said. "Joseph Achak?"

William nodded.

"Oh, man," I said. "This *is* bad."

William started the little engine on his bike.

Uncle Bob took hold of the handlebars. "Where do you think you're going?"

"To find him." William brushed away my uncle's hands and pulled onto the lawn, heading for the forest.

"You'll never make it that way," Uncle Bob yelled. "There's no trail."

Only, there kind of was, I'd been back and forth so often. William pulled a wheelie then disappeared into the trees.

Uncle Bob turned to me. "You lied."

"Not exactly."

"How do you know him?"

"I met him in the woods. I was a wolf."

He grimaced. "Willie knows you're a werewolf?"

"He kind of guessed. There aren't many wolves in South Florida."

"So you've been friends with him? You've been seeing him?"

I thought about the food runs Brittany and I made to the cabin. "Not exactly friends," I muttered.

"How could you do this? How could you let us keep looking for the boy when you knew all along where he was?" He waved his arm. "All this might have been avoided if you had just been truthful."

I wanted to yell back, wanted to excuse my actions. But I couldn't. If I had told him about William a month ago, everything would have been different. William would have been living at Howard's house or back home with his mother. Either way, he wouldn't have been at the cabin–and Joseph Achak wouldn't have set the Everglades on fire.

Uncle Bob took out his cell phone. I assumed he was calling Howard. He listened for a few minutes, then blew out his breath and dialed again.

"This is Bob Nowak. I'd like to speak to the sheriff, please." He waved his arm, pacing. "I understand he's busy, but I have information about the brushfire out on 80. Fine, then give him a message. I believe a man named Joseph Achak started the fire. Yes, ma'am," he said, shooting a glare at me. "It was deliberate."

I opened my mouth to protest. I didn't mean for any of this to happen. But Uncle Bob thought I betrayed his trust. I didn't think he would forgive me.

"Don't hang up," he told the lady on the phone. "I also want to report that Howard Shebala and his son, William, are at that old fishing cabin. You know the one I mean? Yes, ma'am, a lot of people used to party there." His voice rose. "Well, I can't reach him, and if they're still there, they're in danger. Thank you." He jammed his cell into his pocket and headed for his truck. "Let's go."

"Where?"

"To get as close as we can to that cabin. Maybe we can spot him."

"There's a faster way." I kicked off my shoes and unzipped my pants.

"Cody, no. I can't let–"

"It's my fault they're out there. I've got to save them." I took off through the trees, making the shift into a wolf as I ran.

I got a distance away before the pain of my transformation dropped me. A howl burst from my throat. I planted my paws in the dust, head down, a low growl filling my chest. My nose twitched with the reek of scorched grass. The fire was coming.

I fought to keep from running away. I couldn't go into that burning muck. Yet I had to. Howard wouldn't be out there if it weren't for me.

Shoulders hunched, I trotted through the woods. Squirrels and rabbits darted across my path, fleeing a more terrifying threat than a lone wolf. Birds squawked in the trees–I saw peacocks, parrots, and large white egrets hanging precariously from the thin branches.

Monkeys were among them. Their reflective eyes glinted in their small faces. At first, I was surprised; then I remembered Uncle Bob mentioning that monkeys occasionally escaped the local drive-through safari park. I thought about the lions trapped on the pavilion there, thought of the giraffes in the barns, and I hoped the blaze stayed well away.

The whine of William's dirt bike reached me. I quickened my pace, passing through small clearings where smoke hung like fog. There were no longer any animals. Not even insects. I supposed the bugs burrowed underground.

The wind rose. Branches whipped overhead as if the trees themselves were attempting to flee. A hot blizzard of ash and cinders slanted through the air, making my skin crawl and my lungs burn. I flattened my ears and ran in a crouch, trying to keep under cover.

With the sound of breaking teeth, a branch

crashed to the ground. Brown grass burst into flame. I dodged and leaped. More branches fell. The forest filled with a terrible roar. Flames ate the brush and lapped the trunks of tall Australian pine.

It was too hot to breathe, too smoky to see. I ran, and the fire kept pace. It chuckled and crackled, snapping its jaws at my heels until I felt like I sped through a bright, flickering tunnel.

A tree fell nearly on top of me, bowling me over and knocking the air from my lungs. Glowing cinders drifted all around. For a moment, I thought they were stars. I lifted my head dizzily. Then the roar of the blaze thundered in my chest. Embers singed my fur.

With a resounding crack, another tree toppled. And another. Their trunks ruptured as the sap within them detonated. The air wavered with heat. I scrambled to my feet and ran for all I was worth. My eyes stung, and my paws felt blistered.

At last, I reached the forest's end. I burst from the trees, expecting a sea of sawgrass. Instead, I saw a wall of orange flame. Smoke hung like a cloudbank, its underside reddened by flying sparks. The line advanced through the grass.

Cold fear shivered through me. I couldn't fight this. But I thought of Howard searching for his son.

I had only minutes to reach the cabin.

Barking a battle cry, I sped into the grass. The relentless line of fire snapped behind me. Saw-toothed blades whipped my eyes and dragged at my coat.

The haze thickened as I ran, its cloying stench threatening to choke me. Clumps of trees rose like shadowed islands. The inferno roared behind, yet to the side I saw flickers of bright, dancing flame–and I realized that the blaze was horseshoe shaped. Closing in.

Ahead the cabin stood on its stilts at the edge of the dry lakebed. Smoke seeped from its tarred roof, and flame barred the open door.

To one side, William kicked the wall as if to break it down. When he noticed me, he shouted, "My stepfather firebombed the door. I *saw* him." He collapsed in tears.

Gathering my haunches, I leaped onto the dock and barreled into the shuttered window. Its heavy wood splintered. I burst inside and landed in a roll, gasping with blistering heat.

The floor beneath the doorway blazed. Flame licked up the wall and danced upon the rafters. I smelled hot tar.

Howard lay unconscious. Pieces of a wooden chair covered his back. I nuzzled his face.

Wake up! Wake up!

I glanced around the smoky room...

And froze.

A wall of shelves was stacked with old fishing magazines–and row upon row of mason jars filled with gasoline.

Oh, God!

Yipping, I pawed Howard's shoulder. He moaned

but didn't wake.

I couldn't leave him.

Wheezing, eyes smarting, I ducked my head beneath the hefty wooden table and flipped it. With a whoosh, it landed over the flames beneath the doorway, clearing a path.

Almost immediately, a dark form filled the doorway. William the Bear. He lumbered forward, snuffling his father's prone figure.

I sank my teeth into Howard's collar and dragged him onto the upended table. He groaned and turned over, blinking.

His eyes widened in the light of the flame. I tugged harder, and he helped propel himself backwards a few inches.

Then, amid the crackling and popping of burning wood, a loud cr-crack rent the air. A rafter fell. I had an image of us crushed beneath the failing roof.

Suddenly, William the Bear stood over us, catching the beam on his broad shoulders. Sparks showered over him.

Howard cried out, his arms windmilling in his attempt to back away. I doubted that he recognized his son, but he must have noticed the bear wasn't acting very bearlike. With all my strength, I yanked him out the door onto the creaking porch.

What came next seemed to happen in slow motion.

I pulled Howard to the edge of the dock.

William the Bear shook off the burning beam.

He stood on his hind legs, his bulk filling the doorway, his thick pelt smoking.

Behind him grew a brilliant white light.

The brightness encased him.

A concussive boom threw Howard and me off the deck as the jars of gasoline ignited.

TWENTY-FOUR

The cabin exploded. The force swatted me off the dock. Chunks of wood arced into the air.

I hit the ground, ears ringing. Howard landed beside me. He grabbed my ruff, trying to pull me with him as he scooted deeper beneath the porch.

William the Bear flew overhead. His arms and legs flailed. His outline shimmered for an instant, and he hit the ground as a naked boy.

Without thinking, I burst from Howard's shelter to lie on top of William. Chunks of wood rained over us. Much of it was no bigger than kindling–some were so heavy they rattled the ground.

I shuddered with each blow, imagining a big red target painted on my back. William didn't move. He stank of blood and scorched flesh.

A second explosion rocked the air. Howard's truck erupted with fire. The grass around it blackened and curled, sprouting new flames. I cringed and closed my eyes, shutting out the sight, but the afterimage blazed brightly.

Then Howard was beside me. His voice sounded hollow and distant as he called William's name. I rolled to the side. My body ached, and my throat burned. I needed sleep. Maybe I would wake to find this was all a dream.

But the raging brushfire roared toward us over the sea of sawgrass. Superheated air wavered above the inferno. I forced myself up, then shook from head to tail to dispel the lethargy that would kill me.

William lay face down in the dirt.

"William! Will!" Howard turned him over, shaking him.

William groaned, eyes fluttering. "Dad?"

Howard cradled him in his arms. "My son."

I staggered to the boulder that was once a staircase. Moments ago, there had been a cabin on stilts. Now, only the dock stood. Smoking planks and splintered beams drew a large circle around us. Flames grew like little campfires. Fifty, maybe a hundred of them.

Time to leave.

As I returned to my two companions, I stepped on William's magic belt in the debris. The strap was broken, and the bear pelt was singed. I dragged it over and dropped it into William's lap.

He picked it up, staring as if he'd never seen it before.

Howard said, "You were a bear. Do you know how extraordinary that is?"

"Dad..." William shook his head as if to disavow his importance.

"You shielded us from that blast. Only the armor of a bear's thick coat could have saved us."

William closed his fist around the belt then scrambled to his feet. "Come on, Dad. We have to get out of here." He ran to his dirt bike lying unseen in the tall grass. His clothes were there. He quickly pulled them on. Then he righted the bike. It started on the first try. "Come on," he shouted, revving the engine.

"Cody!" Howard yelled.

He mounted the bike behind his son. They took off, lurching over the uneven ground, the bike buzzing like a chainsaw. I sprinted to catch up, dodging debris.

Howard's truck blazed. Fire spread around it, merging with one end of the horseshoe-shaped brushfire. I flinched from the heat as we passed. The old truck groaned. Metal pinged as flame twisted its frame.

The road was nothing more than a pair of tire tracks, but it was easier on my paws than sawgrass. William picked up speed. I ran behind, fighting dust plumes from the dirt bike.

Behind us, the brushfire cackled. Flames leaped and danced beneath billowing clouds of soot. Even at a distance, haze filled the air.

I panted as I ran, my tongue lolling. The smoke tasted awful, but I couldn't seem to keep my mouth closed. The sound of a helicopter eased into my mind. *Thwap. Thwap.*I looked up, but all I saw was the gray sky and a large red sun. Like high noon on an alien planet.

The bike sputtered, and William slowed. It sputtered again. He revved the engine, and it died. He slammed the handlebars with his fist as the bike coasted to a stop.

Howard slid off the end. "What's wrong?"

"We're out of gas," William said as if he couldn't believe the bike's audacity. He climbed off. "We'll have to leave it."

"Are you kidding?" Howard said. "I paid fifty dollars plus trade for this bike."

William snickered. "Fifty bucks? Happy birthday to me."

"There's a big difference between how it looked then and how it looked when I gave it to you. I worked all summer on it." He grabbed a handlebar and started walking.

William held the handlebar on the other side. He limped as he walked, favoring the leg I mangled. Howard moved as if his back hurt.

It was slow going. Too slow. I looked back at the fire. Hazy orange flame engulfed the remains of the cabin. The blaze was moving faster than we were.

Barking, I ran in front of my companions, looked at them, then ran again. They seemed to catch on and started to trot with the bike between them, breathing in ragged gasps.

Howard said, "How did you find me?"

"I figured out what Joseph was planning. He tried

to kill you."

Howard rubbed the back of his neck. "Broke a chair over me."

"Not only that. After you were down, he set the cabin on fire. Molotov cocktails. He even threw a couple into the grass. I guess the brushfire wasn't moving fast enough to cover your murder."

"He was my friend once." Howard sighed. "Thank you for saving me."

"I didn't save you," he said bitterly. "I was *afraid*. I couldn't get past the door. If Cody hadn't busted through the window..." He shook his head.

Howard glanced at me. "Yeah. Cody the dog."

"I know who he is, Dad."

"You do?"

"He's been bringing me food."

Howard stopped walking. Eyes wide, he looked from William to me. "He knew where you were?"

"He promised not to tell. He didn't want to promise, and I'm sure there were times he wished he hadn't. But he honored me with his silence."

Howard stared at his son. After a moment, he took hold of the bike and started walking again. "I only meant that I would've sent food, too. Make you some of my famous tacos."

William scoffed. "Indians can't make tacos."

Howard shrugged. "I make them with buffalo."

Smoke thickened, shrouding the surrounding trees. Sawgrass made way for common grass. Twigs snapped underfoot. Another helicopter flew overhead, but I couldn't see it. I couldn't see five feet in any direction.

It circled again. Probably a news chopper. Did that mean the fire was right behind us? The thought of flames in the fog scared me. I wanted to flee–but in which direction? Any move I made could take me directly into the blaze.

My step faltered. Which way should I go? All I could see, all I could smell was smoke. I had to run–but I couldn't. Couldn't take a step.

Stop it, said a voice inside. *Stay where you are and flames will engulf you as easily as your panic.*

I looked toward Howard and William. They moved slowly now, coughing and wheezing, clinging to the dirt bike more for support than to push it along. They were so frail, so vulnerable.

You have to save them.

The road curved to the right, leading slightly downhill. Smoke lay thick in the hollow. I couldn't go down there. I couldn't see, couldn't–

I lifted my head, ears twitching. Were those voices?

Howard and William stumbled down the road, steering the bike between them. I growled, and they turned to look at me.

Howard doubled over with a coughing fit. He spat in the grass.

I growled again, took two steps into the trees, then looked back at them.

William motioned. "He wants to go that way."

"Leave the road?" Howard rasped.

William shrugged. "Old Miccosukee saying. Never argue with a werewolf."

Howard's laugh ended in another bout of coughing. He helped his son manhandle the bike around and enter the trees.

I didn't wait. I bounded forward, anxious to be out of the miasma. I was certain I could hear voices now, but they were distant. I zigzagged through the trees, nose to the ground, aware of the crashing of the disabled dirt bike behind me.

The trees ended, and I stepped out into a wide field. Patchy smoke hung low over thorny weeds and wild flowers.

About a hundred yards away was a street packed with cars and emergency vehicles. Flashing red lights lit the fog. Several large white tents had been pitched, their sides rolled up to reveal boxes and tables. Someone shouted distorted instructions through a bullhorn.

We'd come out into some sort of staging area. State Road 27. Relief washed through me. I'd done it. I led the two men to safety. I waited for them to catch up.

Their faces lit as they stepped into the open. William whooped and waved an arm.

Howard dropped to his knees. "A good soldier makes a poor scout."

That made no sense. Maybe he was delusional. I wondered if I should run ahead to get help–but I wasn't sure I could. I ached from my battered head to my blistered paws. It would be embarrassing to come this far only to collapse at the end.

I went to Howard and allowed him to use my shoulders to lever himself to his feet. Then we walked.

When we were about halfway across the field, a blue truck broke away from the mass of vehicles, crashed through a barrier, and raced toward us. The sheriff's car followed, lights flashing, but the truck didn't slow down.

It was Uncle Bob.

He swerved to a stop and hopped out. "Are you all right?"

"Thanks to my son," Howard said. "And Cody."

"Cody, I–" Uncle Bob placed a hand upon my head.

Just then, Sheriff Brad pulled up, lights flashing, tires skidding over the dirt as he braked.

Uncle Bob said, "Stay."

Great. The part of the loveable dog will be played by Cody the Wolf.

"This here's restricted space, Robert," the sheriff called as he got out of his car.

"I'm just helping a friend," said Uncle Bob.

"Nonetheless–" He stopped, staring at me. "Where'd that dog come from?"

"He's mine," William said.

"Big."

"Yeah. We think he's part dire wolf."

"What's his name?"

"Tiny," William said without hesitation.

Something in his tone made me think he was enjoying the conversation. With a yawn, I sat in the grass trying to look as doglike as possible.

Sheriff Brad dismissed me. "I received a message from you, Robert. You say you know who set this blaze?"

Uncle Bob nodded. "Joseph Achak."

"My stepfather," William said.

"Now, why would he go and do a thing like that?"

"He hates me," Howard said. "He's jealous of my relationship with my son. Said as much just before he hit me with a chair."

William said, "Then he set fire to the cabin and the surrounding brush."

"That's attempted murder," the sheriff said.

"You're darn tootin'," said Howard.

"Sheriff, we've all been through a lot," Uncle Bob said. "Can your questions wait?"

"Of course," said Sheriff Brad. "There's a couple of ambulances on the street. They can examine Mister Shebala and his son."

"No need." Uncle Bob draped his arm around Howard's shoulders. "I'll take these two to the emergency room then bring them around to your office later on if that's all right. They can make their statements then."

"I'll tell my assistant to expect them."

Uncle Bob walked Howard to the passenger side

and got him buckled in. Howard looked gray.

William opened the tailgate and wrestled his dirt bike into the truck bed. He sat down wearily. “Come on, Tiny.”

I gave a woof like a good little doggie and jumped up to sit beside him.

Sheriff Brad closed the gate and thumped the side of the pickup. “I’ll be speaking to you.”

Uncle Bob got behind the wheel and started the engine. He turned the truck slowly. The trees we’d walked out of hid in haze. Behind them, the sky glowed orange. Helicopters flitted through the smoke like dragonflies.

The truck jounced and squeaked over the uneven ground. At last, we pulled onto State Road 27, leaving the flashing lights and the bullhorns behind.

William scooted toward the cab and tapped on the rear window. Howard opened it. He winced with the movement.

“We need to get our stories straight,” William said.

Howard nodded. “Truth is always sought but seldom appreciated.”

“I can’t be labeled a runaway,” William said. “It would not look good in court.”

“We were all over South Florida searching for you,” Uncle Bob said. “The sheriff is bound to catch wind of it.”

William grimaced.

“I need a story, too,” Howard said. “If I tell them

Joseph lured me to the cabin with lies about my missing son, they'll wonder why I didn't just call the authorities."

"You should have," my uncle said. "Or at least called me."

"Very well," William said. "You searched for me and found me at the cabin. We spent a couple days there to work out our differences. That way I've at least partially redeemed myself."

"Then Joseph showed up, and we argued," Howard said. "The best stories are rooted in fact."

"But the hospital doesn't need to know all that," Uncle Bob said. "Just say you were caught in the brushfire."

"And the roof caved in on us." Howard rubbed the back of his neck.

My uncle glanced at him. "Did it?"

William rolled his shoulders. "Yes, it did."

They drove in silence for a while. I watched fields and trees whiz by. Wind buffeted me from all angles. It smelled like pine and smoldering hay.

"I'll drop Cody off at the house," Uncle Bob said. "Then I'll take you to the hospital."

"I don't need a doctor." Howard groaned.

My uncle snapped, "I said I was going to, and I will."

Howard and William exchanged surprised glances. Howard looked like he was biting his tongue. Apparently, he didn't want to push my uncle further.

Moments later, we pulled up our driveway. A heap of branches and leaves sat to one side. The sprinkler poured water over the roof. It looked like it was raining.

Uncle Bob got out of the truck. I leaped over the edge and walked beside him. The dutiful pup.

I smelled Brittany as we approached the house. My ears perked, and I glanced around. But she was gone. The scent was hours old.

Uncle Bob said, “Stay inside. I’ll come home as soon as I can.”

He stopped walking. My discarded Levis were on the porch, neatly folded on top of my shoes. My cell sat on top. It buzzed to say I missed a call.

“Someone’s been here.” Uncle Bob picked up the pile, breathing deeply. “Brittany.” He opened the door and walked inside. “She’s not here now. You should call her. Let her know you’re safe. Just don’t leave. I’ll be back.” He left me in the silent house.

When the door clicked shut, I shifted back into a boy. With blistered fingers, I picked up my cell phone and gingerly dialed Brittany’s number.

She picked up on the first ring. “Cody?”

“Hi.” I smiled. “Are you okay?”

“Just imagine how I feel for a moment,” she said, her voice rising. “Just imagine there’s a fire, and people are being asked to evacuate. So you call your boyfriend. *Three times*. No answer. Imagine you drive out to his house only to find the door wide open and the TV left on. No boyfriend. Then you find his clothes in the yard."

"Yeah, Howard found out about William, and he went to the cabin, so it was up to me to–"

"You could have called the police," she shouted. "They would've gotten there faster than you. They have copters and ATVs."

"But I had to..." What? Redeem myself? Atone for my sins?

"Wonderful. Now your wolf has you convinced that you're a superhero. Like you're indestructible. And I'm left to worry that you've burned to death."

"I didn't."

"This time."

I hobbled to the couch and sat with a sigh. "I'm sorry."

She groaned. "Why can't you be a regular boy?"

I winced with the sting. "You want me to be... to be–"

"Normal. Yes. If I could have the Blue Fairy wave her magic wand and turn you into a real boy, I would. In a heartbeat."

"Then... You don't love me."

Her voice softened. "I do love you, Cody. With all my heart. That's the problem."

TWENTY-FIVE

The sky was brown, the sun orange. Ash covered everything–a gritty white powder that made it tough to breathe.

Behind me, the morning newsman said, "Stay indoors and keep those air conditioners running."

I stood at the front window with a cup of hot chocolate, watching Uncle Bob fasten a tarp over the debris we'd piled in his truck. I offered to help him take it to the dump, but I was wheezing so bad he told me to get inside.

I suspected he had an ulterior motive; he was still mad that I hadn't told him about William. He didn't say it, but I knew he blamed me for the fire. Or maybe I just blamed myself. In any case, I didn't think he wanted me around.

"The fire is not out, folks," said the newscaster, "but it *is* contained, and that's a good thing. Evacuees can head back home. Schools are closed for the remainder of the week. That's because of the buses, folks. Police want to keep our streets clear for emergency personnel."

I turned off the television and rinsed my cup. The

palms of my hands were red and sore, but the blisters had healed. I wondered how Howard and William were doing. Uncle Bob said the hospital kept them overnight. They were burnt and bruised, but nothing was broken.

My cell rang–Brittany's ringtone. Smiling, I picked it up. "Good morning."

"Hi," she said. "I only have a couple minutes, but I wanted to let you know what was happening."

I frowned. "What's wrong?"

"Grandpa Earle is having trouble breathing. The hospital wanted to admit him, but he said he'd be on his deathbed before he'd let some little nurse give him a sponge bath." She chuckled. "Anyway, Butt Crack and I were elected to drive him up to my sister's house in Kissimmee."

I blurted, "Why can't your dad take him?"

"Dad says he has to finish raking the lawn. Between you and me, I think he's afraid to face her."

"Are you coming right back?"

"No. Since there's no school, we're going to stay over, visit with baby Miley. I should be home late Thursday."

"Oh." I sank onto a kitchen chair. "I was going to invite you for a movie date. You could pick any movie you wanted."

"That's sweet. I'm busy during the day on Friday. Let's plan for Friday night."

I forced a smile into my voice. "Great. Have a good trip and a nice visit."

"I'll call later to let you know I arrived all right. Bye. I love you."

"I love you," I whispered, but she had already clicked off. I stared at the phone for a while, then I crawled into bed and put the pillow over my head.

Uncle Bob got back from the dump around lunchtime. He looked like he'd aged ten years; ash turned his steel-gray hair white and outlined every wrinkle on his face. While he showered, Howard and William showed up sporting bandages, smiles, and two pizzas.

"How'd you get here?" I asked. "Your truck is toast. Literally."

"My mom dropped us off," William said. "She's being cordial for a change."

Howard reached up to clap him on the shoulder. "She's just happy her son is alive."

Just then, Uncle Bob came out of the bathroom, hair dripping, a towel draped around his middle. "Hey. I thought I heard voices."

"Howdy-do." Howard gestured with a bandaged arm. "Lunch is served."

"You didn't have to do that."

"Well, thank you just didn't seem enough." Howard nodded to me.

William set the pizzas on the coffee table.

My uncle headed toward his room. "Don't start without me."

"I'll get some Coke." I pulled a two-liter bottle from the refrigerator and got out four glasses.

Uncle Bob came back, and we sat around the pizzas. They were just the way I liked them: sausage, pepperoni, meatball, and onion. We didn't speak, just ate in companionable silence.

After a while, my uncle said, "When we're done, I'll drive you to the sheriff's office so you can make your statements."

"Not necessary," Howard said. "A deputy interviewed us last night. He even took some photographs of my bruises."

"Is that so?"

"They arrested my stepfather," William said as if he was busting to tell us. "About an hour ago. They caught him riding a stolen ATV, added theft to the list of charges. When they found him, he told them he didn't know I was in the woods. He only wanted to hurt Howard."

Howard laughed. "As good as a confession."

"Let's hope they put him away for a long while," I said.

"They better," William muttered.

Uncle Bob reached for another slice. "So what happens now? Are you going home, Willie?"

His face brightened. "My mother is petitioning the tribal council to allow me more time with my father. I'm staying here until Sunday night."

Howard smiled. "I have much to teach my little one."

"Your little one is almost a foot taller than you," Uncle Bob said.

We all laughed.

The Marlins were playing the Washington Nationals, so my uncle turned on the TV. He and Howard sat back to watch the fuzzy baseball game. William sighed and rolled his eyes. I motioned him into my room.

"Not much of a sports fan?" I asked.

"I like lacrosse. Played it in high school." He sat at the desk, twisting the chair around to face me.

I sat on the bed. "You still go to school?"

"Graduated."

"At seventeen?"

He shrugged. "They have good schools on the reservation, but they only teach you basic stuff, so I finished early."

"How did you learn to be a medicine man? I mean, I remember you saying that the Miccosukee don't have a written language, so you couldn't just pick up a book."

William sighed. "I got much of my knowledge from my grandmother, who was Story Keeper before my mother. We were close before she died."

We fell silent for a moment, then I asked, "How did you learn about the Navajo side of things?"

"Internet." He grinned. "They have a website."

For some reason, I found that insanely funny. I laughed until I snorted.

When I quieted, he said, "We have not always been friends, you and I. But you saved my life and that of my father. I won't forget."

"And I'll never forget how you caught the roof on your shoulders and kept us from being squashed flat. You are major-league strong."

"Fear finds its own strength. In any case, thank you. If you ever need help with anything, just ask."

I had a feeling he'd just made a life-long commitment. I tried to think of an answer, something stoic and impressive, but before I could decide on anything, my phone rang. I didn't recognize the number. I almost let it go to voicemail, but then I thought it might be Brittany calling from her sister's house or worse from a hospital bed. I picked it up.

"Hello, Cody," said Dr. Saarsgard. "I trust you were untouched by the fire."

I felt myself go ten shades whiter. "How did you get this number?"

"Is that really important?"

"Don't call me again. Or else."

"Or else what?"

"I'll... I'll turn you in, tell everyone what you're really doing. I'll have you arrested."

She laughed, sending chills up my arms. "Silly little boy. You can't harm me. My project is funded by many governments, including your own."

"What?"

"No one wants to have filthy werewolves in their country."

I tossed my cell to the end of the bed and stared at it like it was a poisonous snake.

"Old girlfriend?" William asked.

I couldn't even speak. I pulled my gaze from the phone and met his eyes. The smile left him. He leaned forward and gave me a little nod, prodding me.

I never had a brother, someone who'd take my side without question, who'd fight my battles with me. But at that moment, I felt as if William was my big brother.

I started talking, slowly at first then in a rush. I told him everything, things I hadn't told my uncle, things I hadn't wanted to tell myself. William listened, his expression never changing. No disbelief. No criticizing. Even when I told him she called him a shaman and told me to stay away from him, all he did was take in a breath.

When I'd spilled everything, I stood to pace the room. "I can't do it anymore. I can't go through life looking over my shoulder. I have to end this."

"What do you mean?"

"It's like she said. The only way I can make her lose interest in me is to stop being a werewolf."

"Are you serious?" William asked. "Don't you understand the incredible gift you've been given?"

"She'll take me away. From my home. From Brittany." I held out my empty hands. "Brittany is my mate. I can't exist without her. If I'm given a choice between losing my wolf or my mate..." Tears filled my eyes, and I turned my back so he wouldn't see. I waited until my voice felt normal. "It's a moot point, anyway. Brittany's potion for turning a werewolf into a human has to be used on the new moon, and that was last weekend."

William shifted in the chair and cleared his throat. "I could probably tweak that potion for you."

"You could?"

He gave a rueful smile. "Brittany talked about the potion at some length. She seemed to think it was her crowning glory, and that life went downhill from there. I told her it was just one step in a series of many."

I felt as if he'd slapped me. "I never knew she felt that strongly about it."

"You say this doctor of yours believes in shaman magic?"

"Yes."

He stood at the window, staring at the ash-covered trees. "I need a place to work. Somewhere quiet."

"You can use the hidden courtyard that Brittany and I used. It's near an old quarry, so it was probably protected from the brushfire."

"Do you know how to reach this woman?"

"Yeah. I mean, I think so. Her number will still be on my phone."

"Have her meet us in your courtyard Friday afternoon. She'll want to witness your transformation first hand."

TWENTY-SIX

This is the last day of my life.

There was no other way to look at it. If William's potion didn't work, Saarsgard would pounce on me and take me away. If it did work, then I would lose a part of me I would never recover.

I will never be the same.

Uncle Bob left for work early that Friday morning. He had plenty to do in the fire's aftermath–mending fences, clearing debris. I weaseled out, claiming the stomach flu. It wasn't far from the truth.

I dumped my bowl of soggy cereal down the kitchen sink and stared at it, trying to get my nausea under control. Even Lucky Charms didn't make me feel lucky.

I will never be the same.

For the umpteenth time, I took out my cell and punched in Brittany's number. And for the umpteenth time, the call went to voice mail. Why wasn't she answering her phone? She was supposed to be back from Kissimmee late last night. Maybe her battery died. Or maybe she was doing something that was more important to her than me.

When prodded for a message, I said, "I love you." The same message I'd been leaving all morning. There was nothing more to say. I only wanted to hear her voice. Just in case.

The last day of my life.

I left my phone on the kitchen counter. I couldn't afford any distractions either. I walked out the front door into the woods.

The brushfire hadn't come close to our house, yet the trees smelled burnt. Airborne soot covered everything. Birds squawked from the branches. I wondered if they blamed me. Like Uncle Bob.

Everything I did was wrong. Every decision. Maybe I should rethink my plan to banish my wolf. But I didn't know what else to do. I couldn't let Saarsgard take me away. Besides, Brittany herself said she'd rather I was a regular boy.

When I reached the old quarry, the sky was clear. The sun beating on all that white stone made me feel snow blind. I climbed a pile of boulders and stood, shading my eyes.

Part of the forest was green and normal. Part was black, the trees charred and leafless. As if someone had drawn a line.

Was that what I was doing? Drawing a line between Saarsgard and me? When this was over, where would I be standing? Green or black? Life or death?

I sat cross-legged on the sun-heated rock and thought of Brittany–the way her nose crinkled when she laughed, the way her green eyes flashed when she was angry. I promised myself that no matter what happened I would hold those images of her in my mind. I wanted her face to be the last thing I saw.

After a while, I got up and made my way to the hidden courtyard. As I walked, I recognized the growing stench of William's potion. It smelled similar to the one Brittany concocted but with an undertone of wolfsbane. The tweaks he'd promised.

My already queasy stomach lurched.

I stepped from the trees and stood dumbstruck. Despite the tromping of many police boots, the place looked the same. Here was where Brittany first saw me turn into a wolf. Where we had a water bottle fight and fell onto the grass, kissing. Here was where we splashed a killer werewolf with a potion that turned him back into a man so we could have him arrested.

I saw the magic circle Brittany and I carved from the grass. In the center was the fire pit Brittany made out of rocks. Now William's potion bubbled there. It was in a large, dented pot, not a cauldron. The police confiscated the one we used.

"About time," William said. He stepped from the tree line nearer the road. As usual, he didn't wear a shirt. "I put a flag on my bike so your doctor would know where to come in."

"Good thinking." My voice sounded distant, as if I wasn't really there. "Is the potion ready?"

He screwed up his face. "Are you sure you want to go through with this?"

"Can you think of a better plan?"

"Other than killing her?" He crouched to stir the pot. His bare back showed shiny, burned patches from when the cabin exploded. "It's ready. Do you remember what to do?"

"It's all I've thought about." I peered at the thick, greenish-purple liquid. Bubbles burst on its surface. Galoomp. Galoomp. "Does it have to be boiling when you douse me with it?"

"Don't be a sissy."

My wolf roared up at that. This was a trick. His potion was never going to work. He *wanted* Saarsgard to take me. He was eager to get rid of me. He wanted Brittany all to himself.

William placed his hand on my shoulder, and I looked into his eyes. "Trust me," he said.

And I did.

A warm breeze brought an additional whiff of wolfsbane. My throat constricted. "She's here," I whispered.

"Is she alone like we said?"

I motioned with my chin. "There's a werewolf in the trees."

"Figures." He gave a wry smile. "Time to put on my war paint."

He must've meant that literally, because he opened a backpack and brought out a kind of artist easel with little pots of paint. He set it at his feet. Then he picked up a staff with feathers tied to one end and stabbed it into the ground. Eyes closed, he shook out his arms and released a slow breath.

He began to chant. The sound of his voice cut through the silent courtyard. Arms raised, he looked at the clear blue sky as if communing with nature itself.

I turned toward movement in the brush. Dr. Saarsgard stepped from the trees. She wore a pale gray pantsuit that made her complexion look sculpted from snow.

Her eyes narrowed. "What's the shaman doing here?"

I wanted to say something witty and brave, but even if I could have thought of something, I was too terrified to speak. I folded my arms so she wouldn't see how my hands shook.

William chanted as if oblivious to anything but the cadence of his own voice. Crouching, he dipped his fingers in three pots of paint–yellow, red, and blue. He wiped three stripes on each cheek. Then he stood, fingers dripping with red paint. He drew three lines across his chest. It looked like bloody claw marks.

Just then, a dark cloud obscured the sun. Like he planned it that way. It was a nice effect.

"What's he doing?" Saarsgard glanced up.

He was sticking to the plan. My part was to keep the good doctor talking, keep her engaged, so she didn't walk away too soon.

And I was blowing it.

Clearing my throat, I said, "I know that you are

experimenting on the werewolves at your asylum. I saw them on your laptop."

If she was surprised that I'd been in her hotel room, she didn't show it. Then again, maybe her werewolf goon had smelled me there. "They suffer in the name of science," she said. "They die for the betterment of all mankind."

"I'm sure their families would be proud to hear that."

She sneered. "Those people don't care. Don't you understand? They pay me to take their *loved ones* away."

"They pay for the hope of a cure."

"Fools with a bank account."

I smiled. "I could tell them."

"Your government is too deeply involved to allow it. They'd tie a red ribbon around your neck and deliver you to my doorstep."

"Not if I have good news." I spread my arms. "You told all those poor families you were looking for a cure. Now you actually have one."

"What are you talking about? What is going on? You told me you wanted to take me up on my offer."

"That's right. You said the only way to get rid of you was for me to stop being a werewolf. I accept."

Her face fell, and her eyes widened. She stared at William. "Don't do this."

William shook his staff to the beat of his chant. A gusty wind blew. Dry leaves danced across the courtyard.

Saarsgard's silver hair whipped her face. "Cody, stop! You don't know what you're doing."

She took a step forward. I inched closer to the fire, glancing toward the werewolf behind the trees. I figured he was her tailback. Snatch me and run. But he remained hidden.

Voice rising, William danced in a wide circle around me. Saarsgard seemed loath to cross the line. His circle wasn't like the one Brittany and I drew, but it *was* magic. The air hummed with energy. My thoughts flew to the Indian burial ground I'd visited with my uncle.

Saarsgard shouted, "You're both insane."

William the Shaman danced. Abruptly, the wind rose. Clouds raced across the sky like a fast-motion movie. Lightning crackled. There came a boom of thunder.

"Cody!" cried Saarsgard. "Get away from him!"

A bolt of lightning struck a tall Australian pine tree, snapping the top in a shower of sparks. The doctor ducked, although it didn't fall anywhere near her.

William began a second circle around me. His gyrations were hypnotic, his voice steady and pulsing. The sky boiled with green-black clouds. There came another lightning strike. I flinched, wanting to cover my ears.

On the other side of the clearing, Saarsgard's bodyguard stumbled into the open. It was the big goon I saw before–but he didn't look threatening now. His mouth hung open, and his eyes widened as he stared at the sky.

Saarsgard yelled, "Stop them, you fool!"

I could barely hear her. A shriek rose over her words–a high-pitched screech that jangled my nerves and set my teeth on edge. But it wasn't human. It was the wind.

I raised my arm to shield my face, staggering to keep my feet. Saarsgard also stumbled, buffeted by flying debris. Her teeth were bared, her eyes white all around.

William started a third circle. That was my cue. This part of the plan was my idea. I thought it would be more effective if it appeared that William was forcing me to shift into my wolf form. Saarsgard didn't know I could shift on command.

I made a good show of it, grasping my throat and gargling, letting my fangs show. I even stretched out my hand to the big guy. I thought that was a nice touch–one werewolf to another, begging for help.

Then a huge crash stole my attention. And another. It sounded like a giant was thrashing through the forest.

The wind was uprooting the trees.

My momentary lapse of attention cost me my control. The wolf came faster. I threw back my head and howled, clawing my chest, ripping my shirt in two. It started to rain. Fat drops shot at me like bullets. I fell to my knees. Hair sprouted over my body. I couldn't stop the transformation.

Through a red haze, I saw Saarsgard step woodenly toward me, mouth frozen in an unheard scream. In a flash, her werewolf bodyguard was at her side, holding her back.

A tree fell into the courtyard, branches snapping. William ended his dance.

Three times and done.

I snarled, fangs bared, haunches coiled to spring.

Liquid agony struck. The shock turned me instantly into a boy. I screamed, rigid with pain as the scalding potion enveloped my body.

Saarsgard's expression changed, becoming resolute and distant. Lightning flashed, and the thunder was so loud it stole my breath.

Then the clouds opened. Like a faucet. Rain sizzled on my skin.

The last day of my life.

I pictured Brittany, imagined her eyes, her mischievous grin.

And miraculously, she was there. Bursting from the tree line, hair streaming, looking like an angel. Only she was screaming.

Screaming. "No, Cody! Oh, my God!"

Saarsgard looked at her, something like pity in her eyes, then turned and walked away.

I must have blacked out, because the next thing I knew, someone was rolling me onto my side. Raindrops patted my face. Or was it fingertips?

From far away, Brittany said, "Cody? Can you

hear me?"

I blinked, fighting for focus. Brittany's face swam into view. "I thought I dreamt you."

"I came as soon as I could. When William told me what you planned to do–" Her voice cracked.

"I had to do it. I couldn't let Saarsgard take me away from you." I stroked the side of her face. My hand felt fat. My fingers were so blistered they looked like they were made out of bubbles.

Her lip trembled. "You did this for me? Gave up a part of you?"

"I would do anything for you."

I kissed her then, and the world went away. There was only her lips and tears and breath.

TWENTY-SEVEN

Brittany snuggled beside me, filling the hollow carved from my gut. I couldn't help feeling happy when she was near. Yet behind my smiles and banter, I grieved for the death of my wolf.

We sat together in my uncle's recliner in front of the flat screen TV. Every once in a while, Brittany pointed the remote and changed the channel.

She settled on the news. The screen showed a tree on top of a minivan.

A female voice-over said, "A freak storm with winds in excess of one hundred miles per hour uprooted trees and downed power lines yesterday afternoon." The scene changed to a tree blocking a residential street. "Dangerous lightning was reported in the area. One man claims a strike set his stable afire, nearly killing two horses."

The man in question came onscreen. Before I could hear what he had to say, there was a knock at the door.

Brittany hit mute. "Who could that be?"

I lifted my nose–it's funny how quickly things can become habit–but of course, I couldn't smell anything. I shrugged to hide my disappointment, disentangled her from my arms, and climbed sideways out of the recliner. "I'll go see."

It was William and a very pretty girl.

"Howdy," William said in a voice remarkably like his father's.

"Hey," I said. "Come on in. Um, Eileen, right?"

"Right." Eileen smiled with her bright white teeth. As she stepped inside, she tossed her sun-drenched hair, and a flowery scent hit me in the face.

"Nice to see you." My cheeks turned warm. "I almost didn't recognize you with clothes on."

"How tactful," Brittany said as she embraced her friend.

Why did girls always hug?

"I'm taking Eileen to the reservation." William draped his arm over Eileen's shoulders. "I want her to meet my mother."

"Oh," said Brittany. "Then it's serious."

Eileen beamed. "We're ready to take the next step. But we're not sure if his mother is ready to have a paleface hanging around."

William squeezed her shoulders. "You are a healer. She will recognize that."

"Wow. That's great," I said, not sure it was great at all. A witch and a medicine man? Not a safe combination.

"But that's not why we're here," Eileen said. "Tell them."

William looked uncomfortable. "I would like to

apologize. I didn't mean to burn your back so badly. I thought your fur would protect you."

"And," Eileen prodded. When he didn't speak up, she said brightly, "Will played you both."

"What do you mean?" asked Brittany.

"He could've called you sooner, but he waited until just before the ritual started, when it was too late for you to stop what was happening. He hoped, and rightfully so, that you would show up at the end and react just as you did. For drama's sake."

Brittany looked perplexed. "So, I was part of a show?"

"But, it wasn't just a show," I said. "It really happened. My wolf is gone."

"Let me put this in a way you can understand." William placed his hand on my shoulder and met my eyes. "Dude. There is no cure for lycanthropy."

"But... You said–"

"I needed you to believe so you could convince your doctor."

"But, the dance. The wind."

He looked sheepish. "It was a rain dance. It turned out a little more powerful than I'd intended."

"Or maybe *you're* more powerful." Eileen grinned.

"Wait," said Brittany. "Are you saying his wolf isn't gone?"

"That can't be true," I sputtered. "I couldn't even smell you at the door."

"You didn't expect to smell me, so you didn't."

"No." I shook my head. "You said you tweaked the potion so it would work."

"It did."

"I was a wolf, and you changed me back."

"I do not know a lot about werewolves, and I admit that I took a big risk. But it seems to me that even a werewolf will change back to a human when hit with a pot of boiling sludge."

I stared. "But I was prepared. I was *willing.*"

"I know." William looked solemn. "My brother, the last time I saw you, you had third degree burns over most of your body. How do you feel now?"

I rubbed my neck. "A little tender."

Eileen laughed. "A regular person would be in the hospital on pain meds. But you aren't regular, are you?"

I cringed. She knew what I was. Maybe I should wear a sign: Wolf Boy. Get your autographs.

"We should be going," William said.

"Yeah." I felt dazed. "Thanks for stopping by."

The two girls embraced. William said something about a barbeque at his dad's house tomorrow. Everyone was invited.

They left.

I shook my head. My wolf survived? Saarsgard was off my case, and I still had my life? It was too good to be true.

Then I saw Brittany's stunned expression. She took a step away from me.

My elation burst like a bubble.

"I'm sorry," I said. "I tried. I really thought the wolf was gone."

"So did I."

I closed my eyes. "Please don't leave me."

Moments passed, then she sighed. "I don't want to be afraid of you."

"I know."

"Promise you'll work on your control."

"I will. I mean, I do."

She frowned, looking dubious and beautiful. "I love you, and if the wolf is part of you, I guess I love the wolf, too."

"I would never hurt you."

She nodded, then kissed me. It wasn't particularly enthusiastic, as kisses go, but it spread waves of heat over my body. My heart flew.

Brittany pulled away. "Anyway, it explains a lot."

"What?" I blinked, struggling to switch back to conversation mode. "What do you mean?"

We sat on the couch. I could tell she was gearing up to tell me something important.

She prefaced it with a sigh. "Yesterday I was in court for the abduction case against Pascal."

I winced. "Crap! I forgot all about it."

"I figured as much." She chuckled. "You only left like twenty-seven messages."

"I'm sorry. I should have been there."

"Turns out, it was a waste of time. We waited all morning, but Pascal never showed. Finally, they told us that he was transferred to a secure facility, and my testimony was no longer necessary."

"What? Why?"

"Well, you know me. I had to find out." She leaned toward me and lowered her voice conspiratorially. "On April twentieth, Pascal went berserk and killed his cell mate. I'm told it was brutal and bloody."

"April twentieth. That was a full moon."

She nodded. "In light of what William just told us, I think Pascal shifted into his wolf form in jail."

"The potion didn't work," I whispered.

"I did some digging on the Internet. It seems he was sent to a mental health facility in Sweden. Do you think it could be Saarsgard's werewolf asylum?"

"I wouldn't wish that on anyone." Then I thought of the blood in Brittany's car, and my fear that I wouldn't find her in time. "At least we know he will never get out."

"Yeah." Brittany snuggled against me.

I wrapped her in my arms and rested my cheek on her prickly hair. It didn't matter that she had me on double-secret probation. I would take moments like these whenever she offered them.

I could never hurt her.

Late that night, after Brittany had gone home and my uncle was asleep, I climbed out my bedroom window. Heart thumping, I trotted into the forest that bordered our yard.

I could hardly believe what I was about to do, thought I'd never have the power again.

I went to my favorite tree. Its lower branches were broken off, making suitable pegs to hang my clothes. I stripped, then folded my arms over my chest.

What if I couldn't? What if the wolf had given up on me?

But it answered my call as eagerly as if it had been anxious, too. Fierce joy rippled through me. Pride and relief. My flesh tingled as fur clothed my body. My nose filled with a thousand scents–rabbits and flowers and muck.

I lifted my head to Mother Moon and howled.

Excerpt from Book Three of
The Amazing Wolf Boy

WOLFSBANE BREW

ONE

The scent of blood lay thick in my nose. I shouldn't be here. It was too dangerous. I should run.

No. I had to find Brittany. Had to be with my mate during this time of death. But she hadn't passed this way. I couldn't smell her.

There was only blood.

My control slipped. My vision flashed red. A ball of panic exploded in my chest. I staggered into a wall.

I was not a wolf. Not only a wolf. I couldn't shift in this place. But, the moon called me, seductive, tantalizing...

"Sir?" came a voice. "Sir, are you all right?"

I made a show of wiping my eyes, putting on my

best distraught expression. "I'm trying to get to ICU."

"You're headed in the right direction," the nurse said. "Just follow the gold line. The waiting room is on the left."

"Thank you." I nodded, looking down at the floor.

There were several lines painted on the white tile, a different color for different destinations–Admitting, Out Patient, Cafeteria. The same as in any hospital, I supposed. I remembered following colored lines when I was a kid back in Massachusetts. Looking for my mother. The exalted brain surgeon. She was never home. Never had time for me.

When I turned out to be a werewolf, Mom banished me to South Florida to live with Uncle Bob. I'd hoped never to see the inside of a hospital again. Now, here I was. I shrugged. This wasn't about me. I had to find Brittany. My mate. Only she mattered.

I forced my thoughts back to the lines on the floor. My wolf sight picked them out like in a 3D video game, hovering in mid-air. But they were all tinged with red. I couldn't tell gold from green.

I continued forward. Straight ahead. Waiting room on the left. The smell of blood was strong, tainted by the stench of antiseptics and dying flowers. My stomach churned. I shouldn't be here.

My thoughts drifted to Uncle Bob. He would be a wolf this night, running through the woods. His mate, Rita, was in town, and I was sure they'd be together. A glorious reunion. Running.

Running.

A whiff of coffee stirred the conditioned air. My heart quickened, and I stepped faster. The room I entered was dim compared to the hallway. I stood in the entry, breathing deeply, allowing *her* scent to fill me.

"Cody," Brittany said. Her hair was purple, her eyes pink with crying. Mascara smeared her pale, perfect cheeks.

I pulled her close, and suddenly it no longer mattered that there was a full moon or that my inner wolf scrabbled at my gut. I was the amazing wolf boy, but for the moment, I was like any other kid holding the girl he loved.

"Hey." Butt Crack, Brittany's younger brother, stepped beside us. He was short and scrawny with a mop of black hair dangling over his eyes.

I shifted my hold on Brittany and held out my hand. "Hey, man. How's your grandpa?"

He shook with me, his grip firm. "Everything's failing at once, you know? First his lungs, now his heart."

"He's going to make it," Brittany said, her voice muffled by my shirt.

I tugged her gently. "Let's sit down."

The three of us sat on a beige couch in the middle of a beige room. Their parents, Dean and Dalia Meyer, stood at the coffee pot, talking quietly. I was surprised to see them together. He was an abusive man, and it had been an unforgiving divorce.

Grandpa Earle was Dean's father. I gathered the

two of them had had a falling out, and until recently, Dean lived in Georgia. Now, he seemed forever underfoot, like he could worm his way back into the family. Knowing the kind of man he was, it was hard to believe Dean cared about his father. Yet he looked haggard. He kept glancing toward the door as if expecting to see the grim reaper standing there.

"I can't believe this is happening," Brittany murmured.

I kissed the top of her head. "It will be all right."

Butt Crack lowered his voice. "Mom says there's a will. The house goes to his daughter."

"Aunt Lynette." Brittany sighed. "That's better than leaving it to Dad. We'd never get rid of him."

"It doesn't matter who gets it. If Grandpa dies, we're on the street."

My heart gave an uncomfortable lurch. I hadn't thought about that. Would Brittany lose her home? Would she move away?

"He'll make it," Brittany said. "He's not that old."

"He'll be seventy in July," Butt Crack said as if he didn't think a person could get much older.

Brittany shot him an angry glare.

Just then a doctor appeared. We jumped to our feet.

"Doctor Jordan," said Brittany's mother, "were you able to stabilize him?"

"I'm sorry." Dr. Jordon shook his head. "We did everything we could."

Brittany wept into my shoulder.

TWO

"You didn't shift the entire night?" Uncle Bob asked as he drove me to school in his pickup truck.

Uncle Bob had steel gray hair that curled over his collar. When he was a wolf, he was the same color gray. He worked as the local handyman. He knew everyone, and everyone loved him. If he ran for mayor, he'd win, no question.

I shrugged. "Brittany needed me. What else could I do?"

He blew out his breath. "You aren't like any werewolf I know."

I chuckled. "You mean that in a good way, right?"

"I just never heard of one of us being able to choose *not* to shift during a full moon. Either you're the strongest wolf I ever met or..."

"Or, what?"

"Or you're not full blooded."

"You mean I'm not a real wolf?"

"Maybe." He took a left onto Southern Blvd. "Some werewolves hit puberty but only shift sporadically. The rest of the time, they just feel like crap during the moon."

I nodded, remembering my mysterious fevers and unexpected flus. "So they're sick for the rest of their lives?"

Uncle Bob glanced at me. "As they get older, the impulses fade."

"It wears off?" I thought about not being a werewolf. There were many times I wished I could be a regular sixteen-year-old boy. But in the end, my wolf was part of me. I wouldn't be complete without it. To have it fade away… A shudder shot through me. "Let's talk about something more cheerful. Did Rita show up?" Rita was a werewolf and my uncle's girlfriend. They'd been together for almost fifteen years, yet oddly, they didn't live together.

A slow smile creased his face. "Yeah. She was sorry she missed you."

"Me, too. But it was probably just as well. You two deserve time alone."

"On that note, Rita plans to spend a few weeks here in South Florida. She asked if she could stay at the house. I didn't want to say yes without checking with you first."

"Oh." My cheeks became warm, and I turned to gaze out the window so he wouldn't see me blush. It was nice of him to ask permission–it made me feel important. And I liked Rita. On the other hand, the thought of him and Rita in the next room…

"Of course, she can stay," I told him. "She's your mate. I don't know why she doesn't live with you fulltime anyway."

"You sure?"

"Just keep the noise down."

Uncle Bob laughed as if I were joking.

We pulled into the drop-off in front of school.

I hopped down from the truck. "Thanks for the ride."

"Do you need a pick up?"

"No. I'll walk to Brittany's house after school."

"Give her my sympathies. Earle Meyer was a good man. He'll be missed."

"Definitely."

"Let's go out tonight. Just you, Rita, and me. Get us a nice rabbit dinner."

"Sounds good." I thumped the side of the truck in farewell and walked away.

Seminole Bluffs High School looked completely different from my school up north. The building was peach-colored and had a red tiled roof. Instead of a rolling green lawn, it had a cement courtyard with holes cut out to let trees grow here and there.

Inside, it was the same as any school, though—noise and a crush of people. I pushed through the teeming halls, thinking about Brittany, missing her already. Was there a chance that she might lose her home? What would happen then?

The morning dragged. By lunchtime, I had a headache and felt a little feverish. It made me worry that I wasn't a full-blooded werewolf after all. I wondered if my super powers were fading as well, but nope–the cafeteria still stank like the bottom of a trashcan, and I could still hear conversations from across the room.

I grabbed a bottle of water and a cheese sandwich and headed for my regular table. Efrem Higgins sat there. Eff was an ex-football star, and he still ate like he had to maintain his bulk. His tray was piled with sandwiches, fruit, and cartons of milk. Since being kicked off the team, he started working on the school newspaper. It turned out he had a dry sense of humor. I enjoyed his articles.

He looked up as I approached. "Where's Brit?"

"Bereavement." I sat across from him. "Her grandfather died last night."

Eff's face fell. "You're joking. Grandpa Earle? Poor old guy."

"You knew him?"

"Probably every kid in town knew Grandpa Earle. He organized the Kids Parade. Every year for as long as I can remember, he got all the children to march down Southern on the Fourth of July. Even babies in strollers. I guess he was some sort of war hero. He had a chest full of medals. But he always wore a skunk fur hat." Eff chuckled. "What a character. I should do a memorial for the paper."

"Brittany would like that."

"When's the funeral?"

"Not sure. I'm going to her house after school to see if there's anything I can do."

"I'll drive you over."

"What?" I cried. "Your dad got you another truck after you totaled the last one?"

"Hot off the lot." He took a big bite of a turkey sandwich. "Insurance company really came through."

So that's how I found myself in Eff's brand new silver Ford Ranger compact truck. Except for the color, it was identical to the old one. I liked to rib him about being a rich kid, but actually, his parents were paupers compared to mine. If I hadn't turned into a wolf that night in France, I'd probably have my own BMW by now. My father's car of choice.

Loxahatchee, Florida, was a small town. Grandpa Earle had lived there since the beginning. Eff was right–apparently, everyone knew the old guy, and everyone wanted to pay their respects.

As we drove up the dirt road that led to Brittany's house, my mouth dropped open. The front yard was a parking lot. Children and dogs chased among the cars. A line of people waited to get through the front door. They carried casserole dishes and pies.

Eff parked beside an overgrown orange tree. "Maybe I can get some interviews for my memorial." He hopped out of his truck and hurried toward the house without seeing if I followed.

I lagged behind, taking it all in. Along with the kids in the yard, there was a group of men standing outside the kitchen door, smoking. Another group sat in the wicker furniture on the porch. There were so many people either going inside or leaving that someone had propped open the front door.

Brittany's dog, Haff, disappeared along with the other canines in the yard. Animals tended to hide when I showed up.

I climbed the steps and entered bedlam. The living room was filled to capacity. Somehow, Brittany's mother spotted me.

"Cody, I'm so glad you're here." She thrust a tuna casserole into my hands. "I need you on food duty. If it's hot, it goes on the table. Try to fit everything else in the fridge. And make sure we don't run out of cold sweet tea."

I carried the dish into the kitchen. The bright yellow curtains I once found so cheerful now looked out of place. The counters were stacked with two-liter bottles of Coke and jugs of sweet tea from Publix. Bags of ice filled the sink. Around the corner, the dining room table was set up as a buffet.

Eff interviewed people as they circled the food, using his cell phone as a recorder. "What one word would you use to describe Earle Meyer?"

"Loving."

"Funny."

"Cantankerous."

"Hey," Butt Crack said behind me. "Crazy, eh?"

"Hey, man. How are you holding up?"

"Don't know, yet. I'm kind of numb, you know?"

I didn't know. I never had anyone close to me die. Maybe it was like losing my mother in the custody fight–but no, that was by choice. I motioned with the casserole dish. “What should I do with this?”

“Ugh. Tuna. We have three more just like it.”

“In that case, I’ll take it to the garage. Anything else that should go?”

Butt Crack loaded me up with dishes of lasagna, chicken and dumplings, and fried tomatoes. I juggled them out the door to the garage.

Grandpa Earle’s garage was an oversized storage unit. No cars allowed. It was deeply shadowed and had a wet dog smell that always made me crinkle my nose. Among the crates and boxes was a freezer big enough to hold two deer. It was nearly empty, now; he used to joke that he needed the room in case he shot a yeti. A pang cramped my heart as I realized I would never again hear his stories. I put the extra food inside.

I turned to find Brittany standing behind me. She looked haunted–dark circles beneath her eyes, lips pale. I wasn’t used to seeing her without makeup, didn’t like to see her without a smile.

I wrapped her in my arms. “Hiding?” I felt her nod. “Come on. I’ll take care of you.”

With one hand on her back, I guided her into the house. The kitchen table had bench seating on two sides, chairs on the other two. I helped her sit on a bench then slid in next her, holding her close. She felt fragile in my arms.

Her brother spun a chair backward, sitting at the head of the table. “Aunt Lynette’s coming.”

“Aunt Lynette?” I said. “Have I met her?”

"No one's met her," Brittany blurted. "I never even heard of her before now. Apparently, she lives in a commune somewhere in the Blue Ridge Mountains."

Butt Crack nodded. "The black sheep of the family."

"I thought your father was the black sheep."

Brittany sighed. "They both are."

I held back a chuckle. I'd never heard of a family where both children were considered misfits. In my mother's family, Uncle Bob was the black sheep, while my mother, being a brain surgeon, was the good child. I wondered what people said of me. Could you be a black sheep when you were an only child?

"She'll probably sell the house," Brittany whispered.

"Maybe she'll sell it to Mom," her brother said.

"Get real," she snapped. "We don't have any money."

I said, "Maybe whoever buys it will rent it to you and your mom. Don't give up hope yet."

Butt Crack nodded, but Brittany's eyes filled with tears.

"I don't know where we'll go," she said. "And the really worst part is this whole thing has brought Mom and Dad closer together. What if she goes back to him?"

I got it then. She was afraid Aunt Lynette would sell the house to her father just to get rid of it, and her mother would agree to anything just to have a place for her children to live.

I wrapped my arms around her and kissed the top of her head. My wolf sense told me that her father was a broken man, no threat to anyone. But Brittany remembered him from before. She remembered his drinking, his beatings, lying to her teachers about the bruises all over her body. I couldn't let her go back to such a life.

"Cody, please," her mother called from the kitchen doorway. Her face looked drawn and frazzled. She held a casserole dish in one hand and a pie plate in the other.

I took them from her. Suddenly a parade of new visitors filled my arms with dishes. The onslaught of mixed aromas made me want to sneeze. I added the hot food to the buffet on the dining room table and cleared away a few empty dishes. Then I took the cold casseroles to the freezer in the garage. When I got back, Eff was talking to Brittany and Butt Crack.

"I'm sorry for your loss," he said. "Grandpa Earle was a great guy. He'll be missed."

"Thank you." Brittany nodded.

Eff turned to me. "I'm heading out. You want a ride home?"

"I think I'll hang around a while longer," I said. "Did you get what you need for your memorial?"

He brightened. "Got some funny stories. People have good memories of him."

"Okay, then. See you tomorrow."

"See you." He nodded his goodbyes then left the room.

Brittany looked like she wanted to cry again. "He's writing a memorial?"

"Yeah."

I got her a tall glass of ice tea. Then I fielded a few more casseroles and put a load of dishes into the dishwasher.

As the afternoon waned, so did the number of well-wishers. The background roar of voices diminished. I peered around the ruffled, yellow curtains to see a bright orange sunset. My stomach squirmed as if something alive were fighting to get out.

"I have to go," I said. "You understand, right?"

Brittany paused. "It's all right. I'm going to my room anyway." She got to her feet, moving as if she were balancing the world on top of her head.

I wiped my hands on a bit of paper towel, glancing about the kitchen to be sure I hadn't forgotten to do anything. "Get some rest, man," I told Butt Crack.

He nodded. "Seeya."

I put my hand on Brittany's waist and guided her out of the kitchen. Muffled conversation came from the living room.

Two women stood in the hallway. They wore what I considered church dresses–buttoned to the neck and hemmed below the knee. They both smiled at us, and one opened her mouth as if to speak. But she looked at Brittany's face and got out of our way instead.

We reached the bottom of the stairs. We were in view of the living room, so I didn't want to make a big, groping scene.

I hugged Brittany and kissed her forehead. "I'll call you in the morning."

She didn't meet my eyes. "Have a nice night."

I watched her climb the stairs, wishing I could stay with her, wishing I could wrap her in my arms and protect her from the hurts of the world. She climbed to her room without looking back. Her door clicked shut.

I'd failed her. I knew I had, although I didn't know what I could have done differently. With my hands in my pockets, I entered the living room.

It was crowded, but not overflowing like before. Several deputies stood behind the couch where Sheriff Brad sat. The sheriff was Grandpa Earle's best friend.

Brittany's father sat in Grandpa Earle's chair, the one where he used to take his afternoon naps. Dean looked haggard, and I wondered again if he truly regretted his father's death or if it was all an act.

Whether it was or not, Brittany's mother was obviously taken in by it. She flitted about like an exhausted butterfly, refilling drinks from a jug of sweet tea on the coffee table. But she never moved more than three paces from Dean. Her gaze kept going back to him. Perhaps Brittany was right in worrying that her parents might get back together.

I stepped forward. "Missus Meyer, I have to go.

There's more tea in the refrigerator, and I put some of the extra casseroles in the yeti freezer."

She patted my cheek, her eyes sunken, her gaze distracted. "Such a good boy. Do you need a ride home?"

"He doesn't drive?" Dean snapped.

"Stop," Mrs. Meyer said in a placating voice. "He's only sixteen."

Within my pockets, my fists clenched. His tone irked me, but no more than hers did. I didn't need Brittany's mother to defend me.

I smiled, showing my teeth. "That's all right, ma'am. The walk will do me good."

"I'll take him." Sheriff Brad stood, pockets jingling.

I blinked, my mouth dropping open to argue. But, no. You don't argue with Sheriff Brad.

We crossed the parking lot that was once Brittany's lawn. I got into the front seat of his green-and-white cruiser. We drove slowly down the dirt road that ran alongside the house, then pulled into traffic on the long stretch of asphalt that led to my house.

The sheriff said, "It's good that Earle had a chance to reconcile with his son before he went."

"Now I wish the man would go back to where he came from," I blurted, then winced. I expected to get an earful about speaking ill of a man who just lost his father.

Instead, Sheriff Brad said, "Yep."

I glanced at him. Did Sheriff Brad have

suspicions about Dean Meyer, too? "Do you know anything about Grandpa Earle's daughter?"

"Met her once or twice. She's an upstanding citizen. Owns a little shop in McCaysville, Georgia, up by Blue Ridge. Sells candles, of all things. Makes them herself."

Candles? Brittany liked candles. "Grandpa Earle never talked about her."

"She used to call on Sundays, but after the mother died, she stopped. Didn't even come to the funeral. Nothing against Earle. It just hit her hard. He understood that she needed a little space."

He switched on his turn signal and took a left into my neighborhood. The houses were small but well maintained. The setting sun turned their windows pink.

Before long, we turned onto my driveway. Gravel crackled and popped beneath the cruiser's tires. The house I shared with my uncle was set back from the road, hidden by trees and bushes–the perfect place for a couple of werewolves to hide in plain sight.

As we pulled to the house, I recognized Rita's old white van. It might have been shiny once, but now it was dull and spotted, as if the sun had faded even its white paint.

"Thanks for the ride, sir," I said as I opened the car door.

The sheriff grunted. To my dismay, he put on his hat and got out of the car.

Rita burst through the front door, red hair flying

like curls of flame. She stood on the porch, wiping her hands on a dishtowel.

The sheriff said, “Back again?”

“For a bit,” Rita told him.

“Where’s Robert?”

“He’s working late. Is there a problem with Cody?”

“Just giving the boy a ride home.”

She nodded. “I’m sorry to hear about Earle Meyer. I understand he was a friend of yours.”

“That he was.” He tipped his hat. “I’ll be seeing you.”

I skipped up the wooden steps and stood next to Rita, watching the sheriff drive away. “He doesn’t seem to like you.”

“He doesn’t like any newcomers. We upset the status quo.” She turned to me, smiling. Rita wasn’t a pretty woman, but she had a wide, white smile that showed even her back teeth, making her dazzling. “Let me have a look at you. Getting enough to eat?”

“Of course.” My stomach growled, and I grinned.

She scoffed. “If I know Bob, it’s Chinese takeout. Come on. I’ll dish you up some stew.”

She draped an arm about my shoulders, and we stepped into the house. It smelled like dinner. My mouth watered, and I realized I hadn’t eaten since lunch.

In the kitchen, I noticed a few subtle differences. To one side of the sink, clean plates drip-dried in a dish rack that hadn’t been there before. On the other side, a new slow-cooker emitted an enticing aroma. The table sported three wicker placemats and a napkin holder in the shape of a cow. Ah, a woman's touch.

"Have a seat." She lifted the lid off the cooker. Steam puffed toward the ceiling. With a ladle, she filled a soup bowl with her chunky concoction.

Rita's stew was mostly meat–beef, chicken, and pieces of rabbit that I assumed came from their romp in the woods the previous night. I found only a few slices of potatoes and carrots. I groaned in appreciation as I ate, sopping up the gravy with a slice of brown bread.

She watched me, cocking her brow. Then her cell rang, and she smiled brightly. "Hi. Yes, he's here. Really? Okay, then. No, it's fine." She glanced at the cooker. "The longer it simmers, the better it gets. See you in a few." She put the phone in her pocket. "Bob's running late. He says to meet him at Tony's Mound. Do you know where that is?"

I nodded. "I can get us there."

She poured a cup of apple juice into the stew, gave it a stir, and replaced the lid. "Finish up, then, and we'll go."

I wolfed down the remains of my bowl.

Rita's van was so old it had a cassette player built into the dashboard. The last time I rode with her, she played Carole King's Greatest Hits. It reminded me, disturbingly, of my mother as she cruised around in her convertible, singing away–good times long past. This time, Rita played someone called Donovan. I knew she couldn't get recent tunes on a cassette, but his music sounded old.

Tony's Mound was an Indian burial ground out on County Road 835. It was about sixteen feet high. The land around it was flat, and I could see it even from a mile away. A trail ran up its side like a scar. I found that disrespectful. Jogging on top of graves.

But the area was so popular with hikers, it warranted its own small parking lot. We pulled next to Uncle Bob's pickup and got out of the van. The air was heavy with humidity and the fetid smell of muck. It hummed with old magic from the mound, setting my teeth on edge. I doubted the average human would notice it, but my wolf hearing picked it up clearly.

Uncle Bob walked over, ignoring me. "Hi," he said huskily, taking Rita into his arms and kissing her.

I rolled my eyes and moved to the front of the van. Heat rose from the engine.

Rita said, "It's almost time. Should we leave our clothes in back?"

"Sounds good." He gave me a lopsided grin. "See you in a moment."

They climbed into the back of the van. They weren't like me–they couldn't shift whenever they wanted to. They had to wait until the moon rose.

I moved to the side of the van, stripped, and pitched my shoes and clothing through the passenger window. Then I reached with my senses toward Mother Moon.

The change hit immediately. My ears slid upward with a liquid sensation. My teeth ached so bad I couldn't close my mouth. My muzzle grew, feeling like it was pulling off my face. Millions of electric pinpricks swept my body as fur erupted all over my skin.

I fell to my knees, stifling a howl. I heard the familiar pop-click of my joints repositioning. My muscles burned, making me want to run, to work off the pain. I looked down at silver paws.

I was a wolf. Power on four legs. Not a mere human who relied on their wits to live. It made me wonder why I ever changed back. I should remain a wolf. I could do it.

Then an image of Brittany came to me, her green eyes sparkling, a mischievous smile on her lips. I could never leave her.

Still...

I shook myself from head to tail, sloughing off the last of my humanity. Behind me, the van's back door opened and closed. I smelled two humans. Two *naked* humans. No way did I want to see that. I stepped forward into the scrub. There was no game here. Nothing lived near the Mound. Its pulsing heartbeat sent ripples down my spine. That was why Uncle Bob chose this spot–so we could find our way back. But did I really want to find my way back?

The moon rose, and its light bathed my soul in a soft caress. I closed my eyes and lifted my nose. A breeze ruffled my fur. It smelled of sawgrass and the rich, dark earth. Faraway, I heard a peacock call.

Gagging sounds came from the direction of Rita's van. Then two wolves came around the side–one gray, one ruddy. Uncle Bob and Rita. They greeted me with nips and yips. I nuzzled them affectionately–but the reunion needed to wait. I had to get away from the Mound. I led them deeper into the Everglades.

Uncle Bob, the environmentalist, complains a lot about the changes in the Everglades. He hates that housing developments and golf courses encroach upon it on all sides. In addition, he blames the runoff from surrounding farms for introducing fertilizer to the swampland. He says it kills off indigenous plants and allows others to thrive.

Since I am new in town, I don't remember way-back-when. But I do know that, along with deer, gators, panthers, and black bear, the Everglades has acquired a nasty population of python. I thank pet owners for that; some people think you can leave any old thing in the Glades. You never want to tangle with a python. The only way to kill it is to take off its head–and that's where it keeps its fangs.

One animal you don't find in South Florida is a wolf. So imagine my surprise when I entered a thicket and found myself muzzle-to-muzzle with a she-wolf. She was sleek and brown and had golden eyes.

With an alarmed yip, she ran. I barked for the

others to follow and tore off after her. She was smaller than I was, but she was faster than the wind. I had trouble matching her pace. I kept her scent in my nose as we crossed a sea of sawgrass. Its blades swished at my head like serrated swords.

Who was this intruder? I knew she was a werewolf–I glimpsed her short, yellow tail as she sped before me. What was she doing here? Poaching? Scouting the competition? How dare she enter my territory without permission?

My human-side chuckled at that. Who did I think I was? The King of South Florida? I was chasing her because I was interested in meeting another werewolf, right? Not because I wanted to scare her away.

I dismissed the thought. With my ears flat, I ran faster. My back paws dug into the soft muck, sending clumps flying behind me.

That's when I realized that neither Uncle Bob nor Rita was following. Couldn't they keep up? I sighed. Old people.

The she-wolf veered into the forest. Was that where her pack hid? Would they jump me as soon as I entered the trees? Anger tinged my eyesight red. How dare they threaten me?

A low growl frothed my jaws as I raced into the tree line. No one jumped me. I startled a family of rabbits, and they bounded in all directions.

I let them go, focusing on the she-wolf. She was slowing, zigzagging through the trees. After a few minutes, I realized she was running in a pattern:

three tree trunks, turn, five more, and turn again. Like she was playing a game.

My ruff tingled at the back of my neck, standing up in annoyance. I calculated where the pattern would take her then leaped, bowling her over. With a heavy paw, I held her down. My jaws tightened around her throat.

Again, my human flared into being. What was I going to do, kill her for playing hide-and-seek?

A moment of indecision plagued me. Then I released her and bounded away.

Immediately, the she-wolf scrambled up and gave chase. It *was* a game. I darted through the foliage, keeping her close but not too close. She was faster in the stretches, but even though I was larger, I cornered better. I dodged out of her way, then doubled back as she sped past.

Once I lost her completely. I stopped running and boosted my ears. Where could she have gone?

Coming from nowhere, she sailed through the air and hit me with all fours. "Grrruff," she said happily. *Tag! You're it!*

Grinning, I raced after her. It was fun. I forgot all about her being a mysterious intruder. I played as if she were a toy–a chew toy that bit back.

A while later, the howl of a wolf brought me up short. I froze, listening.

Another wolf? Did the she-wolf belong to a pack after all?

She looked at me, gave an apologetic whimper,

and headed in the direction of the howl. I trotted beside her. Each step took me further to the dark side. These wolves were uninvited. I'd marked this land as mine. By the time I was close enough to scent them, I was stoked for a fight.

The she-wolf and I stepped into a clearing. Uncle Bob and Rita stood on one side. Two other wolves stood opposite. The male was black with red eyes. The female was small and brown. All four had their fur on end, trying to appear larger. But bristled as they were, none were as large as me.

I stepped into the center of the clearing, staring down the newcomers. The male met my gaze without flinching. I would take him first, show him how I feel about poachers.

As if oblivious to the tension, the she-wolf walked over, nipped my ear, and nuzzled my neck. Then she crossed the clearing to stand with her... parents. Yes, now I could smell it. They were a family, not a dangerous pack.

I dismissed them with a woof and turned my back. My ears perked up, alert for movement behind me. None came. I nudged my uncle, demanding his attention. The moon was setting. I needed to get him back to his truck.

Relief washed through me when Rita and Uncle Bob allowed themselves to be herded from the clearing. Better yet, the three strangers didn't follow. I didn't want to be known as the bully who beat up a family for passing through.

I kept my group moving until I could no longer hear or smell the newcomers. Only then did I slow to a relaxed trot. Soon I sensed the magical drone of Tony's Mound like the hum of power lines in the back of my skull.

We reached the vehicles as the moon set. Rita hopped into her van to turn back into a human in privacy. My uncle stayed with me. I watched him shift–his face flattening, his spine straightening. It looked painful.

When it was over, he sat naked in the dirt, looking at me. "Your turn."

I gave my best doggy grin, my tongue lolling.

"I'm not kidding, now," he said. "You have school in the morning. Shift back."

I sneezed loudly, hoping to convey that I had other things to do.

Rita rounded the back of the van. She wore jeans and a frilly blouse. My uncle's clothes were folded over one arm. "What's going on? Why is he still a wolf?"

Uncle Bob looked embarrassed. "I told you that he was–"

"You said he was unusual, but I didn't think..." Her voice went up an octave. "The moon is gone."

I snorted at that. The moon was never gone. Even when it was on the other side of the planet, I could sense its presence.

"He shifts at will," my uncle said. "But now is not the time."

Now was the perfect time. I spun about and high-tailed it out of there. I had to hurry or I would miss them. I picked up the scents of the three wolves at the clearing and followed them to a narrow dirt road that wound through the forest. They stood near a charcoal-gray Lexus, all of them human once more.

The father's skin was as black as his wolf's fur had been. He wore brightly colored pajama bottoms, and he was pulling a matching tunic over his head.

The mother wore a long, shapeless dress that split to her knees. Her dark, shoulder-length hair stood out like a frizzy halo, making her head appear two sizes too big.

The girl was not yet clothed. Her smooth body reminded me of a chocolate Easter bunny. She pulled on a pair of tattered cut-offs and a faded blue shirt that had *The Doctor Is In* on the front. She looked younger than my human, perhaps fourteen or fifteen years old.

"You bloody well *do* know what I'm talking about," the father said in a deep voice. "Those wolves might have been dangerous."

"Yes, it's all my fault, isn't it." The girl put her hands on her hips. "I'm in charge. I was the one who should have surveyed the ruddy area instead of assuming we were alone."

"Not to worry," said the mother. "I'm sure they were just passing through."

The father sighed and pinched the bridge of his nose. He looked at the girl. "Ayanna, you are not to leave my side again, do you hear me?"

"Yes, father." Ayanna sighed, rolling her eyes.

Turning, she looked directly at me. I was downwind and hidden in the brush. She couldn't know I was there–and yet... She stood unnaturally still, her eyes glinting gold in the half-light. She looked wild and completely alien.

Then her father called her name, breaking the spell. They got into the car and drove away.

About Author

Roxanne Smolen

Roxanne Smolen became enamored by werewolves after watching the movie Abbott and Costello Meet Frankenstein when she was a girl. The pathos of the wolfman character touched her even then. As she grew into her author shoes, the idea of a conflicted werewolf character grew as well until she knew his story had to be told. Her wolf boy series takes place in Loxahatchee, Florida, not far from her home. You can connect with her on Twitter, Facebook, and Google+.

Books by Roxanne Smolen

The Amazing Wolf Boy

The Amazing Wolf Boy

Werewolf Asylum

Wolfsbane Brew

Werewolf Apocalypse

The Bear, the Werewolf, and the Blogger

The Amazing Wolf Boy Box Set

Dark Angel

Satan's Mirror

Colonial Scouts

Alien Worlds

Alien Jungle

Alien Seas

Alien Beginnings

The Resort Debauch Trilogy

Resort Debauch

The Resort Debauch Trilogy

The Violet Series

Violet and the Missing Laptop

Violet and the Missing Puppy

The Adventures of the Power Girls

Keepers of Magic

Island of Magic

Dear Reader,

Thank you for reading Werewolf Asylum. I hope you enjoyed the adventures of Cody and Brittany and will look for the next book in the series, Wolfsbane Brew.

Readers today have the power to make or break a book via reviews. Without reviews, a book will go unnoticed. Please take a moment to leave a short review. If you have questions or comments, feel free to contact me directly at smolen.roxanne@gmail.com.

Again, thank you for reading.

Roxanne

www.roxannesmolen.com

www.ingramcontent.com/pod-product-compliance
Lightning Source LLC
Chambersburg PA
CBHW071645260626
47170CB00001B/245

* 9 7 8 0 9 9 1 5 6 7 3 2 4 *